Faith & Humor

Faith & Humor

Notes from Muscovy

Maya Kucherskaya

*Translation from the Russian
by Alexei Bayer*

**Russian Life
BOOKS**

The publication was effected under the auspices of the Mikhail Prokhorov Foundation
TRANSCRIPT Programme to Support Translations of Russian Literature

Praise for Faith & Humor

"The most delicate language, deceptively light, deceptively conversational..."

Author Mikhail Shishkin (interview with *Novaya Gazeta*)

"Perhaps there are readers who will find some of Kucherskaya's stories blasphemous. For instance, one priest is a businessman, another is a friend to thieves, a third is a cannibal... Others will be scandalized by other things. For instance, a talented artist abandons the stage for the church, and she is happy! She writes of miracles. In our enlightened age! What are we to make of this work? Simply that there are abnormal (stupid, hysterical, blinkered, tasteless and tactless) people both inside the church and out. But normal people are far more numerous."

Andrey Nemzer, *Vremya Novostey*

"Starting with scandalous tales, the author ably ignites what? Strange as it is to say it: spirituality. She is, after all, not simply a modern humanist, but also a true person of faith. And she speaks of the clergy without catching her breath. For her, they are just a part of normal, everyday life, and not some sort of exotic Orthodox hedgehogs."

Mikhail Vizel, *Time Out*

Contents

"So there you go, for the love of God, there,"
the priest repeated, hopping joyfully.
(Those who saw that particular holy elder remember
that he could sometimes be seen hopping joyfully.)

N. Motovilov, *The Sarov Monastery*, 1844

Foreword

In order to avoid confusion while reading Maya Kucherskaya, the reader would be well-advised to consult a dictionary, preferably repeatedly.

The first thing the reader will discover is that a Paterikon is a book of stories about the deeds of Orthodox priests and/or a collection of their moral sayings.[1] Then, when he realizes that the title is disingenuous and that the author actually intends to confuse the reader rather than help him understand her meaning, said reader will need to resist becoming angry with the author for being a bit too familiar with the reverend fathers, then spend still more time reading appropriate dictionary entries. With a little patience and a few clues, the reader will discover the true meaning of this work.

It will become clear that what we have here is facetia, or light prose, a genre that may not be as spiritually uplifting or instructional as a true Paterikon, but no less useful for that. It is also an extremely amusing genre, which led it to enjoy wild, if short-lived, success among readers and listeners at the time when the Middle Ages was turning into the Modern Era.

Facetiae brought fame and fortune to the Florentine Poggio Bracciolini. His facetiae were translated and widely imitated across

---

1. This book's Russian title was *Современный патерик*, "A Modern Paterikon."

Europe, even reaching as far as Russia, where they were often called "amusing tales." Then they disappeared.

And it is a pity they did. Jokes (facetia is a Latin noun that means "jest, wit or humor") and any frivolous, loving amusement at the expense of the clergy no longer have a place in contemporary literature. Contemporary literature not only grew serious – if not grim – but it split into two distinct strains. One is spiritual literature, which is not at all inclined to amusement, and the other is secular literature, in which the reverend fathers are almost always referred to as priests, and the prevailing tone is either that of denunciation and satire or sarcasm and cold analysis.

In a manner of speaking, the fierce Florentine Giovanni Boccaccio[2] got the better of his gentler countryman Bracciolini. No need to analyze why. It will be enough to admit that this is what sometimes happens in cultural history: one tradition pushes aside another and eventually the latter disappears entirely.

Actually, not entirely, perhaps, as this book attests. I admire Maya Kucherskaya's courage in choosing this genre, as she links hands with those for whom monks and priests were not only the objects of praise or criticism but first and foremost men of flesh and blood – almost like you and me. She follows in the footsteps of Nikolai Leskov,[3] but she still needed plenty of courage – and choosing the genre was perhaps the easiest part. She also had to get her timing right, to find an age in which such a tone and such a form of poking fun were acceptable.

I'm convinced that this idea could not have emerged fifteen or twenty years ago, at a time when even the Bible couldn't be found easily here, when the few existing monks and only slightly more numerous priests seemed if not dissidents or great heroes, then at least deserters from the battlefield of socialist construction. It

---

2. Giovanni Boccaccio (1313-1375) – author, poet and correspondent with Plutarch. Wrote the *Decameron*, among other classic works.
3. Nikolai Leskov (1831-1895) – journalist and author known for his humorous tales. Late in life, he began to question church doctrine and published stories that challenged Orthodoxy and touched on ancient legends of the church.

wasn't the government alone that held this view, and as a result an impenetrable wall separated the Church from society and private life.

That time is now past. It may be too early to speak of a revival of the Orthodox spirit in the nation, but there are numerous signs in daily life attesting to the fact that the Church is becoming for many a source of inspiration. The number of churches, religious shops, Orthodox publishers, candle factories and Sunday Schools is multiplying. Young and old Russians bake Easter cakes, color eggs and come to church to get apples blessed for Easter. Beggars in underground passages in the city have shed their camouflage fatigues, donning cassocks in order to receive more alms. Priests now bless offices, dachas, cars and even, one hears, personal computers.

In a single decade, serving the Lord has ceased being something totally exotic and has become, so to speak, an ordinary profession. If we count not only monks and priests, but sextons, sacristans, church wardens and many others who come together for meals around the refectory table, and add to this number the members of their households, it will turn out that tens of thousands, and perhaps hundreds of thousands actively participate in the life of the Church. It has become a new social class, if you will.

No one really expects that we always hold each and every member of this social class in high esteem, talk of them in reverent whispers, bow to the ground when we meet them and consider each and every one of them a hero and an unmatched paragon of moral and spiritual virtue. That would be silly. Almost as silly, in fact, as to emulate Leo Taxil or Yemelian Yaroslavsky and to see anyone who dons a monastic cassock as a thief, a buffoon, a cynic or a libertine.[4]

It would be more honest, I believe, to set aside both wild enthusiasm and intellectual skepticism and to see those who have

---

4. Leo Taxil (1854-1907), a French writer and satirist (born Marie Joseph Gabriel Antoine Jogand-Pagès) who skewered the Catholic church and clericalism. His works were widely published in the Soviet Union. Yemelian Yaroslavsky (1878-1943), born Minei Israelevich Gubelman, was a fervent atheist, Communist Party activist and editor of the atheist satirical journal *Bezbozhnik* ("The Godless"). He led the League of the Militant Godless and also headed the Anti-Religious Committee of the Central Committee.

taken the orders and their happy flock as ordinary human beings, most of whom often succumb to common human weaknesses. At the same time, it is important to remember that the way of thinking and the way of life of those who have devoted themselves to the service of the Lord do undergo considerable change. Their behavior changes, as well as their values, habits, fears and joys. They even begin to speak differently.

Maya Kucherskaya has attempted to do just that. The result is facetiae, tales that are light-hearted, yet educational. They poke fun not so much at the reverend fathers but at neophites who hide their natural embarrassment by performing with excessive zeal what they feel are the necessary chores of any believer.

I want to particularly stress that the author rarely discusses actual faith. Only in a handful of her tales does her sincere piety, her reverence for the holy miracles and her respect for those members of the Church who are truly deserving of respect come through like a breath of fresh air.

Maya Kucherskaya is young and her development continues. I suspect that she will yet write about her vision of faith – perhaps in another book or even a series of books.

Here she has written exactly what she wanted to write. It's a book written without saccharine sweetness and with a wry smile. She doesn't try to make those who disagree with her change their minds, but invites them to reason along with her. She is not intimidated by her subject matter or her characters, nor does she get too familiar with them.

The most important thing is that hers is a labor of love. It brims with the tenderness and compassion that we reserve for family members, for close relatives and loved ones – even if they may be sinners and at times do awkward things. They may irritate us and make us want to make fun of them, but we still love them because they are family.

I like this book.

I like it because I believe it is very timely now, when Russia is slowly and painfully starting to crawl out of its Middle Ages, leaving behind a medieval, highly ideological, thoroughly outmoded and yet enduring attitude toward faith, the Church and its servants. It is yet to enter a new era, and examples of inner freedom and liberation, presented with delicacy and tact, can be counted on the fingers of one hand.

It is also a good thing that this book happens to be extremely amusing and, once you start reading, it, you will find it impossible to put down.

Sergey Chuprynin
Chief Editor, *Znamya* Literary Journal

Author's Preface

This book was written over a period of many years. The early stories date from 1990, while the most recent ones were finished 15 years later.

The book is also the product of a new era in Russian life, that period during which it was written was also an era marked by the rebirth of the Church.

The Russian Orthodox faith is a distinct branch of Christianity. Formed originally under the influence of Byzantium, the Russian Church gradually evolved into a separate, original, immense and complex world. It comprised holy men of the sort described by Fyodor Dostoyevsky in *The Brothers Karamazov*, hundreds of monasteries and convents, churches, Processions of the Cross and intercessionary public prayers for rain or a bountiful harvest. For most Russians for most of the nation's history, life was hard and poor, and the Church offered a crucial respite: attending services showed people a different sort of life, bright and beautiful and bearing little resemblance to their everyday routine. The light of the candles was a sharp contrast to the gloom of the izba.

It was a colorful, festive world formed over many centuries. And it was almost completely destroyed by the communists. Thousands of priests and monks were executed, died in the camps or were sent into exile. Hundreds of churches were dynamited and atheism became the official state creed. Growing up, we were constantly told that there was no God and there could be none. Only a handful of churches remained open and even they functioned only under close KGB supervision. To be an openly worshipping believer became all but impossible. Still, a genuine life in the spirit endured in some places: holy men lived in remote towns, usually after serving long terms in labor camps. People would come to see them and to ask their advice. But it was a secret, semi-clandestine life.

Then came perestroika. After 70 years of oppression, everything changed once more.

Churches and monasteries were reopened and priests suddenly began to appear on television and even in university lecture halls. The Bible was sold openly. In the early 1990s, people literally flooded the churches, getting baptized one after another and seeking a new life. It was a special, romantic era, a time of hope and revival in the Church. The tree of Christianity sprung a new, fresh, living branch.

Nevertheless, those who joined the Church at that time were neophytes, yesterday's atheists with no experience of religious life, no examples to follow. Some were overly enthusiastic and made plenty of mistakes; the revived Russian Orthodox Church surely had its share of boorishness, hypocrisy and misinterpretation of the Christian commandments.

I too joined the Church at that time, along with many of my friends. I went on pilgrimages to newly reopened monasteries and to visit monks and priests. Soon, there were so many emotions engendered by what I had seen, heard and felt, that I was literally drowning in them. I felt the need to pour them out, to express them and thus to try to make sense of them.

One of the consequences of the 70-year break in our traditions was that we had lost our language for discussing Church matters. There was no linguistic tradition that I could harness and which might carry me along, because modern Russian literature did not have a way of describing the life of the spirit, church services and the lives of monks and priests. Over the previous 70 years, there had been tons of novels, novellas and short stories about love, family, social classes and relations on the factory floor or at a research institute, but not a single work about the Church.

Nevertheless, I took the risk of putting pen to paper and writing my first short vignette: "They were all supping around the refectory table. Suddenly, Father Theoprepus got down under the table..." Then I wrote another, then a third. Short vignettes began to spring from my pen as if of their own accord, their literary form resembling that of ancient Paterika. A Paterikon is a collection of moral tales about Christian fathers, an extremely old genre that had been popular in religious circles since the Middle Ages. My stories combined a wide variety of impressions of the church and church life.

It should be said that this book contains stories about several real clerics, but for the most part it is a work of fiction. Nevertheless, everything in this Paterikon is a true reflection of something I have heard or observed. In short, this is literature supplemented with a few snapshots from real life.

Month by month and year by year my vignettes continued to multiply. Finally they added up to a complete volume. In the end, the book turned out to be an epic about Russian Orthodox believers. It is by turns multicolored, ironic, pious, enthusiastic, grim, sad and joyful. In other words, as diverse as the life of the Church or life in general.

When my Paterikon was published in Russia, it created something of a sensation. Many people felt terribly insulted. "A cannibal priest? An atheist priest? It's blasphemy, that's what it is," they said. At one convent, the book was burned at the stake. Meanwhile, at a seminary in another small town, my Paterikon was added to the curriculum that helps future priests understand problems within the Church. My greatest surprise, however, was that so many people outside the Orthodox Church read this book, and with great interest. They too laughed and cried. So far, the book has been through six printings in Russia.

My great hope is that English-speaking readers will see this book not merely as a window into the mysterious Russian soul or a collection of amusing anthropological facetia about priests (even though it is, in part, both of those things), but as a story about people who ardently believe in something and who carry this belief out into the real world.

Maya Kucherskaya
Moscow, Summer 2010

First Cycle

Readings for the Nativity Fast

1 They were all supping around the refectory table. Suddenly, Father Theoprepus got down under the table. He sat there among the monks' roughly shod feet. The feet remained still. Then Father Theoprepus began to move around and to tug at the monks' cassocks from under the table. The monks were humble and no one dared to reproach him. Only one novice asked him in astonishment, "Father, how would you have us interpret this?"

"I want to be like a child," came the answer.

2 An abbot known for his gift of clairvoyance commanded a novice to cut down a poplar tree growing in the middle of the monastery. The novice, wishing to understand the hidden meaning of this order, inquired, "Father, why should the tree be cut down?"

"I've been laid low with allergies, Sonnie, from the poplar down," the abbot replied, sneezing.

"God bless you," said the novice and ran to fetch an electric saw.

For he had a gift of understanding.

3 Father Stephen pulled a monk by the beard.

"Oy, Oy, Oy!" screamed the monk.

"I thought you'd taken the vow of silence," Father Stephan asked in surprise.

"What of it?" the monk replied and began to cry bitterly.[1]

---

1. The allusion is to the Apostle Peter's repentance.

4 A monk grew despondent. No remedy could be found to cheer him up. But then the other monks gave him a toy truck for his name day. The truck could turn about, blow its horn and blink its headlights.

"Wow, a toy truck," the monk exclaimed.

From that day, he was never again depressed. Every night before going to bed he would load the truck with pebbles, wind up its clockwork engine and watch it roll around his cell, making turns, blinking its headlights and softly blowing its horn.

5 The monks asked their wise elder "Tell us, O Father, where is the best place for us to build a woodshed? Near the fence or next to the bathhouse? Or perhaps on the other side of the fence?"

"Wherever you like," the wise elder replied.

6 Father Yehudiel spilled pea soup all over himself.

"Vasya, why don't you go and wash my cassock," he said to a novice who had recently joined the monastery.

"But I have no idea how to wash clothes," Vasya protested, laughing loudly.

"And so you shall learn," Father Yehudiel replied, laughing louder still.

7 Some monks decided to take a walk in the woods. No sooner had they started on their walk than Father James disappeared.

"Hey, Yasha," the monks called out. "Yasha, where are you?"

But the woods were silent. There was only the sound of a cuckoo calling, and beneath the pine trees, the mushrooms silently grew.

"Why doesn't he answer?" the monks wondered. "Perhaps he has become a hermit? Or has he taken a vow of silence?"

But, Father James had climbed a tall tree, pretending to be a cuckoo, peering through the branches as the monks searched for him. He laughed and gave a cuckoo's call.

8 Father Gabriel was very fat and snored in his sleep. Once, a novice who was not yet familiar with the ways of the monastery heard the snorts and began running about the grounds, looking for a pig. He jumped from bed to bed, poked a stick into dark corners and even climbed the roof and threw pebbles down the drainpipe. But he wasn't able to find any pigs.

9 Monk Stepanenko prayed all night, with prostrations, in his zeal striking the floor so hard with his forehead that he injured his head. In the morning one of his brothers asked him, "What is this, Stepanenko, a bump on your head? You didn't have it yesterday. Did you pray all night?"

"Oh, no. I simply fell down."

"I thought maybe you spent all night praying."

"Oh, no. I simply fell down."

"I thought maybe—"

"Oh, no, I simply fell down."

"The Russian hockey team played Canada last night. Do you know the score?"

"Oh, no. I simply fell down."

10 Once, a monk completely stopped partaking of food.

"Why are you not eating anything?" his cellmates asked.

"Don't you know that my call is to fast?" the monk explained.

"But if you keep this up you will soon starve to death."

"Really?" the monk asked in surprise. "I can starve to death?"

Impressed by their gift of reasoning, he began taking food again, having learned his lesson.

11 A monk once came to the abbot to complain about another monk.

"He is very bad!" he told the abbot. "Many times I have seen him commit a cardinal sin with my own eyes."

The abbot blindfolded the monk with a filthy, foul-smelling rag and said, "Let us punish the two villains. Let them now see and smell their owner's soul."

"Is my soul really so filthy?" the brother asked.

"Much worse. I actually took pity on you."

From that day forward, whenever the monk saw someone commit a sin, he brought the foul-smelling rag, which he always carried with him, close to his face. And he was comforted.

12 One day, participants of a World Conference visited the monastery. Seated around the refectory table, they offered the monks some sausages they had brought from Finland.

The monks deliberately turned away from the sausages so as not to see them or to accidentally eat one of them. But one elder was terribly happy.

"Oh, what joy you have brought to an old man. What joy. I'm so obliged," he kept saying with his mouth full. And he ate and ate and ate. He ate all the sausages from Finland.

The participants of the World Conference were very surprised.

13 An elder at a monastery, wishing to show visitors from a faraway land how far his servant monk progressed in obedience, called him over and, pointing to an orange mutt running in the monastery yard, said, "Can you believe it, Brother John? There is a wolf in the monastery."

"It might kill our chickens," Brother John replied. "Do you want me to fetch the shotgun?"

The visitors from the faraway land clapped their hands in admiration.

14 When he saw a throng of faithful who were waiting for him by his cell, yearning for salvation, Father Paisius took to his heels. The faithful, in their yearning, gave chase, and one of them even caught the priest by the corner of his cassock, but could not hold on to it.

They pursued their recalcitrant spiritual leader for a long time and even trampled two flower beds, but they were quite unable to catch him. They got so upset that they went to complain to the abbot.

The abbot came out onto the porch, gestured to Father Paisius to come over and whispered in his ear, "Why are you running away from your spiritual children, Brother?"

"I am not running away from them," replied the panting Father Paisius. "I am running away from vanity."

15 A monk came to an elder to complain about his hard life. But when the elder began offering him sage advice, the monk responded to everything by saying, "Oh, no. I can't do this."

Or,

"Oh, no. I won't be able to do that."

"Hey, Alexei," the elder called out to his monk servant, "Make this monk a bit of kasha. He is very weak."

16 Father Dorymedontus ate too much chocolate. It had been sent him by his mother, and, on his way back from the post office, Father Dorymedontus secretly ate it all, by accident. At night, he couldn't sleep and lay in bed, holding his stomach. The whole brotherhood, feeling sorry for him, formed a circle around his bed, danced and sang the monastery's traditional lullaby. But Father Dorymedontus continued to suffer.

"Look, he is holding his stomach," one monk said. "He's probably ill from too much fasting. Let's get him some chocolate from the refrigerator. It'll give him some comfort."

"No, please, not that" Father Dorymedontus groaned in horror. "Better to give me some salted water."

When they heard that, the monks were awed by how strictly he kept his fast and made their own fasts even more severe.

17 Father Ambrosius, whose chore it was to work in the refectory, sat down at the table after the monks had finished their meal, took out some chocolate-glazed cream cheese treats and began devouring them one after the other.

At that moment, another monk entered the refectory and saw his brother eating the cheese treats.

"Forgive me, Father. I must remind you that today is a strict fasting day, for it is Christmas Eve," said the monk.

Father Ambrosius raised his eyes to the monk who was speaking and immediately threw up.

18 Brother Anthony was lonely and decided to get married.

"I am getting married," he announced to his brethren.

The other monks were fond of him and could not allow him to go alone into the sinful world. They decided to go with him and to share his fate. At the time, the abbot was away at a World Conference and they had no one to ask for advice.

The monks gathered by the gate, made a sign of the cross and bowed for the last time to the crosses on their churches. At that moment, the abbot entered the gate. He had just returned from the Conference.

"Bless us, Father, for the last time," the monks cried out in tears. "We are going to get married."

"God bless you, Brothers, but—" the elder hesitated.

"What were you going to say? Please, tell us."

"Women, they're all such…"

The monks immediately ran back to their cells.

19 A monk succumbed to temptation and, coming to the abbot, announced, "Father, I have come to realize that God doesn't exist, so I am leaving the monastery."

The abbot burst into tears and replied to him, "Oh, child, my child. You have understood nothing. Go wherever you like."

The monk stayed.

20 A monk came to Father Averian and told him, "I'm so lazy that I find it very hard to get up in the morning to do my chores. Every day is torture for me and I feel I shall soon fall ill from all my chores and labors."

"If it is so hard for you to get up for work, don't," said the abbot. "Stay in your cell and bemoan your laziness. But do so loudly. When others hear how bitterly you weep, they will leave you alone."

21 It was said of Father Averian that he often ran into walls and bumped into various things and had many bruises on his body and even on his face, because his mind was filled with contemplation.

22 Brother Dukitius asked Abbot Pachomius, "Father, I don't know how to behave with other brothers in our common cell and at meals. Everything I do turns out awkwardly and I have become a clown in spite of myself. The monks always laugh at me and ridicule me behind my back.

Abbot Pachomius said to him, "Nothing annoys or provokes other monks more than someone who is different. If you try to be no different from all the others living here, humility will envelop your soul and no one will ever bother you again."

23 Deeply distressed, a brother once complained to Father Pachomius, "Father, I am tormented by devils each and every night. The moment I lie down in my bed and close my eyes, I get a tremendous desire to eat fried chicken. Some crispy fried chicken served with golden potatoes and dill. If not chicken, then fish. Smoked salmon from Finland on buttered white bread. Or else I get up to say my prayers and I am overcome by the desire to smoke a cigarette. Only one cigarette, and perhaps follow it up with a glass of wine. It seems as though all the forces of hell and all the devils are lined up against me."

"Oh, Brother," responded the elder, laughing. "What are you talking about? These are neither forces of hell nor devils. Devils

tormented the reverend fathers, hermits and saints of old. As to us…
No devil would waste his efforts on any of us. These are not devils.
These are simply your desires. To defeat them, you need no great
undertaking. You don't even have to be a monk."

"What do I have to do, then, Reverend Father?"

"Willpower, my dear friend, the power of your will. To strengthen
it, each morning you must do ten pushups and make your ablutions
with cold water. That will suffice."

"And what about the Lord's Prayer? What about prostrations?"

But the elder said no more to the curious monk, declaring that he
was too busy to continue the conversation.

24 Father Plato used to say, "We live in times of great weakness and
enfeeblement. We are not capable of anything and can do nothing.
Let us at least admit it. And may the Good Lord have mercy on us."

25 A novice once asked Father Plato, "What is the best path to
salvation?"

To which he answered, "Go call your mother already."

26 Father Plato also said, "Let us not reinvent the wheel."

27 He also said, "You can't be a believer if you keep your mouth
shut."

28 To women he would say, "Make your oatmeal every day. Toss the
cereal of good deeds into the boiling water of passions. Season it with
the salt of your prayer and sweeten it with love for your neighbor.
Stir it with the spoon of common sense. God willing, you will have a
good meal when the evening comes."

To the men he would say, "Recharge your battery often, or else,
before you know it, your engine will die on you. No 'Angel' will be
able to help you then."

29 An Angel appeared to a monk.

"Are you an Angel?" the monk asked in amazement.

"Yes, I am an Angel," replied the Angel.

"What if you are not a real Angel but only a make-believe one?" the monk asked nervously, making the sign of the cross. "What if you're nothing but a white bird?"

"Whatever do you mean? I am the real thing. If you like, you can touch me."

The Angel stretched out a shining wing.

The monk tried to touch the wing but instead of feathers he felt thin air. Truly it was a real Angel's wing.

30 It used to be said of Father Jeremiah that he had a special monk servant who changed his handkerchiefs every hour – so much did he weep.

31 One novice was very sensitive and often shed copious tears during services. The brethren called him Cry Baby.

32 Two monks had a falling out. As novices, they had been close friends, and after several years of serene friendship they took their orders, first one, and then the other. In their cloister, each was given an individual cell and they had to live separately for the first time. Everything they owned was divided equally, but they could not decide how to divide the video cassette player. It had been given to Father Gennadius, but Father Methodius had it repaired twice, taking it to the repair shop in his car. Besides, there was the question of the tapes, most of which he had bought with his own money. It was because of the player that the two monks nearly came to blows. In their anger, they completely forgot about the television set.

They went to the abbot and asked him to mediate their quarrel.

"Father, pass your judgment," they said, kneeling before Abbot Michael. "We can't decide how to divide the video cassette player. It was given to one of us, but the other got it repaired and bought all the tapes. Whose is it now?"

"Got any good movies?" the abbot asked.

"A whole box full," the monks replied.

"Got *Moscow Doesn't Believe in Tears*?"

"Yes, Father."

"And what about *Office Romance*?"

"We have it, Father."

"And what about Stallone's action flicks?"

"Action flicks, too."

"I see," said the abbot. "Go and bring the player and the cassettes to my cell. And don't forget the TV set. When I decide that I want to see a film, I will invite the two of you to my cell and we will watch it together."

The monks were comforted and did as the elder commanded. They brought the TV set, the video cassette player and the box of tapes to his cell and left it all in his cell.

"Should we hook it up?" the monks asked him.

"Guys, I think I can handle it," the abbot replied, giving them his blessing and bidding them to go in peace.

But to this day he has not once invited them to see a single movie. The monks, on the other hand, have never summoned enough courage to remind him of his promise.

33 Sister Catherine got a letter. She saw the return address and could barely keep from crying out, "It's from Denis. From Denis Grishakov."

The same man who had proposed to her six months before. The same man whom she had preferred less than the nunnery. Catherine's heart was swiftly filled with deep sorrow and longing for Denis. She went to see the abbot.

"You see, Father" she said to the abbot. "When I lived in the world, Denis Grishakov proposed to me, but I refused him and entered the nunnery instead. Yesterday I got a letter from him. I'm afraid to open the envelope, so full is my heart with longing. What if he is summoning me back?"

Father Andrianus lay a hand on the letter and smiled.

"Dionysius, servant of God, you have been blessed! You would have been so unhappy if Catherine had become your wife! Thank God it didn't happen."

Then the reverend father turned to Catherine, "Go on and serve the Lord, serve your beloved, with whom you will dwell in a tent in heaven, wanting nothing of worldly joys, desiring only to be with Him."

"How can I serve Him?" Catherine asked in surprise. "I have at least *seen* Denis. We used to walk arm in arm together, he and I. I have never seen the Lord."

"Help your sisters and be kind to them, then tedium will leave you and your love for your true bridegroom will begin to grow. Leave the letter with me, but remember this day. Come back in a year's time. We'll read the letter and we will know what he has written to you."

Catherine handed the letter to the reverend father and he placed it in the lower drawer of his desk. However, she never got a chance to read it. Several months later, the abbot fell ill and died. It wasn't the right time to look for an old letter.

Exactly a year to the day from the hallowed day when she got the letter, friends visiting the convent told Catherine that Dennis had gotten married.

34 Father John was busy getting ready to go somewhere. He returned books to the library, laundered his socks, mended all the holes in his cassock and shined his shoes.

"Are you leaving us?" other monks asked him. "Are you going home to your mother and father?"

"I am, indeed," Father John admitted with a smile.

"Being a guest is nice, but there is no place like home," he added and instantly expired.

35 A holy man was taking a walk in the woods around the monastery. He saw a little girl standing by the road holding a kitten and bitterly crying.

"Why are you crying, my child?"

"Grandpa, my kitten fell from a tree and died."

"Is this the kitten?" the holy man asked, pointing to the dead kitten.

"Yes," nodded the girl and began to cry louder still.

"Oh, but it is only pretending to be dead. Now, listen up, kitty cat, you know how to catch a rat?"

The kitten remained still.

"Well then," the holy man said, getting angry, his eyes bulging out of his head. He shouted, "Then I'll eat you."

The kitten became so scared it was frightened back to life, meowed piteously and hid in the folds of the girl's dress.

36 Mother Theodosia's chore was to look after the chickens. A university-trained linguist, her previous experience with chickens had been limited to eating them. She had great difficulty doing her chores and endured great distress because of her incompetence.

One day, the Mother Superior as usual berated Mother Theodosia when suddenly loud clucking was heard nearby. A grey wolf had snatched a hen and was running away.

"Go chase it down and bring back the hen," the Mother Superior angrily cried.

Mother Theodosia started after the wolf.

"In the name of my Lord, give me back my hen," she yelled at the frightening beast. "Give it back to me this moment."

The wolf was scared by the pursuit, turned and released its prey. Mother Theodosia picked up the hen and took it to the chicken coop.

Although ruffled, the hen was alive and by the evening had recovered fully. In the morning, it lay a golden egg.

"Come, sisters, let us taste this fruit of obedience," said the Mother Superior at breakfast.

But the golden egg could not be broken. Upon reflection, the nuns placed the golden egg in the convent's Museum of Miracles.

37 It was said of Father Theophanes, who for many years lived as a hermit in the deep woods, that whenever he found a dead beast or bird, he buried it in accordance with Christian rites, prayed for the dead creature to rest in peace and never forgot to put on its grave a little cross fashioned from two twigs.

38 One winter there was no snow. It got to be Christmas Eve, but still no snow had come.

The Father Superior of a small cloister went to a distant hermitage to see an old hermit. Having guessed the purpose of his visit, the hermit came out to meet him and welcomed him joyously.

"O, Father" complained the Father Superior. "Christmas is upon us and yet we have not had any snow. The monks are in despair. They are like children, our monks. They keep saying that without snow drifts and a cover of snow on the ground there can be no true Christmas. Forgive me, Father, and tell me what to do."

"Why didn't you pray to the Lord to send you snow?"

"We did pray, and many times. But not a single snowflake came down from the sky."

"You probably didn't pray well. Do you want me to prove it to you?"

The old man raised his hands to the sky and began to pray. A few minutes later, dark snow clouds began to gather in the previously clear sky and snow began to fall. The Father Superior was awe-struck. He fell to the ground and prostrated himself before the holy man. However, when he raised himself up again, the old man was no longer in front of him. He had run away to the woods.

39 Easter came at the end of April. Hermit Theophanes prayed all night and in the morning he heard birds knocking at his window with their bills. He came out. All the animals of the forest had gathered on the meadow in front of his hut. Bears, wolves, foxes and hares sat side-by-side and stared at him in the thin morning light.

"Christ is Risen!" said the holy man and, bending down to their furry muzzles, he kissed each animal in turn. Then he hugged every tree in the vicinity and kissed every trunk as he kept repeating, "He is risen, He is Risen."

"Truly He is Risen," came the reply.

40 Soon after Brother Daniel entered the monastery, he fell gravely ill. Other monks, who knew about his sinful past, prayed fervently that he might not die but live with them a bit longer, so as to have more time to repent. But Daniel could no longer get out of bed and was at death's door. The monks came to say goodbye. At first he didn't respond to them and lay still with his eyes closed. Then, suddenly, he regained consciousness.

"What is going on, brothers? Is it Easter?"

"What Easter, dear Brother Daniel? It's February. Can't you hear the wind howling outside?"

"I hear voices singing," replied Daniel. "Are you chanting: 'Christ is Risen'? Where is the light coming from?"

The monks fell silent, not knowing what to respond.

That night Daniel died. The storm abated, but snow kept falling in large, thick flakes. It covered the monastery, falling on all the pathways and roofs and sliding noiselessly from the golden domes in soft, heavy clumps.

Second Cycle

Readings for Those Who Have Recently
Discovered the Joy of True Faith

The Writer

Once upon a time, there lived a young woman. She was about to graduate from a literary college. Then she fell in love. The young man dabbled in poetry and had written a four-act play. But the most important thing about him was that he attended church. One thing led to another, and the young man helped the young woman turn to God as well. For a month they went to church together and read poetry to each other. Then, suddenly, the young man received an invitation from Switzerland. Apparently, he had relatives there who were inviting him to come and join them. The young woman remained in Moscow, having been touched by the light of the True Faith. Out of loneliness, she wrote even more. She wrote mostly prose, preferring such modest literary forms as short stories, novellas, essays and, sometimes, short novels. But she continued writing only because she pined for her young man.

One day she went to confession and told this to the priest, "Father, my beloved left me and, distressed and embittered, I have been writing fiction."

"It is not a great sin," replied the priest. "It can happen to anyone. Just don't try to publish it."

"What do you mean?" said the young woman in surprise. "I have been invited to publish some of my works in the journal *Youth*, because I'm still young."

"It may not be such a bad idea in principle," said the priest. "But first you should show it to me. I'm going to read your works and give you my blessing."

The young woman did as she had been told and showed her writings to the priest. In his former life, the priest had been a biologist, and he still liked to glance through the occasional book now and again. As he read the young woman's short stories, he began to cry. The young woman definitely had talent. Her writings were good. But they were not religious writings, not the way Orthodox writings should be. She wrote about profane and sentimental love, describing various kinds of heartache. In other words, it was all secular, and it didn't go in the right direction, so to speak. It was as though she were disdaining the Church and never even mentioned it.

The priest said this to the young woman and instructed her to show him everything she would write in the future. Meanwhile, he told her to tear up her contract with *Youth*.

The young lady was well read and knew that she had to obey the priest. She followed his orders and dissolved the contract with the journal. She went on writing short stories, and even though she didn't forget her Swiss boyfriend, his image began to fade in her memory and a new image began to emerge and shine in her mind – that of the priest. The young woman obeyed him in everything. She showed him her stories. He read them and found that they seemed to have a little more of the divine spirit in them. New, correct images began to appear in them. He praised her and even went over some of them with a pencil here and there, to make corrections. A little more of the same, he assured her, and she would be able to publish them.

A little more of the same, the young woman told herself, and she would be able to publish them.

One day, she ran into a friend who used to work at *Youth* but now moved to a different journal. He read a few of her new stories and hinted that her writing had become worse. He said that her writing was more "unusual." Perhaps he meant that the young woman had gone a little mad.

Three more years passed, then two more, then four more, and the new millennium began. The young woman grew older and began to slouch forward in an unappealing manner.

"I am unhappy," she told herself. "It has nothing to do with publishing my work. I am unhappy, that's all. I feel that I have missed out on something. Maybe I'm not fulfilled. Maybe I miss not being famous, or maybe I should have had kids. The truth is that nobody needs me in this world."

Well, she went and drowned herself in the Moscow River.

The priest said the last prayers over her body.

Dear Brothers and Sisters, what is the moral of this story?

It is that the young woman was unbalanced.

The Actor

Once upon a time, a mother took her son to the theater. The theater stunned him. The actors seemed to be like real animals, and he spent the following week impersonating those animals. The play he had seen was called *The Jungle Book*. At the end of the week, the boy demanded to be taken again to the same performance. A beloved son's wish is a mother's command. His mother called a friend who was connected to the world of theater. Actually, she had a job selling newspapers at a newsstand, next to which was a ticket office, which sold tickets to various performances. The friend was on good terms with the woman who sold theater tickets. The friend was able to get the tickets, paying only a little over the official price, and mother and son went to the theater once again.

The boy watched the performance, his mouth agape, and got angry when intermission came. At home, he again played Bagheera, Shere Khan and the monkeys for days on end.

"Mom, when I grow up I want to be an actor," the boy said.

"You'll need good connections to get into acting school," the mother said. "Because I have no money to pay bribes."

The boy grew up and applied to the State Institute of the Theater Arts. During the entrance examination, he recited a monologue. The jury was dumbfounded. The boy clearly had great talent. There was nothing they could do but admit him. Fedya got in on the first try, then graduated and joined a famous troupe. He also worked in film and was invited to play a gangster in the most popular television series. His mother watched her son on TV and cried for joy. Yet Fedya liked working in the theater the most. He liked to see the dusty curtain roll up and be blinded by the limelight as he entered the stage in costume or even without.

Then, one day, he was on tour in Novgorod. He went for a walk in the city and entered the main cathedral, St. Sophia. He stood inside for a while and stared at the icons. He lit a candle, listened to the choir and all of a sudden – it had to be! – realized that God exists. Fedya became a believer and began to attend the church that was near his house. He went to confession and took communion every two weeks.

One time, the priest asked him, "What do you do for a living, young man?"

Believers don't stand on ceremony, because to them all men are brothers. Fedya actually liked the informality and the straight talk.

"I'm an actor," he replied.

"An actor? What kind of roles do you play?"

"Whatever role they give me."

"Do you do love scenes and kissing scenes?"

Fedya gave an honest answer. "Yes, kissing scenes, too," he said. "There is nothing I can do about it. In one show, we all come out on stage naked. It's the director's inspired idea. We stand with our backs to the audience, but still, it is the main reason why people come to see the play."

"Now, you listen to me," said the priest sternly in a loud voice. "It is all the work of the devil. You must give it up. You're young, and there are plenty of other jobs you can do. You can become a doctor or a construction worker; we need a carpenter. As to your current sinful occupation, you must give it up completely. It is not an occupation for a believer. Did you hear me?"

Fedya nodded. "I did."

He thought it over for a year. It was sad to think of giving it up. But there is nothing you cannot do for your salvation. In fact, they paid him hardly anything in the theater, and the TV show was no big deal, either. In the end, he decided to quit. He spent another year learning to be a cabinetmaker and went to work as a carpenter at his priest's church. He carved such a beautiful iconostasis that it was mistakenly published in a catalog of antiques. The benches at the church were also much more beautiful now, with carved legs and seats in the form of canoes. They were not very comfortable to sit on, but they were beautiful and made in the tradition of Russian folk art. The priest was very happy. He had saved a soul from the pit of perdition and had done a useful thing for the church, as well. Fedya also seemed happy.

Only Fedya's mother was sad. The gangster whom Fedya used to play on TV had to be bumped off in order to explain Fedya's sudden disappearance. After that, his mother became a little strange. Whenever Fedya came to visit her, she wouldn't open the door for him, claiming that he had died.

"Why do you keep coming to see me? I don't like dead people."

But Fedya still came to see her, and brought her food and sat with her, patting her wrinkled hand. Eventually, she no longer objected.

The Masseuse

Tanya Korkina studied to become a masseuse and then found a job giving massages to handicapped children. She was so skilled at what she did that she could literally perform miracles. She could get crippled arms and legs moving again. She could cure high blood pressure. She made premature babies into circus athletes. She even got kids with cerebral palsy up onto their feet. Grateful parents swarmed around her. The list of her clients grew by leaps and bounds, and there was a six-month waiting list to get a massage from Tanya. Meanwhile, Tanya became an Orthodox believer. She now had a confessor. When he got to know Tanya better, he explained to her that children suffer for the sins of their parents. It was God's will when people fall ill. Since her massage restored the children to health, their parents' sins would be transferred onto her.

Tanya was distressed. What was she to do? How could she bear such a burden? So many kids had passed through her hands, she had long since lost count. Thus must her sins be countless.

The reverend father said to her, "No problem. Stop your useless massage work and daily recite three canticles: one to Sweet Jesus, another to the Theotokos and a third to Saint Nicholas the Miracle Worker. This will remove the mountain of other's sins weighing so heavily upon your shoulders." (Indeed, Tanya now felt those sins weighing her down.)

She did as she had been told. She gave up doing massages, firmly refusing all her clients and reciting the three canticles daily. She has lived on her mother's pension ever since, convinced that any day now, thanks to the prayers of her beloved priest, she will meet the man of her life. She has no doubt that the prayers of her father confessor can work miracles.

You don't believe it?

Perhaps you have been reading the wrong books.

The Believer

There once was a man who suddenly believed in God. Thereupon he borrowed a Makarov pistol from a friend and shot himself.

A Wise Decision

There once was a priest who had a special gift from God. Whereas elsewhere the right nave was still being fixed, the roof was on its second year of being patched, and they were using a temporary curtain instead of a good one for the Royal Doors, our priest's church already boasted silver domes with golden stars painted on them, and an iconostasis with sacred sixteenth century icons. He even managed to have a new nave excavated and consecrated, the kind you build underground for special occasions.

While other priests were just beginning to wage a battle with their municipality in order to get a house for their deacons, our priest already had four such houses built. One he gave to his deacons, the other was used to conduct religious classes, the third had been converted to an orphanage and the fourth became a hospice for old women. Every house had antique furniture, eighteenth-century armchairs, marble floors and crystal chandeliers. He felt that while people admired the fruits of human labor, they might also think of the beauty of the Lord's world and, sooner or later, they might even give some thought to the Creator as well.

Once he figured out what to use those houses for, our priest bought three shops, all of them of a religious nature, of course. One sold vestments, the other church literature and the third soy products, to be used during greater and lesser fasts. Once he sorted out his stores, the priest bought a stable, so that he could offer sleigh rides to visitors during church holidays, to make sure they didn't get bored and didn't start bickering with one another. The stable came with an amusement park. In a short order, he had a miniature Disneyland built, with Russian Orthodox saints instead of Mickey Mouse and Donald Duck.

Once he finished the Disneyland, he began building a Russian Orthodox pool, so that he could take a dip after conducting an exhausting service during Lent, or else after a horseback ride or a visit to the amusement park. When the pool was finished, he had a sauna built next to it, as well. And, given that he now had a sauna, he felt he needed a Russian Orthodox sports center. And a sports center naturally required gym equipment. With exercise equipment in place, there was a need for a Russian Orthodox hotel, complete with a conference center. That was because there was now no end of visitors from abroad, eager to learn from the priest how to run an Orthodox parish pastorally. Having had a hotel built, he really needed a Russian Orthodox airport. Once the airport was completed, and a few dozen charter flights were shuttling about, connecting it with 26 countries around the world, naturally there was a need for a small Russian Orthodox airplane of his own, as well as a modest helicopter, of course, to be able to inspect his properties and give rides to visitors.

However, if truth be told, some visitors got air sick. To accommodate those in the spirit of altruism, the priest had a small canal dug, connecting to the Moscow River, with special pilgrimage cruises run by a special Russian Orthodox river fleet. But traveling by water turned out to be too slow. There was nothing to be done but to build a Russian Orthodox railroad. The railroad had to be guarded against bandits and other undesirables, and so the need arose for a special Russian Orthodox Armed Forces, complete with their own gonfalons, banners, a choir, and other requisite props.

The priest eventually realized that now it was time for him to become the Russian Orthodox President. He thought it over but decided against it. If he were to become President, he would no longer have time to conduct services. After all, he was still a cleric, in the rite of Melchizedek. And so he remained a priest, having decided against becoming President.

A Visit From God

There was once a priest who was very poor. He was a third cleric at a parish outside Moscow, a position that provided only a tiny income. If any money came to them, the head priest at the parish took it, and if a believer paid any of the priests to say a special prayer, the head priest demanded a kickback. As a result, the third cleric's kids wore second-hand clothes, his wife shivered all winter in a fall jacket, and the priest had to get around on foot in the dead of winter, ministering to his flock, wearing nothing but a threadbare coat and carrying an scuffed old briefcase. In short, he lived in poverty.

But then, the priest had a blessed visit. An old school friend of his, Yasha Sokolov, came to see him.

"I want you to bless my house," he told the priest. "Trust me, I'll pay you well."

The head priest happened to be away that day and thus would know nothing about it. They got into Yasha's very nice car and set off. Suddenly, they came upon a castle. It had everything a castle was supposed to have, complete with towers, balconies and weathervanes.

"This is my house," said Yasha.

They went into the house and the priest saw that everything was made of pure gold. The chandeliers, the tables and the chairs were of pure gold. The doorknobs were all inlaid with emeralds and pearls. The priest was very surprised to see such splendor, but nevertheless he began to bless the castle. When he finished, Yasha clapped his hands and a table appeared out of a wall, laid with exotic dishes, imported wines and cakes. He clapped his hands again and many people came in, broad-shouldered young men and beautifully dressed young women.

"These are my friends," Yasha explained and invited everyone to join him at the table. The priest didn't know the names of many of the dishes, and he didn't even get to taste many of them, because he soon ran out of room in his stomach.

After a while, the priest saw that Yasha became more relaxed as he kept filling his own glass and pouring more wine for the priest. The priest asked him, "What kind of work do you do, Yasha?"

Yasha burst out laughing and he kept laughing for a long time.

"We are not allowed to work," he said. "It's beneath our dignity. Do you get my drift now, what kind of people we are?"

"No, not really," replied the priest.

"We're gangsters. Got it?"

"I do now," the priest replied, full of fear.

"Don't be frightened. We won't harm you. You're my buddy and, besides, you could be useful to us."

Yasha paid the priest very generously, motioned to invisible servants and they took him home.

After that evening, the priest got to be in great demand. He performed weddings for Yasha's friends, baptized their kids, blessed their castles and even performed extreme unction for some who got wounded in gangland disputes. In short, the priest's life started to improve. He built a new house, bought nice clothes for his wife, sent his kids to a private school, since there was no reason at all why they shouldn't get a good education, and bought a new Skoda. (He chose a white one, which seemed more modest, since the head priest drove a Zhiguli.) However, soon thereafter the head priest was dismissed and the former third cleric became the new head priest at the parish. But, God be my witness, he had not sought that position. It happened all by itself.

As to the gangsters, what of it? Are they not human beings, too? It would be a sin to cut them off from the Lord's grace. Who knows, they might one day repent, like the thief who was crucified with Jesus.

Till we meet in heaven, then.

On the Value of Psychology

Max (a.k.a. Skripa) was not only a highly skilled city pickpocket, but a great student of human psychology. He was especially good with women. He could tell right away, by observing the batting of the eyelashes, the chance smile flitting over the face, or the sudden wrinkle appearing between the eyebrows, whether to swoop in for a kill – inserting his fingers into a pocket or slashing a pocketbook – or whether to wait. He reached such heights of perfection that he not only was able to identify the person in a crowd whose thoughts had drifted far away and who was completely defenseless against his thieving arts, but to recognize those who would forgive him when they discovered their loss. Such people were few in number, but they did exist. On a bet with his fellow criminals, Max played a trick on a number of occasions. He would identify such a forgiving soul and deliberately pull out her wallet crudely, getting himself caught in the act. Time and again, the victim, whom Max had unerringly selected, would not raise the alarm but whisper frantically – not out of fear but out of pity for him, begging him to return the money. Max would return the loot, but he would also smile inwardly and wonder.

Max never got caught, which eventually stood him in good stead. Because by the time he turned 35 he somehow grew horribly disenchanted with his work. By then, he was no longer hustling in the crowd, but controlled one of the city's markets and lived high on the hog. Still, he grew tired and unhappy.

He decided to take up a sport. When he was young, he had spent several years learning karate. At the fitness club he met a man, a wresting coach, who turned out to be a believer. Having thrown Max down onto his backside within 12 seconds, he would then explain to him that victory required not so much great skill as the right inner state. What kind of state, you ask? It's very simple. The most important thing is not to be aggressive.

Over time, Max began to attend not only the fitness club but the church, as well. He read books and tried to understand religion. In the end, he went to confession and repented.

Today, Father Maxim's church is the richest one in the city. First of all, wise guys prefer one of their own as their preacher and come to him in droves, leaving huge alms and solving all the problems the church has with the municipal government. They have even set up a fund to assist prison inmates. But, second, there is the psychology. Whenever a woman comes to see him, before she even opens her mouth, the pastor starts to talk to her about her problems. How her husband, her mother-in-law, her kids or her boss treat her poorly. When they hear this, his visitors become speechless with surprise, so that Father Maxim doesn't even have to tell them how to deal with their problems or offer any sort of advice. What advice could he give them, after all, except to counsel patience and prayer? But that doesn't matter. The most important thing is that the women feel that they have finally found a person who understands them. They leave his church feeling completely comforted.

Thus does Father Maxim have a reputation among the believers as a holy man and a seer, one who has a gift for converting thieves and dispelling women's sorrows.

The Hapless One

There was once a priest who didn't know how to do anything. He didn't know how to fix his church building, and for more than four years his church had been covered in scaffolding. He didn't know how to sell books – how to find the right vending points and start a book-selling business.

He also had no idea how to get a house for his deacons built or even get a classroom for Sunday School classes. He lacked useful connections, didn't have rich sponsors and couldn't boast of hundreds – or even dozens– of devoted followers. He did not own either a car or a cell phone, and not even a computer. He didn't have an email account, nor did he own a pager. He had been born without a gift for debating, a gift for working miracles, or a gift for leading a beautiful service. He conducted services in a soft voice, so that those who stood far away heard nothing. What he lacked completely was a gift for making speeches. He mumbled his sermons and repeated the same thing over and over again. His wife was as good as absent, too, even though he was married. They had no children.

The priest lived like that and eventually died. His funeral service was held on a dim November day, and when the parishioners, according to custom, picked up the candles, the candles lit themselves, filling the church with a heavenly light.

Divine Care

It was said of Father Joannicus that his gift was to get people to confess their sins thoroughly. After going to Father Joannicus for confession, one felt as though one had been to a steam bath, coming out all steamed up and thoroughly cleansed. People signed up to go to confession to him 24 business days in advance.

Varvara Petrovna signed up early, too, but she still had to wait in line and got her turn dead last, at five o'clock in the morning.

Father Joannicus began by asking her a number of questions. Did she spend too much time doing laundry? Had she ever thrown away any food? Any soup, for instance? Any hot cereal? Tangerines?

Beets, perhaps? Poultry? If not poultry, then red meat? What about radishes? Had she ever worked on Sundays? What was it exactly that she had done? Had she washed the floors? Had she ironed? Had she dusted? Did she clean her ears? Had she ever committed sodomy? Did she masturbate? Had she ever eaten in secret during Lent or between meals? Did she suffer from an uncontrolled shopping mania?

The confession went on for two hours, until the matins. Late in the morning, Varvara Petrovna came home, opened the gas burners without lighting a match and lay on the couch without removing her overcoat. However, her husband came back unexpectedly. He had left some important documents at home and had returned to pick them up. He used his own key to open the front door. He shut down all the burners, poured out the holy water from all the jars and threw into the incinerator the chip from the Oak of Mamre, the petrified piece of prosphora from the relics of Holy Martyr Saint Barbara, and one other thing which had a fuzz of mildew growing over it. He broke all the candles, kissed Varvara Pavlovna on her pale forehead and said very slowly, "If you ever set foot there again, I'm going to kill you myself."

Brothers and Sisters. Had her husband not left his documents at home, Varvara Petrovna would have gone straight to Hell. Let us give our thanks to the Lord for his holy loving kindness and the care He always bestows upon us, miserable sinners.

The Abstinent

There once lived a priest who was a cannibal. A person would go to confession and never come home. Or a young couple would come to get married and disappear forever. Or a baby would be brought in to be baptized and both the baby and the godparents would disappear. The answer was simple: the priest ate them all. Only during fasts was all well. People came to confession, got baptized or got their extreme unction administered without ever disappearing. In the Diocese, his dean, of course, knew all about his peculiarness, but used to say that he had no one to replace him. Besides, he was extremely strict when it came to keeping the fast.

A Healing

There once was a woman who fell ill. She went to a priest. Her pastor said to her, "Your illness is not fatal. Pray to Saint Panteleimon the Martyr, drink holy water every morning and, with God's help, you'll get better."

The patient did as she had been told, took home a two-liter jar of the healing beverage and began to drink it and apply it to those parts of her body that ached. But she kept getting worse. Then the pastor suggested that she apply the Jerusalem ointment, which one of the faithful brought back for him every year. The patient began to anoint herself with oil from Jerusalem. She got a little better after that, but did not recover fully. The priest instructed the woman to say forty prayers to saints who had taken the vow of poverty, and to the healers Cosmas and Damian, at the rate of one prayer per day. All went well for a while, but on the day of her thirty-fifth prayer the woman died. The cause of death was rampant cancer in her right lung. A doctor would not have been able to help her in any case. It had been too late. This way, the poor woman at least had time to pray and readied herself to meet her Lord.

A Dialogue on the Uses of Patience for a Lost Soul

"Father, I have a bad headache."

"Patience is a great virtue."

"Father, look, they cut off my leg."

"Patience is a great virtue."

"Father, they cut off my right hand."

"Patience is a great virtue."

"Father, they have crushed the fingers on my left hand."

"Patience is a great virtue."

"They gouged out my eyes."

"Patience is a great virtue."

"They tore out my nostrils."

"Patience is a great virtue."

"Father, they are beheading me!"

"Well that, perhaps, is a bit much."

A head, bouncing off the ground, "Why?"

The priest, "Who will be left to exercise patience?"

Cockadoodledoo

Novice Andrei decided he was a holy fool. He began to speak in the tongues of beasts and birds.

When the abbot passed by, Andrei said to him, "Moo."

When the dean went by, Andrei said, "Baah,"

He said to the cook, "Oink."

He said to the choirmaster, "Meow."

In other words, he managed to annoy everyone. He stopped attending to his chores and didn't want to listen to the voice of reason, responding to everything with mooing, riveting, honking and rooster calls. At first, everyone endured this behavior in silence, sighing and thinking that he might indeed be a holy fool. A holy fool is dear to the Lord's heart. Sometimes he even managed to be funny, providing some comic relief for the otherwise difficult life of the monastery. But eventually the Father Superior grew tired of the joke. He gave Andrei a daily chore beyond the monastery walls: he was required to travel to the orphanage in a nearby town and teach the kids various animal calls.

The Ascetic

There once was a young man who decided to emulate the church fathers of old. He found some old rusty nails in a shed, fastened them together, fashioning shackles for himself, which caused him horrible pain, scratching his flesh till it bled. Two weeks later, the young man was rushed to the hospital with blood poisoning and it was a miracle he didn't die. Since then he has stopped wearing the shackles and every time he looks at the scars that the nails left on his body he says to himself, "Here, you imbecile, are the fruits of your stupidity."

A House in the County

Misha Petrov wanted to experience the bliss of Jesus' Prayer. He decided to go somewhere very far away, where there would be no friends nearby, no telephone and no e-mail. Day and night he would pray, sleep very little and partake of almost no food, just water and a crust of dry bread, while reading the sacred texts.

He had pondered for a long time whether or not to take his cell phone along. After all, he would be far away from civilization. At last he realized that there would be no roaming in the wilderness, so he decided to leave his cell phone at home.

Final exams at his college were over and he would be able to do his internship in September. Misha decided to withdraw to the house in the country. They had bought it the year before from an old woman, on a wager during a school trip to study local dialects. They had paid her 4,000 rubles, which they had collected from other students in their group. In the event, Misha and three of his friends ended up winning the bet and got ten bottles of beer from the girls. The house had belonged to the old woman's late sister. The old woman had been quite happy to get those few thousand rubles. She had promised to look after the house and so on.

Misha told his parents and his friends – the co-owners of the house, that he was going to inspect their property. He didn't say a word about the prayers. His friends were very glad, but none wanted to go along with Misha. They all had other plans.

Misha traveled for two and a half days and finally arrived in Osanovo. That was the name of the village where they had bought their house. He knocked at the door of the old woman who had sold them the house. She had a somewhat literary name, Agafia Tikhonovna[1], but she was nonetheless a true Siberian peasant,

---

1. The name is of the heroine in Nikolai Gogol's story "Marriage."

someone who seemed to have come straight from the pages of a book by Valentin Rasputin.

"Good day," Misha said to her. "How is our little fairy-tale house doing? It has not burned down yet, I trust?"

"Are you kidding?" Agafia Tikhonovna replied angrily. "Of course it is still there."

They went to the other side of the village to look at the house. The house was indeed there, but to Misha it seemed a little smaller than the year before, and a bit more meager. But otherwise it was no different than before. The old woman opened the door and Misha entered. It smelled of the herbs that had been hanging in bunches by the entrance for God knows how many years.

The house was a little dark, but it was inhabitable. The old woman went away and Misha threw down his knapsack, looked around, found a bucket and some rags, got some water from the well and washed the windows. It got much lighter inside the house. Then Misha hung the icons on the wall so that he could pray to them. Next to them he set down a stack of sacred texts and picked up the prayer beads. But then he suddenly realized he was hungry. It was no good to pray on an empty stomach.

He got out the provisions he had brought from Moscow: canned food, sugar, salt and cucumbers, but he saw that he had no bread.

He went to the local store to buy some bread. This was capitalism for you. The year before, there had been no store in the village at all. And look at it now: a brick building, the shelves were neat and tidy and the store carried everything you'd ever need. Even Coca-Cola and Snickers. He bought both, as well as some bread.

Agafia Tikhonovna also came into the store, looking for Misha.

"Come to see me," she said. "I'll give you some potatoes. Last year's crop, as large as a man's fist."

The potatoes were indeed as big as she had described them. On top of that, Agafia Tikhonovna added three eggs, laid by her own hens. At the same time, Maria Yegorovna, a neighbor, came over to visit Tikhonovna and invited Misha over to her house. Misha went with her and Yegorovna gave him a jar of milk from her cow and invited him to stop in and visit her again.

Misha placed his treasures, the bread and the potatoes, on an unpainted wooden table, poured some warm new milk into a metal jug and fried up some eggs, which had abnormally yellow yolks. The house was full of the smell of herbs and, strange as it might seem, completely free of flies.

Misha sat down and said to himself, "My God, how wonderful. I have icons hanging on the wall and sacred texts spread all around. What else would a man need? Let me start by reciting some prayers. From now on, I'm not going to set foot outside. Going out is a distraction."

However, after eating his supper, Misha unpacked his sleeping bag, spread it directly on the floor and fell fast asleep.

He woke up in the morning and felt a pang of conscience. He had spent an entire day eating and sleeping and he had neglected the Lord's Prayer, which was the main reason he had come here in the first place.

However, he could no longer find his string of prayer beads. The day before, it had bothered him to hold them and, besides, he had been embarrassed to go outside with them. He had put them down somewhere before going to the store and could no longer remember where. After searching for a long while, he found them in the entryway, hanging on a nail, having forgotten that he had hung them there. Finally, he knelt before the icons, lit a little oil lamp and settled down. Suddenly, the sky grew dark and it began to pour. Soon, a dark stain appeared on the ceiling and began to spread right over the icons. The roof had a leak and the water was seeping in.

The moment the rain stopped, Misha climbed up on the roof. He barely made it, because one of the boards on the stepladder broke. The roof was completely rotten.

There were also plenty of other things to do. Even though Misha had grown up in a family of intellectuals, he turned down no request and was happy to do the work, assiduously helping the old ladies and taking care of his own property, growing into the role of a true proprietor of his land. A salt-of-the-earth type, like Leo Tolstoy in his later years.

And what about the prayers? Well, everything worked out beautifully in any case. Misha returned tan and a bit thicker about the waist. Agafia Tikhonovna and Maria Yegorovna fed him well.

The Specialist

Once upon a time there lived a specialist in the Russian Orthodox makeover. He did well, because he was never short of clients. Most of his clients were women. They arrived in droves to his modest hut in a village outside Moscow, coming from the four corners of the land of the Rus and begging him to do one thing, "Kind man, please turn me into a real Russian Orthodox. Don't overdo it, though. Do me just right, not too much of an Orthodox and not too little.

"Don't you worry about a thing, Madam," the Specialist would politely respond. "I do a seamless job." Donning his black leather apron, he set about his work. He worked quickly and skillfully, and usually completed the makeover in just a few hours.

He always began with the voice. He implanted an iron throat into his client to make her speak in a soft, strained voice, which was meant not to be really strained but *constrained* by patience. Then he turned his attention to the eyes. He used a pipette to drip a special solution into his client's eyes that clouded her shine. Very lightly, however, so that her eyes looked forever sad, attaining that special expression of secret reproach. Those who asked for it got a bit of a squint. But it was, in reality, neither a reproach nor a squint, but an awareness of one's own sinful nature.

From there the Specialist shifted his attention to the lips. He made injections in the corners of his client's mouth, one on each side, and she was no longer able to smile. Jesus never laughed, after all, and He probably never even smiled. His followers must do likewise. That was how the Specialist explained this procedure.

The right complexion came next. He used a special green facial cream, made with various medicinal herbs, which would get under the skin so deeply that it would stay there for many years. It made the skin sallow, and its hue gave a hint of the secret mortification of the flesh.

Then the Specialist went on to the walk and posture, and after a brief massage session, his client began to walk slowly and with a rather shuffling gait. She hung her head low, so that her sad, clouded and reproachful eyes not only squinted but were downcast as well.

All that remained to be done was for the Specialist to give each of his clients a special kerchief. Once she placed it on her head or tied it around her neck, any clothes she wore lost their shape and began to look exceedingly dour.

The job was finished.

The clients paid the Specialist as much as they could, but usually they rewarded him generously. Country women brought things from their vegetable gardens, as well as eggs, whereas big city ladies (they were in the majority) supplemented the monetary payment with expensive cognacs or whiskeys. In other words, the Specialist wanted for nothing, whereas his clients returned home brimming with genuine Orthodox joy.

The Orthodox Specialist got to be very good by practicing on women, and he got used to working on them. That was the reason why he was a bit at a loss whenever he had a male client, even though he was good at hiding his unease. He used the same tools: the little hammer, the pipette and the face cream. Nevertheless, the men didn't always come out quite as well, and they always acquired some sort of ineradicable femininity – like the ideal eternal feminine – in their eyes and in their look in general. They had long hair, a wandering eye and no willpower. Some even developed a stammer. Perhaps he got his powders mixed up, or wasn't diligent enough, or else he used women's remedies for men. Who knows? Be that as it may, the sickly look, the shuffling gait and the morbid unfocused stare were all typical of his men.

Some parents brought their kids to see the Specialist. But the kids were bad candidates for a makeover. All that happened after a session with him was they became nervous and pale, and some resisted the makeover completely. At last, the Specialist had to ban all children. They had to wait in the corridor for their mothers to be done.

"But what about my heart?" the most advanced of his clients used to ask the Specialist. "The inner self is more important than the outward appearance. Can you make my heart Orthodox, too?"

"I can't change your heart," the Specialist would reply honestly. "Otherwise, the Kingdom of God would have long ago been established on Earth. And such is not part of the Divine Plan."

When he wasn't working, the Master loved leafing through the Book of Revelations by John the Theologian. He was especially fascinated by the descriptions of various wondrous Apocalyptic beasts.

Third Cycle

A Good Man

The Most Important Thing

1 There once was a priest who was a drunk. When not on a bender, he liked to smoke dope.

But who cares? The most important thing is that he was a good man.

2 There once was a priest who did not believe in God. He did everything by the book and was extremely zealous, but he still did not believe in God. Everybody knew this, but they forgave him his small weakness. Like in the old days, a communist didn't necessarily have to believe in communism. That priest was the same way.

The most important thing is that he was a good man.

3 There once was a priest who was a kleptomaniac. He stole gold crosses from the church and even ten-ruble notes from the deacon's pocket. Everybody knew this, but they understood that it was an illness. The most important thing was that he was a good man. The priest appreciated that people trusted him, and whenever the pile of pilfered property at his house got too large, he put it all in a large bag and distributed it as alms to beggars in the vestibule of his church. That's a good man for you.

4 There was once a priest who hated gays. Even more he hated it when people said about priests, monks or even clerics higher up in the hierarchy of the Church, that they were all like that in their monasteries. When he heard something like that, his face would grow dark and he would look the person straight in the eye and say very sternly, "There are no gay priests."

Then he would get up, leave the room, suppress a nervous tic and take his heart medicine.

But why bother about that? Who cares whether a priest is gay or sad. The most important thing is that he be a good man.

5 There once was a priest who loved women. He loved to watch beautiful women and admired the occasional lock of hair that sometimes came free of their kerchief and the sad female eyes that stared at him during confessions, filling with such pure tears. He would fall in love with every decent looking member of the congregation.

He used to say to himself, "I wish I could marry this one."

However, he never got married to any of them and lived with his own God-given wife. He fixed bathroom faucets, hammered in nails when required, picked up his kids from school and led services, of course. That was the most important thing.

6 There was once a priest who hated all people. He didn't get to be that way all at once. At first he loved everyone. Then he stopped loving people and began to feel disdain for them. He who has lived and reasoned, will in his heart hold humans in disdain, to quote Pushkin. He hated them because there were so many people, more and more each year. First, those overheated faceless crowds kept breathing. Second, they pushed and shoved and tried to get ahead, clinking empty jars they had brought with them to fill with holy water, and they stuck palm leaves into his face to make sure he sprinkled holy water over them properly. Third, they asked stupid questions and at confessions bored him with tales of bad husbands and mothers-in-law and demanded advice which they never acted upon, anyway. Fourth, they believed in the evil eye. Fifth, they brought their loudly screaming grandchildren to take communion, on the advice of some old hag doing sorcery on the side. At high holidays, the priest even tried to lead services with his eyes closed. He feared that if he opened them, his hatred would turn them all to ash. Nevertheless, he was a good man and in the company of his friends and family he was actually sweet and kind. He was a little irritable, that's all. But an excellent man for all that. In Sunday School, he made kites for the kids.

7 There once was a priest who couldn't stand Jews. Wherever he looked, he could see that they lorded over ordinary Russians. The movies were made by Jews. All the books were written by Jews. As to music – forget about it. Everywhere he looked, there were those insolent, big-nosed kike faces. Their synagogues were never enough for them. They even managed to sneak into Russian Orthodox churches and push real Russians out.

The priest shared his outrage with his congregation and his congregation paid him very close attention, whereas the kikes naturally wanted to have nothing to do with him.

Time passed. The priest made no secret of his views but, of course, he wasn't disqualified from leading a congregation. He was widely respected because he had served as a priest at his church for many years and because he had rebuilt his church from virtual ruin, setting up a nursing station and visiting jails. Every now and again the priest got various church honors and, to mark the thirtieth anniversary of his ordination, the Patriarch paid him a personal visit.

There was one dark cloud over the priest's life. His beloved only daughter seemed sure to remain a spinster. She didn't like any of her suitors, whereas the men she did like didn't like her. The priest had no male heirs, and he had hoped to at least have a grandson to carry on his life's work. But forget about grandchildren. The daughter turned 27 years of age, then 28 and finally 29. Then, suddenly, she found a fiancé. A true Russian hero, broad-shouldered, tall, with thick black curls and blue eyes. A very hard worker, too. He even owned a car. And, most important, he was madly in love with the priest's daughter. She too, was quite smitten with him, of course.

In the fullness of time, the fiancé came to pay a visit to the priest and asked him for his daughter's hand in marriage. It was a very old-fashioned scene. He wore a tie and was holding a bouquet of red roses in his hand.

The girl's parents were falling all over themselves trying to please him. The priest's wife placed delicacies in front of him, the priest carried on a learned conversation and their daughter sat at the table half-dead with fear and not moving a muscle. Finally, they all shook hands, set the date for the wedding and discussed various practical matters.

The fiancé had put on his coat and was already standing in the doorway when he suddenly said, "Yes, by the way. My mother is Jewish and my father is Russian. I look like my father and my last name is Russian, but my Mom is Jewish. I'm telling you this just in case."

Having said that, he turned around and left.

But in the priest's house all hell broke loose. The priest shouted and stomped his feet. His daughter broke down and cried. Her mother shuttled back and forth between the two of them, applying a wet towel to their foreheads.

Dear reader, you may have guessed what came next, didn't you? The priest spent the entire night praying to the icons in white robes fringed with lace, asking the Lord for advice. In the morning, his face pale and drawn, he called his daughter to the kitchen, hugged her and said, "My dear daughter. Your happiness is most important to me. The most important thing is that he is a good man."

The wedding went ahead and no one ever had an occasion to regret it. Such amazing miracles happen sometimes.

Father Nicholas

1 Father Nicholas lived on an island. Visitors reached him by taking the train to Pskov, then a bus to a nearby village and, once there, going on foot three more kilometers. From there, they took a motor boat or a cutter. In winter, they walked over the frozen surface of the lake or rode in a special car that didn't slide on the ice. The setting sun reflected in the ice.

While traveling, the visitors kept repeating to themselves, "I'm about to see a great holy man. He will explain everything to me."

However, Father Nicholas greeted them all by saying, "Why did you come? I have nothing to tell you."

2 He was a very old, thin man. Only his hands were strong. Father Nicholas used them to hit all stupid and disobedient people on the forehead. He sang in a clear and loud voice, which was like the voice of a young man. His father was a choirmaster at a church, and the holy man loved religious singing.

3 In early fall, when all the visitors had gone away, a silence would settle over the island. Cows lay on the sand and stared into the gray water. Black fishing boats bobbed upon the water and seagulls shrieked in the sky. Large boulders lay along the shore. The largest was called the Lithuanian's Stone. Nobody knew for sure why, but some claimed that at one point Lithuanians used to live on the island. Father Nicholas would show the stone to everyone who came to see him on the island.

4 One day a group of students came to see Father Nicholas. Pasha Andreyev wanted to ask his advice whether or not to get married. But the conversation stayed on general topics and there was no opportunity for him to raise the issue of his marriage. The students asked the holy man various spiritual questions, and he gave them his opinion. At last they began to bid their farewells, and Pasha was in despair. Suddenly, Father Nicholas leaned over toward him and said softly, "Of course you should get married."

5 Once Father Nicholas said to a young man, "You will become a Metropolitan."

The young man got married, had a family, became a priest and soon thereafter the head priest at a large Moscow congregation. Then he was promoted to archpriest. He got various awards and kept rising in the Orthodox hierarchy. But he never did become a Metropolitan.

6 Father Nicholas never said anything about Kostya Trudolyubov's future and displayed none of his gift of clairvoyance with regard to Kostya, even though Kostya came to see him often. Only once did he look at Kostya closely and, patting him on the cheek softly, said kindly, "So, you want to be a modern man?"

Four years later, Kostya stopped going to church, took to drink and started to change girlfriends frequently. He developed the special kind of laugh that was a sure sign of an inveterate marijuana user. He still remembered Father Nicholas and revered him, but he stopped going to see him. But then again, Father Nicholas received almost no visitors in his later years.

7 Katya Yakobinets had wanted to be a nun ever since she was 15 years old. She studied at a music school but spent all her free time attending religious services. She loved to pray and loved Abba Dorotheus the Hermit. When she graduated from the music school, she became the choirmaster of the Convent of the Virginal Conception. Every once in a while she would not go home but spend the night at the convent. The Mother Superior gave her a special cell, because she appreciated good singing but did not want to rush Katya's decision. Katya had a tailor make her two black habits, bought a black kerchief and walked around with prayer beads, eyes downcast. Taking the veil became a foregone conclusion.

Naturally, Katya's parents were horrified. But there was nothing they could do about it. It was the result of an atheistic upbringing. All that was left to do was to obtain a blessing from a holy man. Katya set out for the Zalit Island.

Everything worked out very well. Making the connection between the train and the motorboat went smoothly and the boat brought her to the island. No doubt, Father Nicholas had interceded on her behalf. At the church, Katya was told that Father Nicholas had already begun seeing his visitors and that she was to go directly to his house. Katya easily found his house and joined a short queue of Father Nicholas' visitors. Each one went in to see him in turn, asked him questions and got a brief answer from the holy man.

Soon came Katya's turn.

"Father, I want to join a convent," said Katya. "I have come to ask for your blessing."

Father Nicholas said nothing.

"I have not yet decided which convent to join," continued Katya. "I have even been invited to join the Novo-Diveyevo Convent in America."

"America is far away," said the reverend father with a smile. "There are plenty of good convents here. The best one is at Mount Athos."[1]

"Father, but there–" Katya objected.

"To Mount Athos with you," repeated the holy man firmly and, having given Katya his blessing, sent her away."

Katya cried during the entire journey home. When she got back, she hung her black habit in the closet, left her black kerchief folded on a shelf and soon found other things to do instead of leading the choir at the convent. A year later, she got married and had children. It is no longer possible to look at her with a naked eye: her face now positively glows with happiness.

8 Father Nicholas loved to read poetry. Whenever he discovered that a visitor was a student of philology, he declared, "Always remember: An I before an E except after a C."

Some philologists were puzzled by this little statement of his and tried to uncover its secret meaning. Could those letters be the first initials of their friends' names? Or were the letters symbols for Life,

---

1. On Mount Athos, there are only monasteries (for men) and no convents (for women).

Love and the Lord, and the holy man meant that their order could not be changed except by Divine Intervention?

Those were the kinds of thoughts that rushed through philologists' heads, and one of them even noted that sentence down in a notebook and decided to write a learned article about it. But then it dawned on him that it was just a grammar rule, and that someone had invented a simple way to memorize it.

In his previous, worldly life, Father Nicholas had been a schoolteacher.

9 The reverend father often repeated, "He who does not recognize the Church as his Mother, does not have the Lord as his Father.

10 At the end of each conversation, he used to say, "Remember me in your prayers. My name is Nicholas."

11 For many years, Zalit Island was home not only to Father Nicholas, but to Grandma Dunya. Father Nicholas sent his visitors to her and she put them up for the night. Everyone was welcome. Grandma Dunya was short and stout. She wore a green woolen kerchief slightly askew and had clear, bright eyes. Her son had drowned and her husband had been killed in the war. Her two grown daughters visited her often and looked after her. She was well cared for.

One day Grandma Dunya had to have a major surgery. On that occasion, Father Nicholas opened the altar and prayed at the church. When after the surgery Grandma Dunya was taken to a recovery room on a white gurney, the patients and personnel came out into the hall to greet her, because they had all come to know her and had grown fond of her.

Before the surgery, Grandma Dunya had a dream. She dreamed that she was in a church, and next to her stood a long-deceased relative as well as many other people. The people were pushing toward the altar and Granma Dunya wanted to get there along with the rest of them. But her dead relative said to her, "Stand here. Don't go anywhere."

That was when Grandma Dunya woke up. Later, she realized that those who had been pushing toward the altar were the dead, or at least about to die, and that her time hadn't come yet.

The surgery was successful, all the more so since Father Nicholas had been praying for her. Grandma Dunya told everyone about him.

"Our priest is a holy elder," she repeated solemnly time and time again.

Before going to bed, she always lit up an icon lamp, bowed and then blew out the light. That was her way of praying. Grandma Dunya always fed those who came to stay with her, put them up for the night and in the morning went to see them off, waving goodbye to them from the pier. That's all. End of story.

12 Once, during a winter break, three philology students came to see Father Nicholas. Three young women.

"Thank God you didn't drown," said Father Nicholas and made a sign of the cross.

The young women had walked across the frozen lake, on ice which had large cracks in it. They had been very scared. A small reddish dog had trailed them part of the way, whining all the while, but it had become too frightened and had turned back.

The reverend father took the young women to the church and told them to bow three times to the Heavenly Queen. When he found out that all three were studying philology, he got very excited.

"Remember then: An I before an E except after a C."

Then he told one of them what she would become, describing the two main preoccupations of her later life. He said nothing to the other two, even though both did have a future. One joined a convent and the other married a priest. But Father Nicholas only foretold the future to one of them. Everything he said came true. Every last one of his words turned out to be true. But why he chose her nobody knows. Perhaps because she was the most restless. Her last name was Kucherskaya.

13 Once, Father Nicholas said sadly, "I'm about to leave you."

Everyone was thunderstruck and was unable to breath from sorrow.

"But perhaps not forever," the pastor added with a smile.

14

My life has passed like a day flown by
My life vanishes like a puff of smoke
Death's door and its unbearable weight
Are ever nearer –

This was the poem Father Nicholas recited to all who came to see him. They all imagined that the reverend father was presciently foretelling his imminent demise. But years went by and the pastor went on living. Still, he kept reciting the poem. He used to say that he would live to be 104, but he died at 93. On the eve of his birthday, Father Nicholas took a bath, dressed in a priest's cassock, lay down with a cross in his hands and expired.

Father Tikhon

1 Once upon a time a boy was born in a village. His father was a blacksmith, his mother was a peasant. While growing up, he looked after the chickens, plowed, sowed and watched his father strike white-hot iron, but most of all he loved playing church. He would take a wooden bowl, tie it to a string, fill it with pebbles and pretend to smoke incense all around the house. Eventually, the boy grew up, went to school (he loved learning) and became a teacher. He taught physics and math at school and the kids liked him, but they were not crazy about him. They were more fond of their PE teacher, who played soccer with them. Then that man of ours got married, had a son and a daughter and became a priest. But that didn't happen all at once. By then, he was 50 years old.

Again, he did nothing special as a priest. He only went to church, conducted the requisite services, liturgy and vespers and performed funeral services and the occasional baptism. He had an infectious laugh. It was a little strange, and whoever heard him laugh always joined in and laughed along with him. The pastor had a nice way with people, and his hands had a light, sweet odor, but that was not important. He could have easily not laughed at all and his hands didn't have to smell of anything in particular. The point is that when he looked at a person, that person became extremely happy.

He had a raincoat, a hat and a pair of boots. He wore those to walk from the church to his log house. At home, he was greeted by his wife. In her old age, she sometimes repeated the same question over and over again, eleven or even sixteen times. He answered her patiently sixteen times, never getting short-tempered with her. When he was away from home, he wrote letters to her, signing them Tisha.

2 The Lord answered his prayers and worked numerous miracles. He healed some people and resolved family problems for others. Others still had their greatest wish come true. He made people forgive those against whom they had held a grudge their entire life. He did everything the typical holy elder did, but that was not what mattered.

Fourth Cycle

Readings for Those Who Despair

A Sweet Tooth

There was once a monk who fell into despair and decided to hang himself. He had grown tired of life and bored with it. He removed the light fixture from the ceiling in his cell and tested the hook, which seemed strong enough. He had rubbed soap – Wild Strawberry scented, a strong, unpleasant odor – thoroughly all over the rope, and had even begun to push the table over underneath it when he saw a candy bar on the table. It was a Stratosphere bar, his favorite, which he had liked since childhood. Its wrapper had a picture of pink rockets flying off into the blue of outer space. The candy had been distributed at the refectory after supper the night before, to mark a religious feast. He had saved his but forgotten all about it.

"Fine," he said to himself. "I should eat the candy and then I'll hang myself."

He unwrapped the candy bar and put it in his mouth. The wrapper fell down onto the floor. It would not be proper, he thought, to be hanging in his cell with a candy wrapper littering the floor. The monk bent down to pick up the wrapper and suddenly saw a piece of paper in a crack between the floor boards. It happened to be a list of names a woman had given to him the day before, asking him to pray for them. He had not said the prayers and had misplaced the list, which he had now found between the floorboards.

"Fine," he said to himself. "I'll pray for those people before I die. At least I'll have one less sin on my conscience."

He lit an icon lamp, read out each name in turn and prayed hard for each person. At that moment, the bell rang, calling monks to supper a bit earlier than usual.

In the end, the monk decided not to hang himself after all, but to go to supper. Who knows, maybe he would get another Stratosphere bar, or at least a Polar Bear bar. Sometimes the supply lasted a second day.

A Comedian

There was once a monk who suffered from depression. He fought against it every way he could, but couldn't beat it. Yet outwardly he seemed to be the happiest man alive. He told jokes and laughed all the time. Only in the final year of his life did he become sad and quiet. He no longer suffered from depression and didn't need to tell jokes. He grew weak and died. During his funeral service the church filled with a sweet odor, so that many thought that lilacs had suddenly begun to bloom. This was because Father Basil had defeated the Devil.

Triumph of Orthodoxy

In his past, worldly life, Father Anatolius had been a computer programmer. Some people even thought he was a genius.

At the friary he missed nothing so much as his beloved computer. It had a cache of favorite websites marked by bookmarks and automatically changing screensavers. He had a bubble appear on the screen during the morning boot-up that informed him of the day's weather forecast. Pechkin the Mailman popped up to announce every new email message. The computer had lots of games and other applications, and a whole lot of stuff he had collected during his student days. He left it in St. Petersburg, determined to sever all past attachments and seek salvation for his soul.

Father Anatolius – who at the time was still called Pasha – went about all the customary chores of a novice. He worked on a construction site for a new building, cut grass and chopped wood. In other words, he was mostly doing manual labor. When the trial period was over, the Father Superior, a rather kind man, looked into what else Father Anatolius was good at. He was very happy to discover his computer skills. It was in the 1990s, the time of great technological advances, and two brand-new computers had been recently donated to the monastery. But neither had been unpacked because there was no one who knew how to operate them. The Father Superior gave Father Anatolius a new chore: to load all the necessary software into the computers, to create a personal email account for the Father Superior and to build a website for the monastery. In short, Father Anatolius was tasked with doing everything that at the time was being done in every civilized country of the world, and to do it better.

Father Anatolius became very excited. He convinced the Father Superior to purchase a scanner and went on several business trips in order to get everything else necessary for new cyber-life. Soon the monastery had a modest website, updated daily and containing the news, quotations from church fathers, sermons and a growing library of sacred literature which Father Anatolius assiduously scanned into the database. The computer monk left his monitor only to attend services and partake of meals, and sometimes he even spent the night on a hard couch near his beloved hardware. He was constantly tinkering with his computer.

Soon it came out what it was he had been working on.

Suddenly, an endless procession of monks began paying him visits. Having recited their prayers and bowed to the icons as many times as was necessary, they came together in Father Anatolius' office late at night to challenge each other at a computer game. Often they stayed up until dawn – especially younger monks, of course.

Naturally, Father Anatolius had no use for your typical shooting, chomping games or Tetris. He preferred respectable games like checkers and chess but, most importantly, during his long monastic nights he created two original games as well. Those two games were the most popular among the brethren.

One was called Seven Deadly Sins.

After an opening screen with quotations from the writings of Saint John Climacus, reminding the user how to resist each of the seven sins, a thrilling journey began. The figure of a monk wearing a black cassock mounted a motorcycle and set out to resist a number of temptations, which Father Anatolius illustrated very vividly.

The first stop was Pride. (We mention this for the benefit of the reader. The game provided no clues as to what sin it was that had to be resisted.) An inscription appeared over the entrance to a medieval Gothic-style castle: What Monk Does Not Wish to Become Archbishop?

The creaking gate opened ominously, hinting at lurking danger, and obedient servants led the monk from one great hall to another, all looking like rooms at a museum. In each, an archbishop's vestments and headdresses were displayed, each more beautiful than the last. The monk was allowed to try them on in turn, but if a naive player wanted to leave the castle while still wearing a Metropolitan's mitre or – what a stupid idea! – a Patriach's tiara, disgusting demonic laughter would be heard and the vain loser would be dropped into a river of fire. Only if the player was smart enough to try the vestments on and then remove them before leaving could he get to the next level.

There, the player was tempted by all the riches of the world. He was presented with a comfortable cell, made to look like a nice house with a wooden steam bath, the smoke already curling from the chimney, bank accounts with hundreds of dollars in them, automobiles of all makes and manufacturers, and cassocks of many styles and colors.

At level three the player was tempted by almost heavenly living quarters. Each monk had a separate apartment and did whatever he wished, even ordering the Father Superior around. Only those who revealed no envy for other people's good fortune and didn't want to remain at that level got to the next one, Wrath and Irritability. There, the player was faced with all kinds of insults and bad names shining at him from the screen in bright red letters. The amazing thing was that many players failed at that level, showing themselves unable to bear what really were stupid childish insults, such as "black ass," "stinker" and "klutz," or statements such as "Who do you think you are, you idiot?" and "Do you hope to become Patriarch, moron?" which the screen kept hurling at them. The players knew, of course, that it had been Father Anatolius who came up with all those insults, and they took it personally. They grew angry with him and vengefully pressed buttons to make the appropriate rebuttal. Having thoroughly enjoyed making such replies as "Idiot yourself" or "Get lost," or even "And who do you think you are, you stupid programmer?" they went down the well-trodden path to the river of raging fire.

Those who could control themselves, went up to the next level, where a charming young woman asked them for directions, then another one requested their help changing a tire, then a third piteously implored them to give her a lift, and yet another one, who had been turned into a frog, begged them to kiss her on the mouth and break the evil spell. However, under no circumstances was the player to respond to any of the young women or frogs. Once he survived that level, the player saw a sign announcing that he had grown very hungry. At the same moment, a splendid restaurant appeared on the side of the road. It had a bar stocked with all kinds of liquor and served dishes of every imaginable cuisine of the world. But the trick was for the player to notice a humble place next to the restaurant and to go there instead. There, the starving rider got a glass of water, three dry crusts of bread and the right to go on.

Then it began to rain and the monk was forced to look for shelter, because his motorcycle couldn't ride on the rutted clay of the unpaved road. He looked around and found shelter in his own monastery, which Father Anatolius drew very realistically. The rest was very similar to a typical day at the monastery: very long services, simple meals, irritating petty quarrels with other monks and unexpected new chores. In short, it was their usual boring routine. In fact, that was exactly what it was and the player soon felt that Father Anatolius had made this part far too long. But the moment he agreed to the insidious offer to cut this part short and to go have some fun by playing a computer game, for example, you can already guess what happened to him. Of course. The river of fire awaited the sinner.

It was a very enlightening game.

For those who preferred a more simple form of entertainment, Father Anatolius designed a game called Triumph of Orthodoxy. Actually, it was an ordinary soccer game. The only difference was that one side featured bearded Russian Orthodox Fathers and the other beardless Catholic priests. The computer played for the Catholics. The game was set up in such a way that whenever our side was losing, the Catholics promptly committed a blatant foul and the referee pointed to the 11-meter penalty spot. The Orthodox side couldn't lose by definition and, of course, it always won.

Father Anatolius's popularity in the monastery grew by leaps and bounds. There was a waiting list to play his games, because he could no longer accommodate everyone who wished to play on any given night. Exhausted but happy, Father Anatolius had to catch up on his sleep in the daytime. The Father Superior tolerated it because he knew he would never again find such a highly skilled professional.

Father Anatolius's fatal mistake was to try to create a monastery version of the famous game Civilization. He almost succeeded. While putting his finishing touches on it, he carried on extensive correspondence with colleagues in Moscow and the United States, joined the Computer Genius society and subscribed to several important newsletters.

The point of Father Anatolius's new game was not to build a state, as in Civilization, but a large monastery, complete with agricultural services, buildings and monks. The player was, naturally, the Father Superior, and the computer game had to address him accordingly, as the Right Reverend Father Superior. That was when the real Father Superior told Father Anatolius to get rid of all that nonsense, as he put it, completely and forevermore. Not because the Father Superior was offended or because he had some moral purpose in mind. His reason was simple: enough is enough. The Father Superior had grown tired of his monks carrying on as though they had been afflicted with some terrible ailment, barely able to perform their daily chores after a sleepless night and in general becoming unmanageable. He paid no attention to Father Anatolius's pleas that his games were special and were good for the soul.

Father Anatolius did as he had been told. He erased both games, as well as his unfinished version of Civilization. But he wept for an entire week after destroying his life's labor and, in his distress, even contracted shingles. Then, all of a sudden, he settled down. A visitor told him in secret that his cause didn't die but was alive and well. In Moscow, at the Gorbushka market, one could easily purchase both Seven Deadly Sins and Triumph of Orthodoxy, because some sneaky hackers had long ago downloaded the games without Father Anatolius's knowledge and then copied them for public use.

When he heard that, Father Anatolius thanked the Lord more ardently perhaps than ever before. The strange thing was that after that he took absolutely no interest in computer games. It was as if he had outgrown them.

The Old Man of the Oak Tree

A young novice used to run away from the monastery. Every spring he grew unbearably homesick and began saving up for a train ticket. Before you knew it, he would be back home. Then, after resting there for a little while, catching up on his sleep, eating his fill and doing justice to his mother's pies, he got bored and longed to return to the monastery. There was nothing to be done. He would buy a return ticket, get back to the monastery, go on his hands and knees to the Father Superior and beg for forgiveness.

The Father Superior had a soft heart and, besides, the monastery could always use an extra pair of hands. And he had no choice, really. He gave the young man three extra chores, sending him to the kitchen to peel potatoes or to scrub the refectory, but in the end he always forgave him.

This sequence of events repeated itself several times. Finally, the young man had had enough. After bolting one last time, he came back to the monastery carrying a long thick rope. This time he didn't go to the Father Superior or to his brethren, but he went directly to the far corner of the property and tied himself to a huge old oak tree, securing the rope with a triple nautical knot.

The other monks soon saw him there and asked him to stop acting the fool. But the young man paid them no attention, remained silent and spent his days and nights tied to the oak tree, despite cold weather, rain and, some time later, snow. They tried to take him away by force, made fun of him and even called a doctor. But the young man was firm. The Father Superior only shrugged meekly and told them to leave him alone. The monastery carpenter built him a small house, where he could shelter in extreme weather. The stovemaker made a small stove for his house. The monks brought him plain meals and firewood. Even the Father Superior came to see him in his house, begging him not to torture himself, to think of his health and to go back to work at his shop, since the young man was a good carpenter.

But the young man replied, "If I untie the rope, I will surely run away again, and all the same you won't have anyone to work in the carpentry shop. Forgive, me, Father."

He lived in his little house under the oak tree for many years. Whenever his rope rotted away, he asked the monks to get him a new one. In his old age, his legs no longer served him and only then did he allow them to carry him to a cell. One night, a pair of pilgrims staying at the monastery saw a shining column rise from his cell toward the sky. That only happened once, and no other miracles followed. He had a name for himself. He called himself the Old Man of the Oak Tree.

The Tree of Knowledge

Tanya and Grisha got married the week after Easter and decided to go on a pilgrimage instead of a honeymoon. They took no extra clothing or food, only a little water and bread, planning to walk from one monastery to the next. They were going to spend the night wherever they found shelter, accepting it gratefully and eating whatever they were offered, giving thanks to the Lord.

They set out on their journey early in the morning, a day after their wedding. They traveled by suburban train for three hours, got off and began to walk. Grisha had marked the churches on the map with a cross, and monasteries with two crosses. If all went according to plan, he expected them to reach their first destination, the Monastery of the Ascension, on the first evening.

The newlyweds walked along the road, singing psalms and saying the Lord's Prayer. They rested, had a snack and set out again. By nightfall, they were very tired. Tanya was completely exhausted, and she was hungry, too, because two tiny rolls with water from a creek was not enough food for an entire day.

Tanya said to Grisha in a kind voice, "Look, there are raspberry branches hanging over the fence. Let's gather some berries. And look over there, green peas."

Grisha was also hungry. He kept silent for a while and then replied, "You're a typical woman. If you had been in Paradise, you would have acted just like Eve."

"What do you mean?" asked Tanya.

"You would have picked the fruit of the tree of knowledge and you would have eaten it."

"Me? Never. Adam blamed a woman, but it was his fault, too."

Grisha laughed sarcastically at that.

"Had the Lord forbidden me to eat the fruit, I wouldn't have ever listened to Eve."

Night fell and Tanya and Grisha came to a village.

"Nikishkino," Tanya read on the signpost.

Grisha checked his map and saw that there was no way they were going to make it to the monastery they had planned to reach that evening. Certainly not in daylight. They decided to ask someone to put them up for the night in Nikishkino.

They were turned away at two houses. At a third, an old man wearing a green flannel shirt opened the door. "Come in," he said.

Tanya and Grisha were very happy. Especially since the old man pointed at a table laden with food and invited them to eat.

He was about to go out.

"Are you not going to eat with us?" Grisha and Tanya politely asked.

"I'm going to get the chickens locked up for the night," the old man replied in a fairly friendly voice. "You stay here and eat. There is cereal, potatoes, everything. My old woman cooked up a storm and went to see our daughter at Kotomkino. I don't expect her back tonight. Make yourselves some tea. Just don't touch the aluminum pot on the window sill."

He went out.

Tanya saw a small paper icon on a wardrobe and the couple said Grace before the meal. Then they ate and the food tasted wonderful and fresh. Meanwhile, there was still no sign of the old man. They put up the tea kettle.

Tanya said, "Wouldn't it be great to have some jam-filled pies right now? My Grandma, when she baked pies, would always put them in an aluminum pot just like that.

Grisha said, "My Grandma kept *bliny* in a pot just like that. She used to wrap it in a blanket to keep them warm."

Tanya began to argue with him. "Forget the *bliny*. I'm sure there are pies in there. They are obviously poor and don't have a special dish for pies. They put them into a pot."

Grisha said, "I'm telling you it's *bliny* in there."

"Pies filled with jam," Tanya insisted.

Grisha got angry and said, "Very well then. Let's take a look."

They opened the pot and a mouse jumped out and scurried quickly under the table. At that moment the old man walked in, accompanied by a cat. The cat rubbed its side against her master's leg and meowed. It was obviously hungry. The old man went to the window, lifted the pot's lid and spread his arms wide.

"Shame on you. You've released my cat's supper."

The Very Hairs on Your Head are Numbered

Anna Trifonovna was alone in the world. She had no family and no relatives. Her husband had died long ago. Her son had died in a mountain climbing accident. She lived alone. On Sundays and on holidays she went to church. Anna Trifonovna believed in God and for whatever reason, she became more pious as she grew older. When she turned 74, she became weak but she still attended church. She worried only about being buried without a proper Christian service, like a heathen. Sure, eventually they would start worrying about her at the church and they might even figure out that she had died, mentioning her in their prayers, but she worried about setting out on her ultimate journey without a proper Christian sendoff, because her neighbors didn't care. She explained this repeatedly to everyone. She complained that she might die and be buried without anyone saying prayers over her, wiping her thin, aged tears from her eyes as she said it.

The pastor at the church that Anna Trifonovna attended, the Church of St. Nicholas the Wonderworker, said to her, "Look at the birds in the sky, they do not sow, and neither do they reap, and yet the Lord takes care of them. He will not abandon you, either. Have no fear."

But Anna Trifonovna was worried.

Time passed. One day, the body of an old man was brought to St. Nicholas's. He had not been a believer, and neither were his relatives, but being Russian, his daughters decided to have a church service for him. They thought that it might be a good thing to do and that they would get some kind of a reward for it. For instance, their health might improve, and there could be other good things, too.

The casket was delivered from the morgue. It was taken out of the van and placed upon two stools. The daughters had already started to wail loudly when the lid was opened, and—

It was a wrong body.

"This is not our father," the daughters screamed.

"This not my Grandfather," added the dead man's twenty-year-old grandson.

Indeed, there was the body of an old woman in the casket. There had been a mix-up at the morgue and a wrong body had been sent to the church. The old woman, however, was the very same Anna Trifonovna who had been so concerned about not getting a proper Christian burial. The priest recognized her at once.

Prayers were said over the old woman's body. And the old man's too, since his body was eventually delivered to the church as well.

Love

Riasophor novice[1] Andrei was raised to the second stage of monastic life with the name of Sabbas. On the eve of the ceremony he turned 26 years old. The ceremony was quiet and solemn. The candles burned brightly, the monks chanted movingly and every word reached deep into Andrei's soul, so that involuntary tears flowed down his face. Thrice the Archimadrite threw down a pair of scissors and thrice Andrei picked them up. At last, he heard his new name called, Sabbas.

Having been welcomed by his new brethren and partaken of their modest meal, the monk Sabbas headed to the church where, according to the custom of the monastery, he was to spend three days and three nights engaged in constant prayer, "as long as he could stay awake," as their Archimadrite used to say, being sensitive to the weakness of the flesh.

Father Sabbas read a prayer and bowed numerous times to the icons. Suddenly, he heard a strange sound nearby, in the church, as though there was a living creature stirring.

"Oh, Lord," he said to himself. "I'm being tempted."

He thought of Gogol's story "Vyi," but regained control of his nerves, made a sign of the cross and began to pray even more ardently. He made ten more prostrations before the icons and listened. All was quiet. He was tired and sat down on a low stool, dozing off despite himself. When he opened his eyes, it was dawn and in the far corner of the church there was the same rustling sound, as well as some strange sniffling or snorting.

---

1. This is the first grade of monastic dedication in the Church.

"But it's already morning," thought Sabbas. "Those devilish creatures should have disappeared in daylight."

Still, he was frightened.

Had the rooster crowed already? Who knows? It was so dark inside the church.

Repressing his fear, he stepped out from behind the altar and, holding a candle aloft, went over to the far corner, where there was a counter where they sold books and candles and where he thought the strange sounds were coming from.

He approached the counter and suddenly saw Father Philotheus, his Father Confessor and advisor, sleeping behind it. Father Philotheus was on his knees, leaning against a stall and sniffling like a newborn. Every now and again he made a snorting sound.

Andrei recalled that a few days before the ceremony he had complained to Father Philotheus that he feared dark, empty places and that he was apprehensive about spending a night alone in the church. At the time, Father Philotheus had reprimanded him and instructed him to fear nothing and to screw up his courage. Yet he had secretly come to support his pupil during his night prayers.

Monk Sabbas tiptoed silently back to the altar, so as not to disturb his spiritual father's sleep.

Father Paul

1. About Father Paul

Father Paul was a charmer. He often said "darn" and other unpleasant words. He liked to sing folk songs. He told funny stories about himself. He had completed, as he used to say, lower education. He had only one year of schooling, according to his arrest records. He was 85 years old. He was completely blind, his eyes having been damaged by electric light torture in 1941. He barely had the use of his legs. He had to be held up on two sides while walking. Nun Maria Petrovna, his servant, held him up on his right and a volunteer or two on the left.

"At my age, my whole body is a wreck," the old man used to say.

When people saw him, some began to cry. He didn't like it and always joked about it.

2. Mologa

Father Paul was born in the village of Mologa, on the banks of the Mologa river. The Mologa is a tributary to the Volga, and boatmen used to pulled barges up the Mologa. The village was flooded when they created the Rybinsk reservoir. Paul and his father dismantled their house, had it floated log by log down the river, and rebuilt it near the town of Tutayev. The family went on living in it.

3. Honey Joy

When he was four years old, Father Paul was sent to the St. Athanasius of Mologa Convent, to his grandmother and his aunts, who lived there as nuns. He stayed with them so as not to burden his family, which was poor. At first he did simple chores, collecting thick branches for firewood and looking after chickens, but eventually he started performing more difficult tasks.

One day Father Paul was carrying a barrel of honey from the convent's beehive. The nuns were not supposed to have any honey, but they were young and worked hard in the fields and in the garden, and they were always hungry. Still, the Mother Superior kept a strict watch over the honey and didn't allow her nuns to have any. But Father, although he was still a very little boy, already felt compassion for everyone. When he returned to the convent, he found a rat in a rat trap. He took a clean rag, wiped it on the inner walls of the barrel and smeared the honey onto the rat.

Then he ran to the mother superior.

"Reverend Mother, I don't know what to do. Look, a rat drowned in the honey," he shouted. He held up the rat by its tail, letting a clear drop of honey fall from its muzzle.

The Mother Superior was mad:

"I don't want this ratty barrel of honey anywhere near my convent. Take it wherever you like, only as far away as possible."

The nuns were very grateful to the boy and kissed and hugged him.

But that was not the end of the story.

Little Paul was ashamed of himself for deceiving the Mother Superior. He went to confession and revealed to the priest his great secret about the honey and the rat.

The priest's brow darkened.

"Paul, your sin is very grave," he said. "But if you get me a small pot of honey, God will forgive you, because you have repented sincerely and because you're kind."

Paul brought a pot of honey to the priest and felt great joy in his heart. He felt as though a heavy burden had fallen from his shoulders. The Lord had forgiven him his sin.

4. The Breadwinner

For the rest of his life, Father Paul always provided food to people. At the labor camp he was allowed to go around unguarded because his job was to check train tracks. But while he did his job, he also made sure he took a detour to the woods and gathered some wild strawberries, raspberries, rowanberries and everything else that could be eaten. He brought it back to the camp for the hungry. While in the woods, he also dug holes in the ground, lined them with clay and fired them. They were like clay pots buried in the ground, in which he marinated mushrooms to feed the inmates. Father Paul, who was still called Pasha back then, saved many people from starvation. He had known hunger first hand. When he was four, his mother used to send him to other people's houses to beg for bread, because his family was so poor. His father had been sent off to fight in World War I and his mother had been left alone with three kids. Paul was the oldest.

5. *The Father Paul Station*

When he was released from prison, Paul became a priest. He was no longer young. He spent the next 33 years as a parish priest at the Trinity Church in a rural area. People of all ranks from all over the country used to come to see him. The train station in his village was nicknamed the Father Paul Station.

The priest used to say, "It is the priest who serves the people, not the people who serve the priest. But now, all too often, it is the other way around."

6. *The Holy Spirit Divinity School*

Other priests often came to see Father Paul in order to meet a holy man in the flesh, to pray with him and to ask for his spiritual guidance. Father Paul had a powerful way of conducting services, in a deep voice, speaking directly to the Living God. He would stand in the middle of the church and declare, "I have received quite a few blows across my mug in my day."

That was his entire sermon. But the faithful and other priests, who had come to see him lead a service, had obviously expected more. When they were at a table with him, they hung on every word he said.

Father Paul used to say: "It's the Divinity School for fools."

7. *A Television Set*

When he reached the 25th anniversary of his ordination, the local government presented Father Paul with a television set.

"I shit on your TV set," Father Paul said, shrugging his shoulders.

He believed that a monk had no need for a television and used it as a night table in his cell.

8. *Monks Never Despair*

Once, Father Paul had to spend time in the hospital. He had had surgery and it had been unsuccessful. By then, Father Paul was nearly blind. He became despondent. He lay in his room, old, blind and depressed. It was the first time in his life that such a thing had happened to him. He had been tortured and beaten and starved, but he had never despaired. But now he felt despair gnawing on his soul.

All of a sudden, the doors opened and several men came into his room. They wore mantles and black cassocks.

"Look who is here to visit you," said one of them.

Father Paul raised his head and recognized all the monks he had met in jail and in the labor camp, who had been tortured to death or killed and who had been dead for many years. Such were the visitors who came to see him at the local hospital. Father Paul could see them clearly, their faces and every fold of their cassocks.

"Father Paul," one of them said. "It is not fit for a monk to fall into despair."

Then they filed out quietly. As to Father Paul, he immediately regained his spirit and never again despaired.

9. A Prix-Fixe Meal

One day, Father Paul traveled to a big city. By then he was already very old and half-blind. In the city, he co-served with a certain Metropolitan. The Metropolitan gave Father Paul money for his return trip and they took their leave of one another. There was still time left until his train and so Father Paul decided to have lunch.

He went into a restaurant. The hostess behind the counter said to him, "Pops, you had better get lost. You're not dressed correctly for this kind of place."

She had taken a look at Father Paul's feet and had noticed that he was wearing felt boots. It had been cold when he left his village, but then they had had a thaw and pools of dirty water from his boots were forming on the restaurant floor. The priest's coat was also second-hand and old, and the suitcase he was holding in his hand, which contained his vestments, was scuffed-up. The young woman had clearly taken him for some kind of vagrant. Father Paul left.

He went to another restaurant, which looked more like a cafeteria. They told him that they only served prix-fixe meals.

"I don't mind," Father Paul replied.

Father Paul left his suitcase by a table, picked up a tray and placed his prix-fixe lunch on it. The lunch consisted of soup, the main course and compote for dessert. He placed his food on a table and was about to start eating when he realized that he had forgotten to take utensils. He went back to pick up a spoon and a fork, got back to his table and saw that a stranger had already placed himself there and was eating his soup. Some prix-fixe lunch.

Father Paul sat himself down across the table from the man and, saying nothing to him, began eating his main course. He finished it and stuck the slices of bread into his pocket. The two of them shared the compote.

The man got up and headed for the door. Father Paul looked under the table and saw that his suitcase was gone. The glutton had stolen it. Not only had he eaten half his lunch, but he had pilfered his suitcase as well. Father Paul jumped from his table and started after the thief. But then he noticed his suitcase standing next to a different table. His lunch was on that table, too, completely untouched. He had made a mistake. The man was long gone.

The story gave Father Paul a headache. What a humble man that fellow had been, saying nothing even though Father Paul had eaten half of his lunch.

Fifth Cycle

Parish Stories

The Superman

There was once a parish priest who was a Superman. An old woman called him and said, "Father, I got locked out of my apartment. I left my key inside, and I have no idea what to do."

The priest went over to the old woman's place, broke down the door with a powerful kick, fixed the lock and then departed.

The next day two sisters called him. They had made their way in the world and had become successful businesswomen, but they had received a visit from gangsters who threatened to torch their business. The priest immediately set up a meeting with the gangsters, sneered at the wise guys' bulging pockets and gave them a brief talking-to. The thugs then pledged never to bother the businesswomen and the priest bade them farewell.

On the evening after a service, a mother in tears came to see him. Her son had disappeared. The fourteen year old had fallen in with a bad lot and had spent two nights away from home. The priest immediately got in touch with the appropriate authorities, chatted with the police, said a prayer and by the end of the day a policeman led the boy home by the hand.

The priest even dealt with those who were possessed by demons. One time a woman came into the church in the middle of a service and began to shriek horribly. The priest came down from the altar, took the woman by the elbow, walked her out of the church, returned to the altar and went on with the service. Another time, an old man nearly starved to death at home, because everybody had forgotten about him. But the priest remembered him and went over to give him food, and Holy Communion as well. The old man is alive to this day. Yet another man had a wife who was ill with cancer. Distressed, he decided to go to church for the first time and ran into the Superman priest. For three straight days the priest prayed for the man's wife to get better. A week later, the woman was completely healed, as if she had never been ill. The doctors yelled at her and called her a malingerer, but she got discharged from the hospital all the same and went home laughing loudly and wasn't the least bit embarrassed.

There were countless other stories like this. The priest helped one person overcome despair or saved another from imminent death. He helped numerous couples sort out their marriage problems. One day he prayed for a person and the very next morning that person was presented with keys to a three-room apartment. He prayed for another person, and she immediately found a husband. One person passed a hard exam at school while another was able to at last get pregnant. One person resolved a moral dilemma while another decided against jumping off the roof.

The priest traveled far and wide, preached, helped everyone and comforted the faithful. Twenty three years passed. Suddenly, something happened. He kept doing what he had always done – came when he was called, gave Holy Communion, etc. – but it was as if he could no longer comfort people. It was as though he had forgotten the right words to say. Even if sometimes he could remember the words and mouth them as he had done before on similar occasions, they came out lifeless. The strange thing was that his flock hardly even noticed. It was as though the grace of Holy Ordination hid it from them and the priest remained extremely popular. His church attracted large crowds, confessions went on past midnight and, in all respects, nothing seemed to have changed. Only his servant Misha and his wife knew that the priest was no longer his old self.

But the priest hardly ever talked to them and whenever his near and dear questioned him, he gave the same answer, "It's just that I'm already dead."

No one took him seriously, of course. How could he be dead if he was talking to them. But the priest led fewer and fewer services and eventually stopped seeing people, ignoring even the most ardent pleas. He now began to spend his time in his room. He sat there staring into space. When someone addressed him, he answered, "I'm not in."

Or his usual phrase, "I'm dead."

Still, no one believed him. Doctors paid him house calls and stuffed him with various pills, prescribing him massages and trying to cheer him up. They could see that the man was tired. But the priest was not tired. One day he simply lay down and died.

The Recluse

There was once a priest who began to avoid people, no longer stayed after the service to lead a Bible discussion, didn't visit his flock and stopped taking an interest in their lives. It was as if he could no longer bear it and only wanted them to leave him alone. But people refused to leave him alone. Over the previous 25 years, they had gotten used to seeing him conduct services and they kept calling on him, asking him for guidance and inviting him to visit. Finally, the priest had had enough. He went to the Baikonur Space Center and persuaded the astronauts to make him part of a team training for the next space mission. He was a phenomenally charming man and he could easily make anyone do anything for him. After several months of training, the priest was launched into space along with the others, traveling completely in secret. The spaceship engineers made a special section for him, where he did not stick out so much during live broadcasts from space. This is how the priest got to outer space. He now stares at the blue Earth through the ship's round window, floats in weightlessness, eats, drinks, laughs and implores them to leave him behind to guard the space station, so that he won't have to return to Earth.

A Seance

Father Constantine was a well-known practical joker. Everyone loved him for it and came to him for advice. One day, Pasha Yegorov wanted to ask him for guidance in a difficult situation. Four years before, Pasha had married Vika Kondratieva from the information department, having fallen head over heels in love with her. Vika was not a great beauty, but she had a nice figure, held her head high and had a beautiful walk, especially when high heels emphasized the great length of her legs. In other words, Pasha could not live without her.

What is more, after they were married, his love for her did not diminish, but grew ever stronger. As for Vika, it was the other way around. At first, she seemed happy enough. She made dinners for him and even kissed him now and again, but eventually she got bored. She was never in a hurry to come home from work. Sometimes she went shopping with a girlfriend, which is an easy thing to do nowadays, because stores stay open around the clock and going shopping after work is very convenient. Pasha waited for her at home, almost in tears, staring out the window. His Vika was an honest woman and there was no reason for him to be jealous, still he felt bad. It's unseemly for a husband to sit at home while his wife is out and about.

They began to fight. Vika would hug him and say, "Honey, I get bored staying at home with you. I push paper all day long at work and then, when I come home, there is nothing waiting for me here but housework and you."

Pasha would reply, "Do you think I'm a clown whose purpose in life is to keep you amused?"

They quarreled more and more frequently.

At last, Pasha decided to go see the priest, whom he saw at confession four times a year, at the Great and Lesser Fasts. Pasha was a believer – unlike his wife, it should be noted.

The priest questioned Pasha extensively, yet while Pasha recounted the minutiae of his life, he had to stifle a yawn now and again because he had already heard all the details. Finally, he said to Pasha, "I see. She thinks that you are boring. Now this is what we're going to do."

He explained his plan to Pasha.

The next time Vika came home late and rang the bell, Pasha didn't answer the door. She rang the bell two or three times, but there was no reaction. She used her own key to get in. Pasha's shoes and overcoat were in the hallway, indicating that he was at home.

Vika grew worried. She went to the living room, which reeked of alcohol. She saw Pasha passed out on the floor, completely drunk. Empty bottles and cigarette butts littered the carpet. It should be added that Pasha normally never drank and that he had tried a cigarette only once, in sixth grade – his one and only attempt to smoke. Vika began to kick Pasha, but he only growled in response. Finally, he opened his eyes and shouted terribly in a hoarse voice:

"Oh, my love! You're back!"

He dropped his head on the floor and went back to sleep.

But Vika persisted, getting him up and demanding an explanation.

"My love, I got drunk from despair," Pasha declared unsteadily, staring at her with a stupid grin on his face. "Because you're never at home. And I can't live without you."

Pasha picked up a cigarette butt from the floor and began to look around for matches.

"Why did you throw cigarette butts on the floor?" asked Vika angrily. "You could have set the place on fire."

But Pasha had already dropped the cigarette butt and had gone back to sleep.

With some difficulty, Vika took off his clothes, dragged his body over to the couch, covered him with a blanket, collected the cigarette butts and swept the ashes off the floor, took out the empties (a bottle of Zhiguli beer, a bottle of Neva beer and a bottle of Stolichnaya vodka) and closed the living room door. She settled down in the kitchen to watch TV. Vika's favorite program, *The Woman's Perspective*, was on, hosted by Oksana Pushkina.

The next morning Pasha apologized profusely, kissing Vika's hands and begging her to forgive and forget. He also kept repeating that the reason he had gotten so drunk was his despair. Vika forgave him and told all the girls at the information department how much her husband loved her. But then several days later Olya Motina invited her to check out a sale at the Kopeika store. The store was going out of business, or something like that, and it had dramatically reduced the prices on all of its household appliances. The day before, Motina had bought a food processor and had also wanted to get a juicer, but hadn't had enough money along. Vika needed a new iron.

She came home carrying a box with her purchase and saw Pasha drunk again. This time he was sitting in a chair and cigarette butts floated in a cup of liquid on the table. Even more bottles littered the floor.

After that, Vika always came home on time. Pasha somehow seemed less boring to her. Apparently, he could get drunk and even smoke. She had some stories to regale her workmates with.

But that was not the real miracle. The real miracle was that none of the neighbors told Vika that her husband had spent two evenings walking around the courtyard of their apartment building with two plastic bags and a pair of kitchen tongs. He used the tongs to pick cigarette butts up off the ground and place them into one of the plastic bags. He used the other bag to collect empties.

Father Constantine laughed at this story more than he had laughed at anything before in his entire life. He kept repeating it to people for a very long time, until he found out, rather by accident, that Vika and Pasha had split up after all.

The Flier

Mitya Artyomov loved to go to confession. It was his favorite thing to do in the entire world, even though at times he had to wait his turn until after midnight. He would come to the lectern and confess all his sins. The priest would then give him absolution and Mitya would suddenly feel such joy, it was as if he were walking on air. For a full week afterward, he literally floated through the air, and for the next half-week he felt a spring in his step. By the end of the second week, however, he began to feel as if he were being crushed earthward again. But, thank God, Saturday followed in due course. Mitya's priest heard confessions at night, after Vigil, and after that Mitya would once again feel like he was flying.

It was like this for three years. And suddenly it ended. Mitya still went to confession, but it no longer had any effect. He felt the ground under his feet, the same as before confession. Mitya decided that it was his priest's fault and went to see a different one. But it only got worse. Then he thought that perhaps he had not confessed his sins thoroughly enough. He examined himself closely and tried to repent even more sincerely. But it didn't help. It just didn't work any more.

Then Mitya applied to a flight school, which he finished with honors. He stopped going to church entirely, but whenever he flew over our darkened Earth, he would remember the distant days of his youth and his feeling of weightlessness and joy, and he would smile and make a sign of the cross at the night sky.

His copilot had long since gotten used to this.

Simple Ivan

There once was an artist who loved Russian folk art. She often went with her restorer friends to remote, abandoned villages in a UAZ all-terrain vehicle, searching through crumbling houses and scouring forgotten attics. She had discovered lots of interesting things. For example, she had found a broken spinning wheel, a colorful straw runner, a cast iron pot, a rusty sickle and a worn quilt. The artist took it all home and restored it, cleaned it and patched up the holes. In one place, she fell in love with a wooden cupboard, which was all scuffed up and broken-down, but was a nineteenth century piece with handcarved bits. Another time she found a dining table, which had no carvings but was very solid. Her friends the restorers understood the artist's passion because they knew that if such things were not preserved, all of the good they represented would fade away. So they carefully loaded her finds into their UAZ and took them to her dacha. Gradually, her dacha came to resemble a true peasant izba. It had a plain country dining table, an old cupboard, a worn runner, a patchwork quilt on the bed and a pot by the stove, along with a dried-up, crack-filled wooden trough.

The artist was very good with her hands. Most of the time she painted pictures – which, incidentally, were very much in demand, hung in several major museums around the world and commanded impressive prices – but she also did embroidery and ceramics, using a potter's wheel to make plates and cups and then coloring them by hand. She worked in the same plain folk style, making designs of berries, leaves and circles.

Needless to say, the artist was a believer. One day she decided that it was time to get her izba blessed. She invited a local priest to do the blessing, since there was a church near her dacha. The artist cooked a sumptuous meal, baked pies, swept and washed her house and awaited the priest's arrival. The priest, whose name was Father Basil and who was a hoary old man with a crooked back, eventually came. He set his walking stick aside, donned his liturgical vestments, said the prayers, sprinkled the walls and the floor with holy water, then got ready to leave. The artist naturally invited him to stay for supper and to partake of whatever the Lord had provided for her. She also gave him a generous donation stuffed in an envelope. But the priest turned down the meal and the donation. He made his excuses very politely and with a great show of humility, bowing low and begging her to forgive him. He was firm and left without taking any food or accepting a single kopek for his labors. The artist was upset, but there was nothing she could do. She ate the festive meal all by herself and saved the leftovers for her supper that evening. In the morning, she got on her bicycle and went to church, since it was a Sunday.

Father Basil completed the liturgy and held up the cross for the faithful to kiss. The artist approached the cross in a line of other believers. When she kissed the cross, Father Basil stopped her and gave her something wrapped in a piece of paper.

"Here is something for you. Open it at home."

The artist took what she had been given, got back on her bicycle and returned to her ethnographic paradise. When she opened the letter she found – oh, my God! – five hundred rubles.

What is the meaning of this, she asked herself. And then it hit her. When Father Basil saw her ancient cupboard, her table that lacked a table cloth and her bed covered with an old quilt, he must have thought that the artist was very poor. She even had to do her laundry in a cracked wooden trough and eat off homemade dishes. She didn't even have a rug on the floor, just a rotten old runner.

Clearly, the priest had been touched by her plight and, being compassionate, wanted to provide a bit of relief for her poverty.

A Tree Stump

There once was a young woman who was infatuated with her spiritual father. She attended all the services, listened closely to all his sermons and recorded them with a tape recorder so that she could listen to them again at home. She came to confession every week and tried to lead the kind of life that her priest had taught her – in short, she was his true spiritual child. It all went very well for several years, but then things began to go wrong. At first there seemed to be no outward change. The young woman went to confession and listened to sermons, but the sermons began to bore her and after going to confession she no longer felt the same transformation in her soul as she had before. The young woman began to pray, asking the Lord to enlighten her, to tell her what had gone wrong. Should she perhaps have kept a stricter fast?

Then she had a dream. She saw her church, the one where she usually went, except that in the corner where her priest usually heard confessions there was a tall, completely rotten tree stump crawling with red ants. People took turns approaching the tree stump as though they were going to confession. The young woman was frightened and woke up.

To get her dream interpreted she went to an important monastery. The Elder there said to her, "My child, your dream surely is an omen, but your priest has nothing to do with it. The rotten tree stump is something that has grown within your own soul. You shouldn't go to see your spiritual father any longer, because your spiritual relationship has become too twisted up with human emotion. It would be better for you to turn over a new leaf and find another church, with a different priest. And take care, my child. You should watch yourself more closely in the future."

The Seer

Lenya Andreyev was addicted to drugs. His addiction happened gradually and for a long time he wasn't even aware that he had become an addict. He sometimes injected heroin, but more often he used meth. A close friend was very good at cooking meth and he eventually taught Lenya his art. Lenya began injecting drugs. No big deal, of course. Everybody does it nowadays. Lenya continued to attend lectures at the Chemical Engineering Institute and took tests and make-up exams while visiting his drug buddy only once a week. Then one day his buddy had to go out of town on business and Lenya realized that he had become addicted to meth and could not live another hour without it. He immediately called a friend of his buddy's who agreed to help him. Together they found a dealer, bought the ingredients and cooked some meth. When the original buddy came back, all went on as before. The only difference was that Lenya now visited him more often. He was an addict, so there was no reason why he shouldn't visit more frequently. Things were more honest this way.

One day, however, when Lenya was under the influence of meth and had passed out, he had a vision. It was a terrible vision, as a matter of fact. Lenya screamed, wept and begged to be released from it. He never told anyone what he had seen, but when he came to his appearance had changed somehow and for the first time in his life he decided to go to church.

There they told him that drugs are a path to perdition and that he had to kick his habit. It was easier said than done. Withdrawal pangs were one thing, but coming off drugs meant that he had to think of a purpose in life. He didn't know how to do it, yet he also couldn't imagine life without a purpose. Then they told him – at a special group meeting for former drug addicts at the church that he had joined – that the purpose of life was salvation of the soul. But Lenya didn't give a rat's ass about that. What was this salvation of the soul anyway? It meant getting closer to Christ, cleansing oneself and freeing one's soul of passions. He had no interest in that.

Lenya even considered leaving their Twelve Steps program, but his new friends from the drug addicts' group pulled him aside and said, "Sure you can quit, but just go see Father Vladimir first. He's a cool guy. You'll like him."

"I don't wanna see no Father Vladimir," said Lenya, who was no pushover himself. "What I want is some meth."

But as he said that, he suddenly winced, having remembered his vision.

He went to see Father Vladimir because he felt like he was up to his ears in all this anti-drug stuff and there was really no other way out.

Father Vladimir listened to him for a bit, then began to describe to Lenya his vision. Lenya was somewhat dumbfounded, but Father Vladimir, except for a few details, described his vision almost perfectly, generally getting everything right.

Shaking, Lenya asked, "How did you know?"

The priest grinned at him, "I read it in a book. What you saw was Hell, pure and simple. I know about it from books. And not just from books," Father Vladimir said, face growing stern.

After that, Lenya was his for the taking. Father Vladimir had won over his young soul either by his gift of clairvoyance or through his erudition. He became Lenya's spiritual father. Lenya forgot all about a purpose in life and began to help Father Vladimir do various chores at the church. He finished college, founded a construction company and quickly made a fortune. Father Vladimir's church then also became new and shiny. It was renovated: the floors were paved with real marble, antique icons were purchased, and the walls were painted with murals and covered with mosaics.

Yet, it all began with meth.

Ten years later, the prosperous Lenya moved his family to Norway, where he happened to meet another Russian businessman, also the owner of a large company. They struck up a conversation and soon their families became fast friends. Lenya noticed a photograph hanging over his new friend's desk. It was a picture of the businessman as a young man, standing next to another man. The other man looked very familiar. My God, of course! It was Father Vladimir, except he didn't have a beard.

Lenya's heart skipped a beat.

It turned out that the businessman and Father Vladimir had gone to college together and had taken the same classes. The two experimented with meth, but not for long.

"One time Vovik had a really bad trip. He began to scream as though he had been stabbed, he wept and kicked everyone around him. He barely came to," the businessman told Lenya over a glass of good Scotch. "He told us that he had seen live devils and they had taunted him. After that he quit meth. As you see, he even became a priest. We should invite him over here. We could reminisce about the old days and have a drink or two."

"Sure," Lenya readily agreed.

Father Metrophanes

1 Father Metrophanes was the Father Superior of —sky Monastery. He was tall and had a thick black beard and bushy eyebrows. His eyes shone fiercely from under those eyebrows and his fists were like kettlebells. In his youth, he had been a boxer and even as an old man he retained great physical strength.

Father Metrophanes never said to anyone, "Do as I tell you, my child."

Nevertheless, everyone did exactly as he suggested. If a reader was not prepared and fumbled during the service, Father Metrophanes would strike him on his head with the Typikon. Eventually, his church had only one reader left, but he never made any mistakes.

2 Despite the Father Superior's terrible temper, many people still came to his monastery to ask for instruction or advice. Those who loved him said of him, "After talking to the abbot, I feel like I've been to the banya."

Those who hated him shook their heads and said, "He is rude and has no manners."

3 Nastya Sakharova, a student at a teacher's college and a faithful devotee of Father Metrophanes, used to say, "When Father Metrophanes gives you his blessing in the morning, you feel for the rest of the day as though you're wearing a fur hat."

"Why a fur hat?" they asked her.

"Because the father's blessing keeps you warm."

4 Once a woman came to church for only the second time in her life and she happened to come to confession before Father Metrophanes. She said to him, "I have committed every sin in the book."

The abbot wanted to help the woman overcome her dangerous delusions and asked, "Have you committed adultery?"

"I don't remember," the woman replied, surprised.

"How come? Were you drunk?" the abbot insisted.

At first the woman came to church because she liked the priest, but in time she became sincerely devout and began to attend church regularly, though, true enough, she went to a different church, not Father Metrophanes'.

5 Once a young woman came to see Father Metrophanes. She was very young, no older than eighteen.

"Forgive me, Father, for I have sinned," she said and began to cry.

Her face was nice and pure and it was obvious that she could not have committed any major sin. Of course, most other people, when they said that, told the truth. They had indeed sinned, but this girl was clearly innocent.

Nevertheless she kept repeating, "I have sinned, Father. I have sinned terribly."

The priest tried to comfort her, but she would not calm down. At last, she declared through her tears, "Father, last night during vespers I felt such repentance and divine love that I started to cry and I cannot stop. I feel like such a terrible sinner. No matter what sin I think of, even though it is only in my thoughts, I feel as if I have committed it..."

The priest asked her no further questions and simply placed his vestments about her neck.

And somehow, since that day, he has become considerably more relaxed. If you say to him now: "Father, I have sinned," he no longer asks whether you have killed or raped someone, but just nods peacefully. It is unclear whether this is due to the influence of the young girl or if he has simply become weary.

6 Olga Petrovna, a great admirer of Father Metrophanes, once approached him and said, smiling shyly, "Father, you are..."

She stumbled momentarily, searching for words.

"...You are like Saint Seraphim of Sarov."

The priest shook his head from side to side and stared intently at Olga Petrovna.

"Wait a moment and I'll explain why you think this," he said and went behind the altar.

He didn't come back for a long time. Olga Petrovna even became a bit nervous and wondered what the priest could be doing behind the altar. She wondered whether he was back there praying for divine inspiration and tried to guess what he might say to her. Would he explain to her, perhaps, in what way he was like Saint Serafim?

Finally, the priest came back and said, "It's because you're an idiot."

7 When women complained to him about their father-in-law or mother-in-law, or perhaps a neighbor, the priest gave them all the same advice, "Go ahead and kill him. Or her."

"What do you mean, kill him?" the women shrieked in horror.

"Smother him with a pillow or perhaps put arsenic in his tea."

Sometimes he would also add, "Or else send him to a meat packing plant and let them make sausage out of him."

After this, they stopped complaining to him about their family or friends.

8 Of course, not all complaints made Father Metrophanes angry. But if a woman told him that her husband had physically abused her, Father Metrophanes' brow would suddenly darken. He would then ask the woman to tell her husband that, if he didn't stop it, he would have to deal with Father Metrophanes personally. Such warnings had little effect on most men. The poor wife would usually come back to Father Metrophanes some time later, after another beating.

Father Metrophanes would then ask her where she lived. He would put on his coat and go to her house. There he would wait for the husband to come home, stand up before him in the full magnificence of his height and say sternly, "Just you touch her one more time."

He would raise his enormous fist and smash it through a wooden door. Or else leave a huge dent in the wall. If he was dealing with a drunk, he would take a bottle and crush it in his clenched fist. A few times he leaned his shoulder against a wardrobe and toppled it to the floor.

It was such a terrible sight, that some women would run out of the room in terror. As to their husbands, they stopped abusing them after that, even when they were drunk. They also hurried to fix the holes in their walls and the broken doors as quickly as possible.

Father Metrophanes said on such occasions, "If a man hits a woman he is a coward. It is enough to give him a bit of a scare."

9 To those who wanted to have an abortion, the abbot would say, "You should give birth to the baby and then leave it in a carriage out in the cold, as if it were an accident. It will scream for a bit and then freeze to death, and all will be well. It's a lesser sin than abortion."

"Why is it a lesser sin?"

"Try it, you'll see."

But no one tried.

10 He also used to say: "A guy may go to church for fifty years and have no idea what prayer is. Another may never set foot in a church and yet find salvation."

11 He said also: "Our soul is a stinking pot. We must pour out the nasty bile and transform it into a chosen vessel."

12 This was how he would talk to his disciples: "Come over here, you soggy floor mop from Kazan Station." Or: "You are a squashed toad that can still, for some reason, hoarsely croak."

13 And also: "You're a goat." Or, "You're a moral cripple." Or else: "What do you think you're doing, you idiot?" Many disciples left him, complaining of his rudeness and un-Christian language. But others persevered. They loved their teacher and believed that, in the end, they would be crowned with martyrs' crowns.

14 One monk could no longer bear the abbot's insults but he didn't quite want to leave because he felt that there was a clear spiritual advantage in staying. For a number of weeks he prayed to the Lord, asking Him for guidance. But the Lord was in no hurry to give him an answer. Then, one day in the woods, the troubled monk found a chickadee with a broken wing. The monk saw it as a sign from God and smuggled the bird into his cell. He spent his evenings teaching the bird to speak.

On Father Metrophanes's name day, as the monk walked from the church to the festive meal, he set the bird free. But the bird had gotten used to its master and didn't want to fly away. Instead, it began to fly in circles over a group of monks.

When it saw Father Metrophanes' shiny gold cross, it gently alighted on his hand and suddenly said very loudly, "Don't be rude."

And again, "Don't be rude."

The monks were in no doubt that they were in the presence of a divine miracle. Father Metrophanes merely sneered and tossed the bird up in the air. It flew off, landed on the shoulder of its former master and shouted into his ear, too, "Don't be rude."

That evening, Father Metrophanes told the monk who had saved the bird to leave the monastery. He now seeks his salvation elsewhere. As to Father Metrophanes, from that day forward he stopped calling his monks goats or toads. Now they are only "dear little goats" and "dear little toads."

15 There was the time when Father Metrophanes was invited to a large church in Moscow to mark its patron saint's day. Father Metrophanes decided to go. The Patriarch personally conducted the service, assisted by a pair of Metropolitans. The liturgy was very solemn, with a great number of people in attendance. At the end, there was a procession of the cross. The Patriarch's private secretary, Father Abercius, formerly a military man, was upset that the priests walked around the church haphazardly and he kept trying to keep them in line. He made them march single file and kept pushing them back into the ranks. Father Metrophanes got a nice strong push from him, too. At first he said nothing, but when the priests returned to the altar, he came up to Father Abercius, grabbed him by his vestments and said slowly and distinctly, "You do that one more time and I'll kill you."

16 Whenever people complained to Father Metrophanes about the monks in his monastery, he would deny even those things which were self-evident.

For example, when he was told that Father Eugraphos had asked for an enormous sum to perform a religious rite, Father Metrophanes declared that Father Eugraphos was the world's least venal man. When he heard that Father Zosimas kept a woman in town and had even fathered a child by her, whom she, having for some reason fallen out with Father Zosimas, was now ready to present to him as proof of their relationship, Father Metrophanes replied, "You must be crazy."

When people whispered in his ear that yet another monk had done such totally outrageous things that they couldn't even commit them to paper, Father Metrophanes laughed at those bringing such bad tidings and sent them away in shame.

Many people were upset and thought that Father Metrophanes was a liar. But the monks at his monastery lovingly called their abbot a priest on a barrel, recalling an olden time when an elder, in order to hide another monk's sin, sat on top of a barrel in the other monk's cell, under which a woman had been concealed.

17 Some people said that Father Metrophanes had charisma. Others claimed that he had a magnet in his chest that attracted the hearts of men. When the priest began to grow old and to show the infirmities of old age, people said, "The magnet has become rusty, but it continues to draw people to him all the same."

18 When Father Metrophanes grew very old and his black hair had turned completely white and when his straight back became crooked, he changed. He didn't hit anyone any more, he didn't curse and he hardly ever said a word while hearing a confession. He only listened in silence and sometimes nodded slightly. He kept nodding no matter what was being said. Some people thought that he was hard of hearing. They asked, "Father, did you hear me?"

"I heard you. I hear everything," Father Metrophanes assured them and continued to count his prayer beads and ignore all the questions that people put to him.

But when someone kept insisting that he absolutely give him his advice, he raised his eyes and said softly, "Dearest child, Christ is Risen."

Love of Children

There once was a priest who kept hearing news reports that the Russian population was declining and he made an urgent decision to increase the size of his congregation. He stopped giving communion to young couples who had no children. Unless they produced a child, they could receive no divine blessing and would not be allowed to partake of Christ's mystery. Less than a year passed and his congregation got much smaller. Now only old ladies came to his church. Young couples, even those which had children, moved to a different parish with a more tolerant priest. The strangest thing is that this story is absolutely true.

No Way Back

This is how it happened. Andrei Grigoriev was ordained in Moscow, at the New Convent of the Virgin. His wife Nadya, seeing the freshly ordained priest come out from behind the altar to hold up the cross for the faithful to kiss, was speechless. Andrei's eyes seemed different. They shone with the light of eternity. Nadya didn't approach to kiss the cross. It was as if she were glued to the floor.

"How will I be able to live with him?" she asked herself.

They were sent to Kolomna region, to the village of Proshino, where they were tasked with rebuilding a half-ruined church. They lived in a crooked, abandoned house. Father Andrei relaid the stove in the house with his own two hands. Even though it smoked a little, it kept them warm. His wife made and hung blue calico curtains, put a tablecloth on the wooden table, and the house suddenly became a bit cozier. The priest went to the church every day and cleared a patch of ground. He came home for lunch in the middle of the day and then went back to clear more rubble. His wife did household chores, planted a small vegetable garden, put in a flower bed and admired her husband.

In the evening, Father Andrei and his wife sat side by side, drank tea with pies and talked. There was silence outside and the snow fell softly, since winter had come. The priest cleared pathways in the snow and covered the cracks in the church building with tarps, to keep the snow out. He placed a wood-burning stove in the vestibule and continued clearing away the rubble.

Villagers stopped by the church, marveled at Father Andrei and commiserated with him, but at first no one wanted to help him out. Sometimes they brought the priest food – cookies, potatoes or eggs. But one day an old woman had a grandson and Father Andrei baptized him. Then someone else's mother died and Father Andrei led the funeral service. Soon he started getting requests to baptize a child or bless a house or administer last rights or conduct a funeral service. Gradually, people got to know him. He had a cheerful disposition. He didn't like long conversations and preferred to stick to the business at hand. He would say a brief sermon and leave. He also joked along the way, but nothing fancy. He and his wife didn't have any children.

In the spring, a team of volunteers got together and began to fix up the church. A year and a half later, a new floor was laid, an iconostasis was erected, and regular services began.

Seven more years passed. Two brick buildings had been built near the church. One housed a Sunday School and the other was for deacons. It also had a refectory, a sewing room, an icon studio, a small chapel and a baptistry. All this had come into being thanks to Father Andrei's indomitable energy. He always managed to find the funds.

As luck would have it, a daughter of the famous movie director Nikita Mikhalkov had a dacha nearby. Mikhalkov himself came to visit her three times and even visited the church, to pray and to attend confession before Father Andrei. During confession, Father Andrei didn't say a word, only listened humbly, which made sense, of course: it wasn't he who had come to confession, but Mikhalkov. Nikita Sergeyevich lit candles, made a sign of the cross and then piously accepted communion. In short, he acted like a good Christian, as if he were a regular mortal made of flesh and blood. After his visit, the reconstruction project began to move forward much faster. On his next visit, Nikita Sergeyevich didn't forget the church nor Father Andrei. And, a month after his third visit, the Sunday School got modern, soundproof windows and parquet floors.

But when the church was completely restored, both brick buildings were completed and the church yard was planted with wonderful rose bushes, Father Andrei grew sad. He had done everything, had completed construction and had raised the buildings. He had grown deadly bored with illiterate hags, country women each with two dozen abortions in their past, the talk of evil eyes and spells, the fleeting flash of young men and women, whom Father Andrei had encouraged to go study in Moscow, and country wakes and weddings. He was nauseated by all of it. He felt as if he were at an impasse. Was he to pray more earnestly? But he couldn't pray any more earnestly than he was required to by his duties. He just couldn't bear it. He felt that he no longer had a purpose in life.

In his boredom, he became addicted to television shows and spent entire evenings in front of a TV set.

One day, however, Nikita Sergeyevich came to visit the village yet again. On Sunday, he accepted an invitation to come to lunch in their modest refectory for the first time. At lunch, he spoke a great deal and very well. It was, no doubt, the work of Divine Providence. When Nikita Sergeyevich paused, having just quoted the philosopher Rozanov and clearly intending to quote Ilyin as well, the priest said with an air of assumed indifference, "Sooner or later the life of a village priest comes to an impasse."

Nikita Sergeyevich immediately understood him. He heard him, as they say nowadays.

"We're going to send you to Moscow," he said. "A highly placed person..." Nikita Sergeyevich closed his eyes and lowered his voice. "...a very highly placed person is looking for a personal confessor."

"Oh, no," the priest objected, but Nikita Sergeyevich was already pressing the buttons on his silver cell phone, which glowed with an unearthly green light.

Father Andrei's life changed in an hour.

Soon he joined the Department of External Relations of the Russian Orthodox Church and was immediately given a very high post. He moved to Moscow, drove a shining black car and met with clerics from other denominations. He attended formal dinners, special concerts and court balls.

He was a good-looking and well-built man. He had a blond beard and clear eyes and he was well-spoken. After all, he was a graduate of Moscow State University with a degree in philosophy, no less. He became a guest of honor at formal events. He was asked to cut ribbons, bless mansions, send delegations off on important missions and award church medals to Mayor Yury Luzhkov and Prime Ministers Sergei Stepashin and Yevgeny Primakov. The recipients would fix their dull eyes on the priest. But he kept smiling as he gave each of them a firm handshake and not a single thought passed through his head.

"Obedience and duty," he repeated to his wife after every prolonged Duma or government reception. "Obedience above all."

For the first time in their long marriage and their close intimate union, he didn't want to hear what she had to say. But she had begun saying very strange things, like, "We should return to Proshino."

"The plush life has made you fussy," the priest replied through clenched teeth. By then they had traveled all over Europe and had visited Brazil, Australia and New Zealand as part of high-level delegations of the Moscow Patriarchate.

Many people were envious of them. They said nasty things about them and wrote denunciations to the Partiarchate. But Father Andrei was unassailable. The highly placed person whose personal confessor he had become was no less a personage than... Well, it was a state secret, of course, and probably also part of the privileged relationship between a confessor and his spiritual child. The only problem was his wife, who kept throwing him off his stride. She had managed to lose a great deal of her humility and tried to shake Father Andrei out of his complacency and to open his eyes. But her husband saw everything and understood everything, too. What he didn't see and didn't understand were things he didn't want to see or understand. He mostly held his tongue when he heard his wife's complaints.

The priest's wife began to waste away. It was as simple as that. She began to waste away. Her husband took her to see the best Kremlin doctors. But the doctors merely shrugged. There was nothing they could do to help her. She had rampant stomach cancer. It was too late to treat her. Soon, she passed away. Before she died, she made peace with herself and with her husband. Thank God she didn't suffer terribly, but merely wasted away and grew weaker with every passing day, until she could no longer get out of bed. As she lay dying, she said nothing grand to her husband, she didn't even give him her blessing or make any last testament. All she said was, "This is the end, my dear Andrei." And she never regained consciousness.

A week after her funeral the priest received a letter in the mail. The envelope had no return address and it was long and bluish. Inside he found a black and white snapshot of their crooked old house in the village with calico curtains over the windows, half-buried in the snow. The smoke was rising from the chimney. The ruins of the church could be seen behind the house.

Father Andrei looked around his beautiful brand-new apartment with the reassuring, blinking green light of the burglar alarm on the electric panel in the hallway, listened to the soft footfalls of well-trained security guards behind the front door, peeked out the window where his personal driver was idling the motor of his black Audi, glanced at his wife's portrait hanging on the wall and said softly, "It's too late, my dear Nadya."

Paradise Lost

There once was a priest at a small village church in –sky Region. His parish was tiny, consisting of ten old ladies and a few vacationers who came during the summer. His wife was his reader and his choir. Rarely did anyone join her in her singing.

The priest's wife was a very sensitive soul, one of those we call "always close to tears." Whenever he conducted a service and came to one of her favorite passages, she began to softly sob. She mourned the Loss of Paradise, and it was at moments such as these that she felt the loss especially keenly. At first she wept softly and continued singing, and that was alright, but as the service went on, her crying got progressively worse. Sometimes she could no longer sing because she was choking back tears. Yet, someone had to continue singing and reading the prayers, loudly and clearly. But how could she continue, when her soul was drowning in tears?

The priest was upset. He had to stop the service, leave the altar, and give his reader and singer a stern talking-to, telling her to immediately end this hysteria. But it was to no avail. Or rather, it helped a little, but only for a short while, until his wife again began to think of the Loss of Paradise. It was lost and gone for good.

One day, the priest's patience ran out. He came out from behind the altar and gave his wife a slap to the head. Then another one, and then a third.

And what do you think happened next?

The priest's wife didn't take offense, but from that day forward learned to weep silently. She kept her tears to herself, so that no one could see them. She still wept, but the service went on as usual. It was a steady and dignified service. The priest was very happy, because there were no more interruptions or distractions due to her sobbing. The faithful prayed, lit candles and kissed the icons. Everything was fine.

There was just one thing wrong: Paradise was now truly lost.

What a Man Needs is a Nice Holiday

Lenya Korotkov seemed to have it all. He had everything a man could desire. He had a wonderful family. His wife was the same age as he, but she looked fantastic, like a college student. She had retained a youthful sparkle in her eye and she could still laugh like a young girl. They had two great kids, aged three and five, both boys. Both had red cheeks and were sturdy little tykes. He got plenty of sex. His wife was a passionate woman and they could get into it pretty well. Every man cares what he does for a living, and Lenya had a great job. He headed a small computer company, which had only four employees, all of them his old friends from college. Another one, also a classmate, was their bookkeeper. A few years after starting the company, each had made enough money to buy a large apartment and a car, and had plenty of spare income to travel to any point on the globe. Moreover, Lenya loved his job because he loved computers. He wrote software and knew hardware. He was the kind of man who, when he heard the words "reformatting hard disk," began to shift impatiently and rub his hands in anticipation.

In short, he had everything his heart desired. And then he got bored.

"Aha, the Church! Faith!" cries any reader raised on the works of Tolstoy and Dostoyevsky. But Lenya had also been raised on this literature and so he already had God in his life. He went to church twice a month, like clockwork. Every Easter and Christmas he went to confession, repented his sins and received Holy Communion. After that, he gave thanks to the Lord by saying a special prayer from a prayer book that he owned. He also had icons hanging over his computer at work. There was nothing amiss from this point of view. Nevertheless, he got bored.

Lenya saw no other way out but to visit Pechora Monastery to see their elder, Father Ivan Krestyankin. He spent two days there, prayed in the caves and, lo and behold, a miracle occurred. He saw the holy man, even though the holy man had not received any visitors for a long time. As an extraordinary, amazing piece of good fortune,

Lenya met an old friend, Irka Kozlova. It turned out that she too had found God and had moved there ten years ago from Moscow in order to be close to the holy man. She painted icons and knew all the ins and outs at the monastery. Irka remembered Lenya and used a secret passage to take him to the reverend father, directly to his cell. On that day, Father Ambrose was the one serving the holy man and, as Irka explained to Lenya, Father Ambrose was somehow forever in her debt.

Indeed, Father Ambrose let them in to see the holy man. Not for long, just for five minutes. The holy man was very ill. Lenya entered the cell and almost had to sit down. The holy man was not only ill, he was barely alive. His face was very kind and gentle, of course, and he looked a bit like Father Frost, yet he was extremely ancient. Lenya didn't dare to ask Father Ivan anything. His couldn't screw up his courage to speak. Or rather, when he looked at the monk sitting there in a large armchair and unable even to stand up, Lenya had a revelation. He put his hands together and came up to the monk asking him for a blessing. Father Ivan called him by his first name, even though Lenya had not had time to introduce himself, but that was not important. The monk blessed him and said with great emotion, which was especially striking in such an old man, "Let the Lord bless you, my son. He will give you everything that your soul needs and desires. Don't interfere with Him."

Lenya gave the monk a shy smile, nodded and went out.

"Why did you come out so soon?" Irka asked, clearly disappointed.

"There didn't seem to be anything else left to talk about," Lenya shrugged.

Before leaving Pechora, he brought Irka a cake that he had bought at a local store, but he didn't stay for tea. He was in a hurry to catch his train. He wanted to get back home, and there was a train leaving that day, and the next one wasn't coming for another two days. He felt a little stupid, but he was happy nevertheless.

The meeting with the holy man lit up his life for a while and for several weeks he was not bored. His life was once more filled with joy.

This was how he explained it: he had met a very nice man, and that was what was important. He even said to his wife, Larisa, "That was what I needed, to go and see a nice man. You see, I'm happy again."

Larisa nodded in agreement. She had also found religion and had begun attending church soon after Lenya, except she attended much more frequently. It had been her idea for him to go and see the holy man, and she was glad to see that everything had been resolved so easily.

But then it turned out that nothing had been resolved. Soon Lenya again felt that his life was gray and bleak. He no longer smiled, not even to his kids.

Lenya went to see a psychiatrist. The psychiatrist told him that he had to visit him once a week and that, God willing, they would be able to get to the root of his depression.

But they got to the root of his depression much sooner, thanks to the approaching New Year's holiday. One day, Lenya was walking past an optician's shop when a man wearing a funny red hat and no beard stuck his head out and pulled from a large bag a tiny chocolate bar with the store's business card attached to it. It was a promotional campaign.

Lenya suddenly remembered something and went straight to the psychiatrist.

It was just before the New Year's holiday and he had turned six. At the time, he still believed in Father Frost. That year, his parents had solemnly promised him that Father Frost would not only come, but he might even stick around until Lenya woke up, in order to chat with him.

Little Lenya scratched at his stomach to keep himself from falling asleep. He stayed up until he heard midnight strike in his parents' bedroom, but then immediately fell fast asleep. He woke up early the next morning to find a large pile of gifts under the tree, but he didn't so much as glance at them. He called out to Father Frost. But instead of Father Frost, his mother came into the room. She smiled sheepishly and said that Father Frost had just left. He was not able to wait any longer and had to visit other kids with his flying sleigh.

Lenya didn't believe his mother. Surely she was wrong and Father Frost hadn't left yet. What if he was hiding somewhere? Lenya quickly checked all the places he would hide while playing hide-and-seek: behind the curtains, inside the wardrobe, under the bed, behind the bathroom door and even on the landing outside their front door. But the landing was empty and quiet. Suddenly, a door slammed somewhere on the stairwell. It was their downstairs neighbor. She buzzed for the elevator and it rumbled as it moved. There was no Father Frost anywhere. Lenya cried and stomped his feet, and his parents were at a loss because they had never seen their son in such a state.

Eventually, they managed to distract him by opening his gifts, and Lenya calmed down. A year later, he overheard his parents discuss whether they should hire a Father Frost from an agency. He came into the room and told them that he no longer believed in Father Frost, because there was no Father Frost, only actors wearing costumes. His parents were reassured and the story was soon forgotten.

Now 32 years old, Lenya suddenly remembered how bitterly he had cried, how he had tried to bite his mother when she tried to keep him from going out onto the landing. He remembered feeling miserable and lost.

The psychiatrist shifted in his chair a few times from the sheer pleasure of hearing Lenya's story.

"Now everything is completely, utterly, thoroughly clear," Joseph Samuilovich said, adjusting his glasses.

He advised Lenya to hire a Father Frost for his kids, since New Year's was just around the corner, and it was extremely easy to find one. When Father Frost came, Lenya should try to transform himself into a child, too, at least in his mind, and feel joy at the arrival of a bearded old man. In other words, he should try to feel now what he had not been allowed to feel as a child and thus recover his loss, albeit many years after the fact.

Lenya did as he had been told. Father Frost came. His kids promptly hid behind their father's back and Lenya was left on his own. When Father Frost chanted "One-two-three, let's light up the tree," the tree didn't light up right away, despite Lenya's best efforts. But eventually it did light up. The boys overcame their shyness and each read a poem for the old man, danced around the tree and received their gifts.

Larisa, being a good hostess, invited Father Frost to sit down and have some tea with them, but Father Frost whispered to her that he would then have to remove his beard. He would have been happy to do this, but Lenya shook his head vigorously. No. Instead, he stuck an extra hundred-ruble bill into Father Frost's deep red pocket and walked him to the door.

After that, everything changed. The treatment worked well. Lenya is never bored. On New Year's Eve he raises his glass and says the same toast every year, "My friends. Therapy can sometimes work. And New Year's is not a completely useless holiday."

Father Valerius's Dreams

1 In the beginning, Father Valerius was just Valerka. He was very good at frying eggs and he adored his chatty wife to distraction. But then he graduated from the theological seminary, was ordained and became Father Valerius. He and his wife had a daughter and then, many years later, they also had a son.

Once, Father Valerius had a dream. He dreamed that he was conducting a service and behind the altar stood two altar boys holding candles. The priest woke up. Soon, his wife presented him with another boy. Both the ultrasound and the midwife had told them to expect a girl, but the priest merely smiled into his graying beard, "All women are good for is making noise."

He had no dreams about his next son, but he was born anyway. In total, they had a girl and three boys.

2 Another time Father Valerius had a dream about Father Serafim of Sarov, who struck the floor with his walking stick and declared, "Cousin, why are you conducting services so poorly?"

When Father Valerius woke up he inquired what it could have meant. It turned out that his grandfather came from the Kursk Region, which was where the Reverend Serafim was from, too.

3 Before being ordained, Father Valerius had been a reader at a church. It was a small church, something like a village parish, but there was a long tradition that on feast days the local bishop came to lead a service. That bishop set great store by church services and disliked it when they had errors and mix-ups. Father Valerius always did his preparations for services and was a good reader. The only problem was that he was a smoker. He worked hard to lose this vice, but there was nothing he could do about it.

Then God sent him a dream.

He dreamed of being at vespers and standing in his usual spot at the lectern. The choir members finished their chants and it was his turn to read, but he couldn't figure out what he was supposed to read. He had everything in front of him, the Octoechos, the service book, and the Festal Menaion, and he had had the Sticheron for the vespers psalm all written down on a separate sheet of paper, but it had all become mixed up. He had no idea what to read. He leafed through one book, then another while the choir stood silent. A minute passed, then another. The silence stretched on and on. Father Valerius was terrified.

At that moment, the bishop came out from behind the altar, approached Father Valerius, tapped him on the shoulder and said, "Shall we go and have a smoke?"

Father Valerius woke up in a cold sweat and after that night lost all desire to smoke.

Fir Trees

Father Valerius was fond of Russia. But he lived in America. It happens like that sometimes.

Everybody has illusions of youth and, besides, there was perestroika, youthful romanticism, and so on. Father Valerius did his job honestly and passionately and in a few years built a large Russian Orthodox congregation – members of the intelligentsia, computer programmers, historians, what have you, all from a large university nearby – and he was much loved by everyone. But it was not Russia. In the end, Father Valerius returned to Russia with his large family and became a village priest in a remote region of his enormous homeland.

One day he came to Moscow to run some errands, shop and visit the Patriarchate. In the evening he stopped by to see some old friends. They were his old classmates, a married couple. He had some tea and was relaxing. The hostess, who liked exotic things, began to question him:

"Tell me, Father, what kind of miracles have occurred to you lately? After all, you have come back to Holy Russia."

"Oh, my" replied the priest. "I've got almost nothing to tell you. Maybe just about those fir trees?"

The hostess was excited. She put her hands together and prepared to listen to his story. The priest began, "I planted some firs in the village, to serve as a hedge around the church."

"What for?"

"The house next door had indoor plumbing put in, but the sewer burst and raw sewage is now seeping onto the road and flowing into a ditch just 200 yards from the church. Besides, there is a grocery store next door, and local drunks hang out there all day. It is a nasty place, completely barren. In short, I planted some firs around the church. There's a man there, a drunk. He's not rich, so he buys a bottle of some nasty stuff for 10 rubles, which is good enough for him. His name is Sasha. He often comes into the church, stands there swaying back and forth for a while and then leaves.

"'You're a good priest,' he said to me. 'But I don't much believe in God.'

"I planted the fir and the next day, when Sasha saw me, he started to complain:

"'Why did you plant those firs, Father?'

"'Why not?' I asked him in surprise. 'They look nice.'

"'You've gotta pull them out. It's a bad omen. If you want, I can come around tomorrow and dig them out for you.'

"'Have you had one too many?' I asked him sternly. 'Fir trees bring joy.'

"'Fir trees are a bad omen,' insisted Sasha. 'A bad omen.'

"'What's so bad about them?' I asked, trying to reason with him. 'A nice row of fir trees. A joy to behold.'

"'No joy whatsoever,' replied Sasha stubbornly, staring at the ground. 'It's a bad omen. They mean death.'

"'Look,' I said to him. 'You believe in bad omens but don't believe in God.'

"So, I sent him away," the priest concluded.

The hostess waited for him to go on, but he didn't. The host was also a little surprised. There was neither a moral to the story, nor any miracles. Sewage and firs, nothing else.

"Is that all there is?" the host asked the priest.

"That's all," the priest sighed. "I praise the Lord if I get a dozen old women for a Sunday service. But I'm glad we returned."

Father Artemius

Father Artemius graduated with a degree in philology from Moscow State University, which is named after the great Russian scholar and educator Mikhail Vasiliyevich Lomonosov. Whenever the priest opens his mouth, silky soft grasses spread upon the ground, sweet-smelling flowers bow their heads, young leaves dripping with sap cling to their branches in silent admiration, birds in heaven fold their wings and fall silent, daring not to go on with their wonderfully sweet songs, wild beasts, thick of fur and long of tail, freeze mid-stride and sniff the air, pricking their ears in awestruck surprise, and creatures of the sea lay motionless, moving their tails ever so slightly as they emit tiny air bubbles. Humans record the priest's sermons on tape and video cassette recorders and print his books in the thousands. But some were bewildered and rubbed their temples, trying to grasp his meaning.

"It's very simple," an admiring member of his congregation said. "Our reverend father is under a lot of pressure and he is very busy. He has forgotten plain Russian words and is using only old Russian ones, because at the university he used to get straight As, both in Old Russian and Church Slavonic. It would be better if we had a translator for him. For instance, when our reverend father says: 'Be it known to Thee that Thou hast to shake from the soles of Thine shoes the dust of atheism even as Thou sheddest pride and dangerous self-regard,' he simply means that we must give up our sinful ways. See how simple it is? Nothing to puzzle over."

A Chance Meeting

Father James Potter didn't believe in miracles. Whenever he heard about an icon shedding tears or a person having a vision, or about a prophetic dream or people hearing voices, he grimaced and sighed, "Guys, let's be reasonable now."

Whenever the conversation touched upon holy men or, worse, seers, he promptly got up and left the room.

Not long before he died, he had a visitation. He was visited by a woman dressed in white, pale and wearing a plain, long canvas dress. Father James was quite ill by then and could barely get out of bed. The woman stood at the head of his bed. She had come in unexpectedly, simply materializing out of the wall. Her hand passed through the wooden headboard and Father James concluded that she was not of flesh and blood. The priest pushed a chair against his visitor but she didn't even move. He managed to gather up enough strength to ask her, "You want me to believe that you're not a hallucination? You want me to believe that you're a miracle?"

"No," said the woman simply. "I'm not a miracle. I'm death."

Father Alexander and Poets

Father Alexander Men was asked:

"Why do you praise all poetry people show to you, even if it is often the work of graphomaniacs?"

"It is far better to write poetry and believe in your higher calling than to drink like a fish," Father Alexander replied.

A Light for the World

Father Alexander used to say: "All we can do is give off light."

The Best Looking

Father Metrophanos used to say: "Father Alexander is the best looking man I have ever seen."

On Idiots

One pregnant woman often fell ill. She got one disease, then another and then a third. She suffered terribly. The doctors said to her: "You must have an abortion immediately, or else you will give birth to an idiot."

Her family was also distressed and they said, "Think of it. You will have a retarded child. Where will it live? We have no room for it."

Indeed, they were a large family sharing a two-room apartment.

But the woman was stubborn. She was religious and she didn't want to have an abortion. Her clever relatives encouraged her to talk to Father Alexander, because they knew him to be an open-minded and modern priest, not your typical obscurantist cleric. He spoke foreign languages and read books. He held scientific notions in high regard – so they hoped that he would encourage her to have an abortion.

The woman came to see Father Alexander and explained to him her problem. Father Alexander said: "If you give birth to an idiot, it will be an idiot you'll love."

She had a son and he was not an idiot at all. In fact, he is grown now and attends university.

No Holy Man

Father Alexander never had the ambition to be a prophet, like the preachers of old who were true shepherds of human souls – allowing them one thing and forbidding another, ruling on matters of life and death, barring them from receiving communion and preaching. He was very different. He mostly comforted the faithful and talked to them about the philosophers Vladimir Soloviev and Pavel Florensky. But those who came to see him were not looking for anything else.

When he died he could not be replaced, because no other priest ever read either Florensky's nor Soloviev's writings.

Where Sickness and Sorrow Are No More

When Father Ivan Krestyankin turned 90, he stopped seeing his flock. His followers, who were used to receiving spiritual nourishment at his feet, began to complain, "He nurtured us for so many years, leading us on the path to salvation. What now? It is not his fault. It is the evil men in his entourage. Why are they not letting us see him?"

But Father Ivan's servant, after turning away those who wanted to see him yet again, said to another monk with a smile, "Father Ivan has opened the gates of heaven for the people so wide that they have forgotten that old age and disease still afflict this world."

Father Misail

Father Misail had known Anna Akhmatova and was a great raconteur and an excellent speaker. He collected stories about priests. They were all true stories, and very funny ones, too. Those stories were collected in a book and the book went through several printings. Readers sent Father Misail fan mail, television channels invited him to debate the future of the Church and newspapers fell over each other to interview him. Everyone was very happy.

Then Father Misail had a strange dream. He was sitting at his desk leafing through his book about priests. But instead of his texts, the book had photographs of his characters, and they were all completely naked, like newborn children.

"What is going on?" Father Misail exclaimed, closing the book in horror. But on the cover there was another priest, a friend of his, and he was wagging his finger at him. He was also stark naked.

"Do not expose your father," the priest sternly admonished him.

The Good Shepherd

Soon thereafter, Father Misail discovered that he had a rival. It was a lay person and, moreover, a woman. A certain Kucherskaya who, so it was rumored, had also written about priests. Father Misail read a few of her stories in the *Literary Gazette*. He went to the trouble of getting the aspiring writer's telephone number and calling her.

"Mrs. Kucherskaya, I have heard that you mock priests in your writings," Father Misail said after a short and generally pleasant preliminary chat. "I have even read some of your stories. Some are amusing, but most are sad."

Kucherskaya trembled and remained silent. Think of it, a friend of Akhmatova had telephoned to give her literary advice.

"Writing about priests is a dangerous and ungrateful task," Father Misail continued. "I have learned this through personal experience. You had better apply yourself to childbearing, my lady. Unfortunately I am unable to do likewise, otherwise I swear, I would have quit writing and raised children. You, on the other hand, must never forget that bearing children leads a woman to salvation far more surely than does writing."

Kucherskaya was taken aback by such close scrutiny of her personal life and by such fatherly concern on the part of a priest. So much so that she began to have children. First she had one, then another. After the second one, however, childbearing hit a snag. She had to choose: either go on bearing children or go back to writing about Fathers. As a result, she went back to writing her tall tales about priests.

"I can't live without them, it's as simple as that," she said.

And so, while her kids were in daycare, she wrote all day and read her stories out loud to herself. In the process, she slapped her thighs, laughed, hopped about, and on occasion cried.

Volume Nine

The Paterikon was published and many copies were read all over this great land of ours. At one convent it was subjected to an *auto da fe* and burned as a piece of writing that damages the soul and is generally undesirable, while at another the nuns read it in secret and praised its unknown author. At one monastery, monks read the Paterikon openly and quoted it. Father Theophanus said, "This book should by published as Volume Nine of the Priest's Reference."

Sixth Cycle

Readings While Waiting in Line for Confession

Beauty Will Save the World

Asya Morozova was an extraordinary beauty. Her eyes were dark and seemed to look deep into one's soul. Her eyebrows were black and sharply arched, as though they had been drawn on her face. She had a straight nose and a tiny birthmark on her cheek. Not to mention her eyelashes, which were so long they covered half her face, or her thick, light-brown hair, so soft and gently curling.

Asya was bored with her studies and quit school at the age of 19. Teachers always gave her Bs because of her unearthly beauty, except for her computer science teacher, a single, 52-year-old woman who made trouble. Asya didn't want to make up a failed exam and so she dropped out.

She had so many admirers that she had long since turned off her cell phone and walked around with her hat pulled low over her eyes, so as not to attract additional attention. But it was no use.

Naturally, she didn't like anyone. Guys were jerks. She had no interest in their money. What on earth for? But she did enjoy the good life. Her parents lived in another town. They were no longer young. She had two sisters, which meant that she had no one to rely on. How can a nice young woman make a decent living? Asya became a prostitute.

Naturally, she didn't have to turn tricks on Tverskaya Street, but instead worked at a small private establishment. She made huge amounts of money. She could set any price she wanted and never did anyone refuse to pay her whatever she asked. The clientele at this establishment was well-off and background-checked; services were rendered only by appointment. Drug use and excessive drinking was not encouraged. In short, the girls were taken care of as well as if they lived in their mother's home.

It would have gone on very well had not that cozy little brothel received a visit from a very strange person.

It was a rainy day. October was at an end and the girls were yawningly bored. It was noon, which in their line of work was the slow time of day. Besides, it was raining hard outside. Suddenly, the doorbell rang. A stranger stood at the door. He was dripping water on the floor and looked miserable and wet. But even through the raindrops it was clear that he wasn't at all like their regular clients. He was about 40 years old, and he looked melancholy and pale. He wore his beard waist-long and water was dripping from its end.

Asya laughed at the sight. She had never seen such a funny bearded guy before.

"Hey, are you a professor of some kind?"

The bearded man stared silently at Asya and said nothing. The madame winked at Asya and whispered a few words into the bearded man's ear. He nodded and Asya took the new client up to the second floor.

In her room, the man thoroughly dried his beard with a towel and opened a large black bag, which he had brought with him. He put on a long black coat, over which he hung a gold cross, then took out a long narrow apron made of golden fabric and placed it around his neck. He added stiff golden cuffs held in place by strings, which he then laced up. Asya stared at him in silence. The man turned out to be a priest. He took out a pencil and drew tiny crosses on every wall of the room.

Then, he asked Asya to get him a bowl of water. There was a bathroom with a shower attached to her room and so Asya promptly got him some water. The priest opened a thick purple book and began to chant prayers and sprinkle water all around. Asya sat in an armchair and listened to the prayers. In addition to "Lord have Mercys," she made out another strange word, which sounded as though the man was trying to clear his throat: Zaccheus. A little while later, the priest stopped chanting, replaced the book in his bag, along with the small brush which he had used to sprinkle the water, took off his cassock and his cross and bowed low to Asya. Asya started in surprise. Of course, many people had gone on their hands and knees to her, but this situation was obviously different. This man straightened up easily and got ready to leave.

"What did you mean by all this?" Asya asked.

"Do you really want to know?"

Those were the first words the bearded man addressed to her. He was smiling and looking at Asya differently than any man ever had. His eyes had such an effect on Asya that she was unable to reply. His eyes were very gentle and there was no desire in them. Asya couldn't utter a single word.

"Come to see us at St. Peter's Monastery. It's on Kaluga Ramparts. Ask for Father Luke. I'll explain it all to you," said the man.

"Like hell I'm going to come to see you," Asya shrugged, returning to reality. "Not bloody likely."

Father Luke left. Asya asked them not to charge him any money. The madam did as Asya asked: Asya had a privileged position in her establishment, being its chief source of income.

But from that day forward Asya was no longer her old self. She wanted to see the bearded priest again. It was, more than anything, that strange look in his eyes. The way he looked at her, which didn't frighten her and, on the contrary, cheered her. For some reason she had a strong desire to speak to him again. She could barely wait until her next day off. She usually was free on Tuesdays or Wednesdays, the days of lightest customer traffic. She dressed as modestly as she could, hailed a cab and gave the Kaluga Rampart address. The taxi took her to the white walls of the monastery. There, Asya got cold feet for a second, but when she saw that people entered the wide-open gate freely, she screwed up her courage and went in as well.

A monk stood at the gate and Asya asked him for Father Luke. Soon she saw the familiar bearded man walking towards her. He was wearing a long cassock and a small black cap, and he had no cross on his chest. Father Luke didn't seem at all surprised to see Asya and took her to a large church with golden domes, which stood in the middle of the monastery. There, he sat next to her on a bench and began to talk to her as though he had known her for a long time.

"I'm glad you came to see me," the priest said.

"I have no idea why I came," Asya sighed. "After your visit, I missed you. I began to hate my life. It is a terrible life. I want something different."

"What is it that you want?"

"I want you to get me out of there."

"Isn't it your own choice?"

"No. The income I bring to the establishment is so large that they won't let me go as long as I'm young. They'll find me anywhere."

They spoke for a long time, discussing how to rescue Asya and talking about Christian virtue. When they spoke about lust, Father Luke told Asya his own story.

"You see, at one point I lost my faith. I will not burden you with details of how it happened, because it happened slowly, step by step, and in the end I almost stopped believing in God and doubted everything the Church tells us. The soul never remains empty for long, it yearns for sustenance, any sustenance, and if you don't give it divine sustenance it will find earthly sustenance in the pleasures of the flesh. I came to see you for the same reason everyone else does. The temptation of the flesh had tormented me since before I began to lose faith. At first I fought against it with all my strength, but the further I moved away from God, the more defenseless I became before such thoughts and sinful passions. I found the telephone number of your establishment in a newspaper. The advertisement described it as a place for 'respectable' people. It made me laugh and

I liked that description. I was, in fact, a 'respectable monk.' I called your madam and got directions to your establishment.

"I told the Father Superior that I had been called away to conduct a special service, to bless an apartment. It is usual for us monks to go into town to conduct services. To allay any suspicion and to silence my own conscience, I took with me my usual equipment, a bag with vestments and all the necessary wherewithal. That was how I set out into the arms of the Devil.

"For a long time I wandered around your neighborhood. I could not find the right address, despite the directions I had received. It was raining hard and I was soaked to the bone. I was ready to give up my adventure. It was as though the Lord had protected me from sin. But just as I had decided to return without carrying out my plan, I found the place. I had passed your two-story townhouse a number of times, but I could have sworn it was some kind of nice office or a branch of a bank, until I happened to glance at the windows and saw the white curtains with colorful butterflies printed on them. That made me realize that I was in the right place. I rang the bell and said the password, and the door was opened. That was when I saw you. I was blinded. Could a human being be so beautiful? If there was such beauty in this world, then God absolutely had to exist. All my doubts about Him and His infinite mercy and warm and merciful love for us were dispelled at that very moment. I felt the presence of the Lord. And yet, I had been tormented by lack of faith for many months. I had been despondent and melancholy. I had dreamed of possessing a woman for a long time – I'm sorry I speak to you so frankly – and then, from one moment to the next, all my doubts and sinful desires were banished from me. I felt some kind of stunned exhilaration.

Asya laughed, "Yes, I remember how you stared at me."

"I said to myself that as long as I was there, I had to conduct a service," Father Luke continued. "I went in and I blessed your room. Then I returned to the monastery. This is my entire story."

"Why didn't you speak to me then?" Asya asked.

"I was afraid to dissipate the joy I felt so suddenly. Then again, what could I have said? That I'm ten times worse than you, that I'm a lustful hypocrite and apostate?"

"Why didn't you stay and get what everybody else comes there to get? Your joy would have been even greater."

"When you feel the presence of the Lord, there is nothing else that you ever need. Your carnal desires leave you and you become impervious to sin."

"What do you think of my trade? Is it a deadly sin?"

"I say to you truly that it is the worst sin there is."

They spoke like that for many hours. Asya never returned to the brothel. Father Luke baptized her on that same day and dressed her in a modest cloak that greatly changed her appearance. For three months Asya lived in a cell at the monastery with women who did the cooking for the monks. She went to confession, talked to Father Luke, repented and cleansed her soul. In the end, she went to a remote convent with the intention of remaining there forever. At Christmas, Father Luke received a moving postcard. At Easter he got a telegram: Asya had been found in the woods near the convent, her skull crushed. The murderers were never found.

When he got the sad news, Father Luke could not recover from the shock for several days. He went to the police and told them about the establishment which he had once visited, but when he went to show them its location he could no longer find it. The cozy townhouse had simply disappeared.

There is another version of this story. After he converted Asya to the path of goodness and universal love, Father Luke could not resist her beauty and asked her to marry him. They were soon married. Father Luke left the priesthood and was defrocked. They had beautiful kids, albeit not quite as beautiful as their mother. Other monks at the monastery at first thought that Father Luke had been lost to them forever and his brethren and his spiritual children grieved greatly for his lost soul, until one day the abbot declared at supper, speaking distractedly and using Father Luke's worldly name, "Do not mourn Boris. He'll live."

Metamorphoses

Marina was a "hostess" at a well-known casino. She lived with her two younger brothers, her mother and a paraplegic grandmother. Her father had left them a long time ago, her mother drank and the family had no money. All young women want to be happy and Marina began to earn a little extra money. At first she turned the occasional trick at a nightclub and then, for three months, she had a permanent job at the casino. She enjoyed a measure of success and acquired some wealthy patrons. Soon, her family's fortunes began to turn around. Marina hired an attendant for her grandmother, sent one brother to a different weeklong daycare which had better food, and got the other brother, a first-grader, transferred to a program that offered computer classes and cost an additional 300 rubles per month. Her mother now could afford to drink Moldovan wine instead of the cheap swill sold by the liter. Her mother was not such a bad lot, really. She had been a typist at one point, typing banned samizdat literature and had even dabbled in poetry. However, she had taken to drink and, like many poetesses, had become a wino. Marina's family had once been part of the intelligentsia. In fact, Marina started to put aside money to pursue her own studies. She wanted to take classes to become a masseuse or a cosmetologist, she hadn't yet decided which.

One day at school, while Kolya took part in a computer game tournament, Marina started to chat with the father of a large family. He was waiting for his own twins. He had kids in every grade, eight all told. The father offered to take Kolya to a Sunday School that he ran.

"We have excellent teachers leading the classes," the father of the large family said. "We have a sculptor who teaches the kids to sculpt, an artist who teaches them to draw, a singer leading the choir, and a deacon teaching religion."

At first Marina didn't think much about their conversation. But the following week the paterfamilias repeated his invitation. On a lark, Marina took Kolya to the Sunday School. While Kolya was in class, she sat in the hallway alongside grandmothers, mothers and the occasional father, listening in on their conversations, which revolved around their kids, the church, priests, temptations and sins. Marina found it interesting. She had never seen so many religious people in one place. At the casino, many girls wore crosses around their necks, but they didn't attend church and if they did, they only went every once in a while, to light the odd candle. The following Sunday Marina would have overslept, were it not for Kolya. He grabbed her shoulder and shook her energetically, because he wanted to go back to that damned Sunday School. She had no choice but to get up.

Several Sundays passed, during which time Marina discovered that all those who were waiting for their kids in the hall attended services on Saturdays and Sundays. At church, they spent two hours at a time standing on their feet and then took their kids to Sunday School and waited for them half a day in that airless hall. In other words, they were completely weird.

Whenever Marina took Kolya to Sunday School she thought it was going to be the last time, because taking him there was very inconvenient. Saturday nights and early Sunday mornings were the busiest time at the casino, but Kolya begged her to take him, crying. Their mother was hungover and didn't react at all to his appeals, so Marina, although she was severely sleep-deprived, dragged herself out of bed to take Kolya to study sculpting, drawing and religion. The one saving grace was that the classes began at 1 p.m. At least there was a little time to sleep in. Besides, she eventually made new friends in the hall, especially Lenka, a young mother of two children. At least she didn't have eight kids – a measure of her relative normalcy. But Lenka was a cool gal in other ways. In short, they became good friends. Naturally, Marina never disclosed to any of the hallway crowd what she did for a living.

Lenka gave Marina idiotic religious books to read, about what you needed to know when you went to confession, the mystery of baptism, the Antichrist in Moscow and other religious propaganda. Marina put the books in the bathroom and read them only while sitting on the toilet, because they were dead boring – no real story line, and not a word about love or passion. Nevertheless, Lenka didn't leave Marina alone and kept urging her to meet the priest and to ask him about anything that bothered her. But Marina had no questions for the priest. She was bored as she sat waiting for Kolya to finish. Kolya couldn't even be trusted to travel three stops by bus to get back to their house, because Kolya was a little slow.

Then, one day Marina had a major fiasco at the casino. Somebody was stealing her rich clients from her, right under her nose, and Garik, their dispatcher, had given them a green light. Then Garik hinted to Marina that she had better stay away from the casino. She had to kiss all the extra money goodbye. Marina became so distraught that she agreed to meet Father Maxim. Father Maxim – she had to laugh – was only 25 years old, almost the same age as she. She had just turned 20.

Father Maxim suggested to Marina that she should be baptized. Yet Marina had already been baptized. A million years ago, before she had been struck by paralysis, her grandmother had had Marina baptized.

"Repentance is a second baptism," the priest replied and somehow managed to persuade Marina to go to convession.

Marina went to confession and, while confessing her sins, she grew so ashamed of her life that tears began to roll down her cheeks like water and she could not stop crying. In fact, she did stop in the end, because she passed out. She passed out because she felt as though her heart was filled with some kind of heat or fire. She felt as though she was going to suffocate. They gave her rubbing alcohol to sniff and she came to. After that, her life began to move in a totally weird direction.

Marina liked to feel the fire that had nearly burned her, but she could only feel it – albeit much weaker than the first time – when she went to confession. She tried to go to confession as often as she could. The casino had become off limits, but she had not yet saved up enough to go to school. Instead, she began to make some money by cleaning the church. Despite her previous occupation, she actually liked cleaning the church. She was much happier doing this. But the money wasn't enough. Father Maxim, despite being so young, kept giving her all kinds of bonuses and told the kitchen to supply her with food every week. One member of the congregation came by their house regularly to help with their grandmother. The priest had sent her, and she didn't charge any money, of course. She worked for the salvation of her soul. The grandmother soon died, in any case, and the priest conducted a funeral service for her. Marina's mother got so drunk from sorrow that an ambulance had to be called, but after that she stopped drinking for two full months.

Six months later Marina took the veil. She went to the New Golutvin Convent at Kolomna. She had no desire to get married, she had had her fill of men, so that side of things is pretty clear. Her family could manage without her. Her little brother continued to attend the same weeklong daycare, but he returned home on his own on Fridays, and went to school on his own, too, because there was no one to take him. Marina's mother resumed drinking cheap swill, but she now drank more moderately, perhaps as a result of Marina's prayers. Kolya continued to attend Sunday School on his own. His developmental problems became less severe and he almost completely lost his stammer, even though Lenka and her two daughters still had to walk him home from school. Kolya in fact became the mainstay of the family. He always put in a good word for his sister when their mother cursed her and complained that they had no money in the house because of her. He always said to his mother, "When I turn ten, I will start selling newspapers on commuter trains. They say I'm still too young now. Wait a little while, Mom. Wait until next year."

The Homeopath

There once was a priest who was a homeopath. He treated the faithful successfully and always accompanied his ministrations with a bit of common-sense advice. He told women that all female troubles came from wearing mini-skirts. Thyroid problems came from wearing low-cut dresses. He said these things not as a joke but in all seriousness, so that members of his congregation would dress very modestly, wearing skirts that dragged after them on the ground. They also preferred turtleneck sweaters.

Murderers

Father Aphanasius's chore was to hear the confessions of nuns at a convent. One day Father Elijah came to see Father Aphanasius. They had been close friends from their seminary days.

"Oh, how I wish a nun would turn out to be a murderer," Father Aphanasius said to his friend after they had been sitting at the table for a while and had had some refreshments.

"My God, what are you saying, Father?" Father Elijah said, shaking his head.

"I can't bear it any more. It's as if they've all part of a conspiracy. They come to me one after the other, saying, 'Father, I ate a sardine on a Wednesday.'"

Mandelshtam Street

Deacon Gregory, a Literary Institute graduate, adored Pushkin. No, he absolutely worshipped Pushkin. Sometimes, when he had to deliver a sermon, he would insert a quote from his favorite poet. He spoke of Eugene Onegin and Masha Mironova as though they were real people. At night, after saying all the prayers and bowing repeatedly to the icons, he would pick up a volume of Pushkin's verse, read a few and then invariably weep with emotion. Pushkin wrote so beautifully, the son of a bitch. Other monks had a nickname for Gregory. They called him Pushkin.

One night Father Deacon had a dream. He saw a huge field, yellow and bare. The rye had just been harvested, with a stem or two still standing here and there. He saw Alexander Sergeyevich Pushkin in person, walking toward him across that stubbly field, wearing a coat and holding a walking stick. His hair was curly and he was very animated, looking very familiar and perfectly recognizable. The wind played in his hair, blowing a forelock off his forehead. But to Father Gregory Pushkin seemed very sad.

The deacon sat down in surprise.

"Alexander Sergeyevich, is it really you?" he asked.

"Of course it's me," replied Pushkin.

"Why are you so sad then?" Father Gregory asked, nearly crying from sorrow.

Alexander Sergeyevich said nothing but looked at Father Gregory with even greater sorrow.

"Alexander Sergeyevich, I wish you knew how famous you have become on Earth," the deacon cried out.

"Ah, what is fame?" Pushkin replied forlornly, hanging his head even lower.

"But if you aren't the greatest, who is?" Father Gregory exclaimed in surprise.

Pushkin suddenly raised his head and squared his shoulders. He smiled mysteriously and looked up, staring at something behind the deacon's back, as though meaning to say: "Come now, take a look for yourself."

Father Gregory turned around, looked up and saw a birch tree. Osip Emilievich Mandelshtam was perched atop the birch tree. Mandelshtam seemed very happy. He laughed, waved his arms as though he were a bird and had wings. He even chirped like a bird, not a human being.

At that moment the priest woke up.

After that night he gave up Pushkin and read exclusively Mandelshtam. He is now committing his entire collected works to memory.

Seventh Cycle

Bedtime Readings at a Convent

Mother Gregoria in the Animal Kingdom

Mother Gregoria entered the convent in the romantic 1990s and over the course of the next fifteen years was transformed from a naïve young woman into a mature nun. She used to say: "There is nothing worse for a convent than to claim that obedience is better than fasting and prayer. By following this dictum blindly many nuns lose their love. And their human form as well."

She also used to say, "You enter the convent as a fluffy bunny rabbit, but over the years you become a prickly hedgehog. Otherwise you can't survive here."

When she said that, she usually frowned and spread out her fingers toward her listeners, like hedgehog quills.

Divine Mercy

Mother Philareta worried that the nuns at her convent were progressing poorly toward their salvation. The nuns themselves stoked her fears by complaining incessantly that they spent all day doing chores and had no time to attend services or to say their prayers. Those who were given chores in some quiet place were fortunate, at least. But what of those who worked in the barn? The lowing of the cows, the piles of manure – how could one concentrate on prayers in such an environment? Returning to their cells late at night, they complained, they barely had time to take off their clothes and go to sleep. There was no time even to read the evening devotion before bedtime. What kind of convent life was this? The holy men of old had so much more time on their hands.

The abbess spent a long time pondering the problem. At last, she made a tour of the convent and stopped at the abandoned bathhouse. The bathhouse had been built by the previous owners. It was no longer in use and was filled with trash. The abbess ordered the bathhouse cleared of the trash, cleaned up and washed. Everything was done as she requested.

"This will be your place of retreat," the abbess announced during evening meal. "Start signing up."

Each retreat was to last one week. The retreating nun received a copy of the Scriptures, a prayer book, a book of psalms, the Festal Menaion of the week, and a Typikon, along with a wool blanket. The hermit could lie under the blanket or spread it over the hard wooden bench of the bathhouse. The nun's arm, bent at the elbow, would serve as a pillow. No other bedding was provided. Sleep was allowed for three hours at a time, whereupon they had to wake for prayer. The regimen was enforced by two nuns specially placed to guard the penitent. They kept watch in turn, observing their charge through a key hole. If she fell asleep, they banged on a bucket to keep her awake. The same guards brought her food once a day.

A schedule was set up so that each nun was cloistered at least once a year. But it didn't work out that way in the end. Mother Juliana, who worked at the refectory, was the first to be locked up in the bathhouse. She had been a journalist in her past life, and very beautiful, too. She was also the most vocal among the nuns and often expressed her outrage about convent procedures. The abbess decided it was a top priority to heal the suppurating wounds that pride and excessive self-regard had inflicted upon Juliana's soul. However, on the fourth day of her retreat Mother Juliana began to make strange noises, which grew louder as the hours passed. What she meant by them was unclear, since talking to the hermit was forbidden. Yet she herself was not likely to start talking, because she was simply emitting a terrible howl. The guards reported this to the abbess. The abbess ordered them to wait another 24 hours, and in the meantime instructed the nuns to pray for the hermit that entire day. But before the day was over Mother Juliana fell silent. Apparently, the nuns' prayer had had the desired effect. But in the evening Mother Juliana didn't come to the window to take her food rations, nor did she appear the following morning. They grew concerned and opened the door a day early. At first, Mother Juliana refused to come out. She kept shaking her head and seemed to have forgotten how to speak. At last she had to be led out by the hand, and she came out willingly. She didn't react to the Mother Superior's questions, entreaties or threats, merely staring back through frozen, blue eyes. There was nothing to be done but send Mother Juliana to the infirmary and to continue praying for her unhappy soul. Two days later, in response to the nuns' prayers, she came to and became almost herself again. But from that day forward she shunned closed spaces and always tried, at the least, to keep a window vent open. But even normal people can be afflicted with this problem. It goes by the name of claustrophobia.

While Mother Juliana was recovering, the next nun was sent into retreat. This one volunteered ahead of her scheduled turn, in order to put the Devil to shame after he had so clearly had his fun with Juliana. Mother Mastodonta came through her cloistering with flying colors. She prayed, fasted and emerged completely normal, if only a bit thinner. She gained all the weight back quickly and as to the question of whether she had suffered any temptations, she replied that she had had just one temptation – towards the end she just wanted to go to sleep.

After Mother Mastodonta's great success, the Mother Superior took heart, but the next nun was another disaster. By all appearances, she came out of the bathhouse perfectly normal, but almost immediately thereafter was rushed to the hospital with a heart attack, of which she eventually died.

That was how it went. One or two went through the ordeal without incident, but a third would either go mad or become ill, or leave the convent altogether. Or else she would laugh all day long after her release, and no one could make her stop.

The Mother Superior then gathered together all the nuns at mealtime once more and declared, "It's clear that you're not ready to pray. Better to keep doing your chores as usual and stop your complaining."

That was how the Lord, in His infinite wisdom, put an end to this affair.

La Dolce Vita

Before the bathhouse retreat was shut down, but while the penitents were no longer watched closely, Mother Sophia's turn came. She was a graduate of the Shchukin Theater School. A few days later, her two best friends, Mother Georgia and Mother Hope, decided to help the prisoner survive her solitude by buttressing her spirit and, more important, sustaining her flesh. They found the key that fit the lock and, taking along as many sweets, candies and sandwiches as they could carry, along with Mother Sophia's favorite treat, tomato juice, sneaked in for an evening visit. But as soon as they unpacked their treats and started to enjoy them, there came a knock on the door. What to do? They quickly tossed all the sweets back into the bag and pushed it under the wide bathhouse bench, hanging a blanket down to the floor to hide it. Being very slim, Mother Hope slipped in behind the blanket as well, while Mother Georgia hid behind a curtain.

In came the nun who was in charge of discipline and scheduling, and whose job it was to give the penitent the proper prayers to read. Stiff with terror, Mother Sophia greeted her. It should be noted, however, that Mother Hope, who was crouching underneath the bench, was a giggler. She sat there biting her fingers to keep herself from bursting out in laughter, which made her want to laugh even more. Finally, she snorted. The nun was greatly alarmed.

"Oh, Mother," Mother Sophia exclaimed. "I've been so scared, so terribly scared. I hear strange noises here all the time, as though some evil spirits keep knocking on the walls, sighing and moaning. It is only by praying that I have been able to keep them away. Some even grab at my feet."

This time a noise, very much like a grunt, came from behind the curtain. That was Mother Georgia, who was unable hold it in any longer.

The scheduling nun had started to back away slowly, but she hit her leg against the high bathhouse bench. Mother Hope couldn't resist the temptation – which is always strongest in places of penance – and pinched the visitor's leg ever so slightly. The scheduling nun screamed like a stuck pig. She ran from the bathhouse and headed straight to the Mother Superior.

"Evil spirits inhabit the bathhouse," she shouted. "They're snorting, braying and pinching people all over."

Out of the corner of her eye, she had seen the curtain in the bathhouse sway in a very strange manner.

The abbess was instantly suspicious and promptly went out to investigate, with the scheduling nun close on her heels. Unlike the scheduling nun, however, the Mother Superior pulled at the curtains and took the trouble of bending down and looking under the bench. Nothing. The bathhouse was quite empty. By then the nuns had already fled, of course. Instead, the scheduling nun got a dressing down.

"What kind of trouble-making is this? Who will ever agree to be cloistered here if you go around spreading old wives' tales?"

In vain did the scheduling nun try to defend herself, blaming it all on Mother Sophia and throwing up her arms in despair. Next time it was she who was sent into retreat. As to Mother Sophia, she soon agreed to do her penance again, out of turn.

"Those were the sweetest moments I have had at the convent," she thought as she recalled her period of retreat, shaking her head thoughtfully.

The Frog Queen

There once was a Mother Superior whose name was Raisa. She had once been a kind, gentle woman, but since she became Mother Superior she was completely changed. She no longer loved anyone and had cut off all her friendships. Her nuns had a difficult time with her and suffered great hardships. But not every nun. Raisa had an inner circle, consisting of the deaconess and treasurer. They knew how to please the Reverend Mother, even though they too suffered much abuse at her hands. But the worst lot befell the pariahs who had at some point run afoul of the abbess, or had failed to please her, or had contradicted her in any way, or had not bowed promptly enough before her. Mother Raisa hated such nuns with an intense passion and pursued them with a relentless fury. She banned them from receiving packages and letters from the outside world, kept them from seeing the doctor in town, set other nuns upon them, and made them do man's work, such as carrying logs and chopping wood. She didn't allow them to come to services until they had finished their chores, so that they didn't attend church for months on end. Whenever anyone complained, she replied, "Obedience is more important than fasting and prayer. Are you nuns or what?"

Some of the pariahs went to live in other convents, others went home and, their hearts hardened, left the church altogether. Others still fell ill from the back-breaking work and became disabled for the rest of their lives. There was also a small group of nuns who had earned the Mother Superior's forgiveness, but earning it was no easy task.

Such was life at the convent, hidden from the prying eyes of outsiders and to all appearances peaceful and harmonious. Then, one day, a nun whose name was Anna entered the convent. The hour had struck for God's Will to be done.

Anna came from St. Petersburg, where she had been a physics teacher. At the age of 30 she took the veil and joined the convent as a novice. She had been there for two years and had performed various chores, the latest of which had been working as a seamstress. She was known for her even-tempered, cheerful disposition. She was well-behaved and had a good record, and it was time to find her a permanent position at the convent – either to promote her and to make her a nun, or else to demote her and not make her a nun.

One day, the Mother Superior summoned Anna into her presence.

"You have been at the convent for a long time but you are still a novice. That's because you have not received proper supervision," the Mother Superior explained to her. "I want to take you under my wing. I want to hear your confession – what your thoughts are, what weighs upon your soul and what sins you have committed. Now, speak."

Anna remained silent.

"I am all ears," said the Mother Superior sternly.

"Reverend Mother, I'm grateful to you for your concern and motherly care, but I attended confession last night and revealed all my tempting thoughts and confessed all my sins to Father Anatolius. There has not been enough time for me to accumulate any fresh temptations as yet."

O, silly, silly child. What deplorable lack of common sense. What naiveté. Was this any way to speak to your betters? Did you need to talk back to the chief caretaker of your miserable little soul, who only wanted to be a mother to you? It was all your own fault. You had no one to blame but yourself for bringing ruin upon your head with your false honesty (which was, in reality, nothing but disguised pride), and with your supposedly unequivocal answer.

"Not enough time, you say? You have not had any fresh temptations yet?" the Mother Superior shouted in anger, stomping her feet.

"You say you want to learn to sew nuns' habits," she continued shouting, recalling a conversation she had had with Anna some time before. "You'll learn it very well indeed. Starting tomorrow, you'll be sent to the barn to look after the cows."

She continued screaming quite a while longer, citing Church Fathers and calling Anna a pig, a miserable creature, a criminal and other such names. But she couldn't make Anna shed a single tear. The pig-headed wretch!

The next day Anna cheerfully headed for the barn and all went well. The cows got to like Anna very much. Whenever she entered the barn, they began to moo in unison, as though they were giving her a greeting. The calves licked her hands and mud-boots.

Several months passed like that. The hard work didn't seem to tire Anna at all but, on the contrary, to fill her with joy.

Then she was transferred to a damp cell, with moisture dripping from the ceiling and plaster peeling off the walls. At first, Anna placed a bowl under the drip and then she got her hands on some plaster and patched up the ceiling. Then Mother Jehosapha was told to release surreptitiously some cockroaches into Anna's cell, entire families of them, one after another. But Anna called the cockroaches good boys, gave them bread crumbs and once Jehosapha secretly observed the cockroaches line up and march single file to the open window on Anna's orders. They climbed a tree growing outside her cell, where they settled in for the night. When she heard Jehosapha's report, the Mother Superior smashed a vase on the floor and shouted, "It's an old wives' tale and nothing more. It's November. It's freezing outside."

She then sent Anna to a construction site, to work as an assistant. Anna did well there, too. She carried buckets of cement and looked happy, as though she were at some resort and not doing hard labor. Nor did she ever get so much as a stuffy nose. Not even once.

The Mother Superior then told a nun who had been a doctor in her previous life, and who was the convent's medic, to examine Anna and to find out whether she had any ailments. It turned out that, when she was young, Anna had suffered from a weak heart. So the Mother Superior sent her to the laundry. Few nuns could bear the heat and humidity there for long. Nuns worked in the laundry according to a strict schedule, and no more than one month per year. But Anna worked there for six months straight and nothing happened to her.

Mother Raisa became obsessed with her inability to reduce Anna to the same miserable state as all the other pariahs. The other pariahs at least looked pale and exhausted, and whenever they saw Mother Raisa they trembled and promptly fell on their knees, even if they had to kneel in the mud or the snow. Only by bowing low or prostrating themselves whenever they saw her could they earn her forgiveness. It was a well-known fact. Those whom she forgave made the best spies.

But Anna never fell on her knees, and even though she bowed low to the Mother Superior, all the way to the ground as all other nuns did, including those who were not pariahs, she still smiled gently as she did so. The Abbess sent out an order to check if perhaps the novice had gone crazy, but her most trusted spies reported back that Anna had spoken to them like a normal person. When asked to give the reason for her joy, she replied that, while her body endured hardship, her conscience was clear.

At that point the Abbess decided to do away with Anna once and for all. She summoned her into her presence and said, "Here is a chore for you, Anna. The construction workers don't seem to be able to finish the bakery. They may have been led astray by the Devil. He's leading them away from their holy task and won't allow them to complete their work. There are only a few hours' worth of work left on the site. I feel that you'll be able to put up a good fight and defeat the Evil One. Go and finish the bakery. I'm giving you until next morning. Are you up to it?"

"Bless me, Reverend Mother," said Anna, not uttering a word of objection, even though she had a very good reason to object, since the work on the bakery had started only recently and there was at least two months' worth of work left to complete it.

"God bless," replied the Mother Superior and made a sign of the cross over the novice. "But if you fail—"

She let the sentence trail off. It had been rumored at the convent that two nuns who had made the Mother Superior especially angry had disappeared. Their relatives raised a stink, and the police were called in to investigate, but no trace of them was ever found. The Mother Superior told their relatives, "Russia is a big country." As to the police, they visited her briefly in her office, then came out and were never seen at the convent again.

The night passed and in the morning the Mother Superior came out of her chambers. Jesus Christ! The bakery was there, all done and finished. Next to it, Anna was sweeping construction debris with a little besom broom.

The Hegumenia grew even madder at Anna.

"Here is another task for you, my dear," she said. "After this, I will put in a word for you with the bishop, to make sure you become a nun. All you need to do is to dig us a new well, because the water in our old one is starting to go stale. Do it overnight. You understand, don't you, that the nuns should not be made to drink bad water."

"Bless me, Reverend Mother."

"God bless."

When the Hegumenia woke up next morning, her chambermaid brought in a dipper full of clear fresh water.

"Reverend Mother, the well is finished."

The Mother Superior rose from her bed, threw the water into her maid's face and shouted in a terrible voice, "It's witchcraft, of course. She has been getting help."

The Mother Superior called her most devoted nuns, the deaconess and the treasurer, and told them to spy on Anna at night and to find out who was helping the accursed woman.

Meanwhile, she gave the novice a new task: to plant an apple orchard in the field next to the convent, and to make sure that the apples matured overnight, so that she, the Hegumenia, could have apples for her breakfast.

Anna said nothing and bowed to her. Late at night she set out for the field, followed by the two camouflaged nuns. One crawled on the ground, her head covered with tree branches, while the other wore military fatigues.

The nuns saw Anna kneel in the middle of the field and begin to pray fervently.

"O, Thou, All-Holy and All-Powerful Universal Lord, do not forsake me, give me time to repent my sins and do not let my soul be lost. O, beloved sweet Jesus, be merciful to me, for I am weak. Send me Thine Sacred helpers. Help me plant an apple orchard."

As she said these words, the night sky was lit by a heavenly glow, the heavens opened and the field was filled with winged young men. Each held a shovel in one hand and a small apple sapling in another. The young men began shoveling soil and planting the apple trees. They worked at a strange, angelic, superhuman pace. In less than half an hour the entire field was planted with saplings. Then the heavens darkened and it began to rain. The rain stopped after only a few minutes, having sprinkled the ground lightly. The saplings began to grow and soon became beautiful young trees. Black buds began to swell on their branches, then the buds burst into white blooms and the orchard was instantly in full flower. Anna, meanwhile, continued to pray and to cry bitterly.

The apple blossoms soon lost their petals and the fruit began to ripen on the branches, growing from small green specks into large, green spheres.

Anna continued to pray. Then, suddenly, the green spheres became golden right before the eyes of the two shocked spies.

Morning came and the winged men suddenly disappeared, as though dissolving into thin air. The treasurer and the deaconess didn't even see them go. Only one young man, or rather an angel, stayed behind. He headed straight for the shrubbery behind which the two were crouching. When he came upon them, he declared in a voice that was as loud as thunder, "Tell Mother Raisa that she has made the All-Merciful Lord very angry and that she now has but a few hours left on this Earth in which to repent. If she does not, horrible tortures await her soul. And before departing this Earth, she must go and take a look in the cellar of the far apiary."

Once he uttered those words, the young man also disappeared.

Half-dead with fright, the nuns ran back to the convent and recounted to the Mother Superior what they had seen and heard. She couldn't bring herself to believe them and shouted at them, slapping their faces and demanding to know how they had found out the truth about the apiary. However, the Treasurer and the deaconess insisted that they were only repeating what they had heard from the bright young man in the apple orchard.

Still, Mother Superior wanted to hear none of it and, as she insisted, "I have no sins to repent. No sins at all."

Then, suddenly, she turned black in the face, fell down and died.

That same evening, once the news of her death got out, the guard at the far apiary came running to the convent and fell on his knees before the nuns. He then led them to a small cellar near the apiary, unlocked the door and set free the two nuns who had gone missing a year before. They were singing and their faces shone with heavenly joy.

The treasurer and the deaconess fled the convent, after unlocking all the cellars and leaving behind the keys. The nuns spent a number of days celebrating and treating themselves to a nice big supper. Then they got together and elected Anna their new Mother Superior. Her rule in the convent was long and happy.

Her apple orchard became famous throughout Russia. It produced large, sweet apples of a previously unknown variety. Even scientists from the Timiryazev Academy of Agriculture came to see the new Hegumenia and consulted with her. The head academician was so impressed by her story that, in spite of his advanced age, had himself baptized on the spot.

A Resort

Mother Anastasia was very worried about the nuns at her small convent. They were lackadaisical, constantly asking to go on leave and to have time off, or were off bathing, doing the laundry, or falling frequently ill. Only six or seven of them out of the hundred-lot were worthy of the name. It simply wore out the Mother Superior.

She called the nuns into a general meeting and asked them, "Do you want me go to the bishop and to ask him to declare this convent a resort?"

The nuns began to clap their hands, shouting, "Yes, please."

Poor Quality

Once upon a time there were two novices, Ira and Lena. They were best friends, and had been since sixth grade. Together they started attending the Petrochemical Institute, together they became disillusioned with it all, and together they took the veil. They were placed in different cells, but they remained friends, even though a little less so than before. They no longer had much time on their hands and, besides, friendships at the convent were not encouraged.

One day Ira grew sad. And so did Lena. They slipped away to a grocery store located not far from their convent and bought two bottles of vodka. They put one aside for later use and decided to drink the second one right away. They met after vespers in the showers, having told their sisters that they wanted to wash. They spread a newspaper on a bench, got out bread, a can of salmon which they had also purchased at the store, and two plastic cups. They untapped the bottle, poured the first glass and drank. But the vodka had a strange taste, Ira thought. And so did Lena. They poured another glass but something definitely was wrong. Ira was the first to see what the problem was. Despite the label and the golden cap, the bottle was filled with ordinary water. They had purchased fake, counterfeit vodka.

But the Devil, the father of perdition, wasn't napping. He had laid his trap cleverly and with skill. The two novices promptly went to fetch the second bottle, which was very easy to do since their hiding place was also near the showers. But the second bottle also contained nothing but water, which tasted a bit like "Holy Springs" brand water. There was nothing else to drink.

Only then did the scales fall from their eyes and the young women began to shed the bitter tears of remorse, soon to be followed by the joyful tears of gratitude to the All-Merciful Lord, who had saved them from committing a sacrilege and a sin. After that, they never let a drop of alcohol pass their lips. Well, for the past three months at least.

The Telephone Nun

Mother Anthesa's chore was to watch over the telephone. The convent was in such a remote, godforsaken place that to reach the nearest post office you had to travel an entire day. The convent had only two telephone receivers. One was located in the Mother Superior's office, the other in a room next to the refectory. Anthesa's responsibility was to stay near the refectory telephone and keep the nuns from making telephone calls. Calling home was allowed no more than once a month. Anthesa had a neat, handwritten schedule detailing whose turn it was to call and when, and everyone followed her schedule. Only on the rarest of occasions, by making a special request to the Mother Superior or the deaconess, could an exception be sometimes made.

Anthesa was always in the room, as steadfast as Christ in the world, even after his Ascension – only to a different purpose, answering calls and guarding the telephone. During services and at night she kept the room under lock and key. There was no other way to enter the room or to use the telephone. Anthesa was the third most important person at the convent, after the Mother Superior and the deaconess. Nuns feared her.

Her power over them came to an end with an almost frightening swiftness. All of a sudden, the nuns began to miss their scheduled calling days and didn't stop by on the long-awaited day when they were allowed to call home. First one, then another, then a third failed to show up to make their call. The nervous tension that had always been felt in the telephone room eased a bit, and then dissipated completely. Of course, the nuns continued to bow to Anthesa, but it was very obvious that they did so without the old reverence. They addressed her with less and less respect, whereas the most insolent ones all but laughed in her face. Anthesa couldn't understand what was going on. Indeed, what was the matter?

You have probably already guessed. The age of the cell phone had arrived. Every nun now had her own tiny phone. They guarded them closely and kept them in secret hiding places, taking them out late at night and using them to write text messages to one another, both in prose and in verse.

The Mother Superior declared war on all cell phones, naturally giving her blessing to Anthesa to join the fight against the spirit of this world. Anthesa conducted searches and whenever a cell phone was found it was put into the trash before its owner's eyes. She promised the guilty eternal perdition and expulsion and, with the abbess's blessing, imposed severe penances. It was to no avail. The nuns performed the penances but replaced lost phones with new ones, finding more sophisticated ways to hide them. At last, the Mother Superior sounded a retreat because she realized that this was the sort of evil that cannot be excoriated.

Anthesa returned to the telephone room, because a handful of nuns still came there to make calls, seduced by the fact that it was free. But there was no longer a schedule. All scheduling had been abandoned. Anthesa sat at her desk, her face as dark as a storm cloud. Sometimes she could even be seen crying. She began to come to confession more frequently and attended all services diligently. Suddenly, to the amazement of other nuns, this sturdy, energetic middle-aged woman was transformed into a thin, melancholy grandmother. Over just eighteen months, Anthesa literally faded away. Father Ambrosius, the convent's confessor, conducted the funeral service. May you rest in peace in the Heavenly Kingdom. Glory Be to the All-Merciful Good Lord, the Keeper of Our Salvation.

The Abbess' Blessing

Novice Nastia Arbatova started to gain weight. Five months later the truth came out. It was too late for remorse. Nor was abortion an option. Nastia stopped going out and pretended to be ill. She was afraid to go to the Abbess because their Abbess was extremely strict. But such things could not stay hidden for long in a convent. No doubt someone had already informed the Abbess, but for some reason the Abbess had not yet summoned Nastia; she agonized while her girth continued to expand.

Finally, the young woman could bear it no longer and went to the Mother Superior's office. The Hegumenia barely glanced at her and asked, "What are you planning to do?"

Nastya sobbed and wiped her tears with her fist.

"Did you find a midwife yet? How are you going to raise the child?"

Nastya said nothing.

The Hegumenia imposed a penance on her.

"You will have to leave the convent. When you have the baby, I want you to raise it a Christian. We will help you with money."

Nastya shook her head but the Mother Superior went on, "Do not refuse. It is my fault, too. I failed in my duty to protect you and it is my foremost debt to the Lord. We will have to support you both. When your child comes of age, he or she will have to take the vows in your place. This is my penance on you. Do you understand?"

Nastya understood, thanked the Hegumenia and promised to do as she had been told.

She had nowhere to go, for she was an orphan from a family of refugees. She settled in a small town not far from the convent.

Soon she gave birth to a boy, and an amazing boy he was. From a very early age his favorite game was to play church. He pretended to be a deacon. His second passion was for books. He loved reading about history and biology. On the Abbess's orders, the convent supported Nastya financially, so that mother and son did not want. There was peace in their small household and every Sunday they attended services at their local church. Nastya adored her Alyosha. The older he got, the more deeply she loved him. She feared that her son would one day find out about her promise to make him a monk. She had no wish to send him away to a monastery. She wanted to be a grandmother and to play with her grandchildren. She wanted to have a normal life.

Time went on. The boy was about to graduate from high school and he was attending a tutorial for college in Vladimir, where he commuted twice a week from their town. Soon Nastya found out that the Hegumenia who had imposed the penance on her had died. She felt as though a heavy stone had fallen from her chest.

But when Alyosha turned seventeen, one day after graduation, he rose from the dinner table, bowed to his mother and asked her for her blessing to become a novice at a monastery.

Nastya went cold with horror. How had he found out about her penance? Had somebody been talking?

"Who told you about it?"

"Nobody told me anything," replied Alyosha. "I want to be a monk."

Then Nastya revealed to him her terrible secret and her penance, which she had kept secret from him for so many years. Alyosha smiled gently at her.

"It is the Hegumenia's blessing," he said.

A week later he left for a remote monastery, which had recently been reconsecrated. Nastya, still a relatively young woman, never returned to the convent. It was not to be her path in life, after all. She moved to a village not far from Alyosha's monastery, where she lived long enough to see him wear an Archbishop's mantle and she passed away quietly, at peace with herself and the Lord.

The Ballerina

"You see, Reverend Father," a novice once said to the confessor at a convent. "I'm bored at the convent. I started to dance at the age of four and I almost became a ballerina. When I took the veil, I threw away my ballet slippers and my tutu, as well as all the photographs which showed me dancing. Yet now I have such a strong desire to dance."

The priest said nothing to the novice, but a month later, on her name day, he gave her a gift of pink satin slippers and a real tutu.

The novice was overjoyed. She tried on her new slippers and they fit her perfectly.

"When you think of your past," said the priest, "and you get the desire to stand in third position or sixth position, I give you my blessing to put on your slippers and your tutu and to dance as much as you wish. You can use our conference hall. Get the key from Mother Eustaphia.

After that, the novice lost all desire to dance. She never asked for the key to the conference hall. She put the slippers and the tutu away in the corner of her trunk and didn't think of them for months on end. But every year, on the evening of her old name day (she had by then become a nun and had taken a different name), she would open the lid, look at the priest's gifts and remember his warmth and infinite love, and she would pray for the soul of Hieromonk Andrianus, because the priest had long since passed away.

Eighth Cycle

Seminary Tales

Clowning Not Encouraged

Father Athenogenes taught liturgy at the seminary. He was thin and tall and had a dark beard and thick, bushy eyebrows. He had a nasal voice and spoke slowly, pronouncing words in a singsong manner and pausing after each one for nearly a minute.

"Let us start. Without haste." A pause. "The Holy Liturgy." A pause. "Must not. Be celebrated." Another pause. "In chapels." A pause. "Homes." A pause. "Or cells." A very long pause.

At his lectures, students literally choked on their laughter.

One day, Father Athenogenes called a student to the front of the class. The student began to recite the lesson exactly as Father Athenogenes had presented it, repeating it word for word and using the same expressions and making the same long pauses.

"The Holy Liturgy." A pause. "Must not. Be celebrated." Another pause, etc.

Father Athenogenes listened to him for a long time, apparently unaware of the joke. The students were literally groaning, holding back their laughter. At last, Father Athenogenes frowned, bringing his his bushy eyebrows together and saying calmly, "Clowning is not encouraged."

How to Relate to the Clergy

Denis Skvortsov, a first year student at the seminary, was ignorant of the customs of the institution when one day he entered the office of the Dean, Father Eupsychius. Denis wanted to ask permission to go home for the weekend.

The moment he came in and before he could utter a single word, Father Eupsychius asked him, "What do you think of the clergy?"

"I respect them," Denis replied, surprised.

"Then get out and close the door behind you."

Denis got out and immediately knocked on the door again.

"Good day, Reverend Father Eupsychius," he said. "May I ask you—"

"What do you think of the clergy?" Father Eupsychius again said, interrupting him.

"I revere them."

"Get out and close the door behind you."

Denis was in despair. He knocked on the door a third time. This time he didn't even have time to open his mouth.

"What do you think of the clergy?"

"Very highly. They're absolutely wonderful," responded Denis, completely confused.

"Get out and close the door behind you."

The poor student got out and stood at the door of the Dean's office lost in thought. He wanted to go home very much. At that moment, an older friend of his, second-year student Levka Ovchinnikov, happened to be passing by. Virtually in tears, Denis told him that Father Eupsychius seemed to have lost his mind. In reply, Levka laughed.

"Did he ask you what you thought of the clergy? Next time when you come in, ask him to bless you and grant you permission to enter."

Next time, Denis did as he had been told. An hour and a half later he was traveling by suburban train, comforting himself after his terrible misadventure with an excellent, ripe apple, given to him by Father Eupsychius.

Hair Length

While the seminary students were having their breakfast, Archimadrite Benjamin, who in his past life had been a policeman, walked around the dining hall and inspected their heads. Whenever he saw someone with longer hair than permitted by regulations, he would address the transgressor in a loud voice:

"Who are you?"

"I'm Alexander, sir," the student would reply, half-choking and jumping to attention.

"You must reply, 'Student Alexander.'"

"Student Alexander, sir."

"Now, Student Alexander, take a look at the back of my head."

Father Benjamin would turn his back on the hapless student.

"Are you seeing what I want you to see?"

"I am, sir," the student would reply uneasily.

The Archimadrite would then touch his neck with two fingers, indicating how short his hair was cut. Then he would compare it to the length of the student's hair and say:

"I'm an archimandrite while you're merely a student, Alexander. But my hair is shorter than yours. I'm going to check again before supper whether or not you have understood what I'm telling you. If you have not, you will have to go without supper."

Needless to say, the student came to supper the next time with his hair cut short. Years passed, and in due course Archpriest Benjamin became a bishop. Some of his former victims, when they got together at some conclave or public procession, liked to joke about him and to wonder whether the bishop checked the length of his diocesan priests' hair, telling them, "I'm a bishop whereas you're a mere archimandrite. Yet, my hair is shorter than yours."

Fat and Thin

There once were two seminary students, Cyril and Vitya. They went to school together and together they hated the communists. They read underground samizdat literature and admired Father John of Kronstadt and prayed to the martyred Russian Emperor Nicholas II, in secret of course, keeping a strict fast on July 17, the anniversary of his execution. Everything was clear to them and their life was uncomplicated. Eventually, the boys got married, and each was best man at the other's wedding. Soon they were both ordained as priests. Father Victor was sent to a parish near Moscow, while Father Cyril went to a remote place in the Moscow region, to a church that had been abandoned for a long time. Father Victor became the third priest at his parish, whereas Father Cyril became the parish priest.

Both were happy. Father Victor commuted to his church from Moscow by bus. He was easy-going and accessible and had a gift for speaking smoothly and clearly. He was compassionate and kind and soon earned the affection of his congregation. He was also on good terms with his superiors and, when the parish priest at his church died, it was natural enough that he would take his place. Moreover, he turned out to have a knack for building. He had an excellent house built for his deacons, where a charity meal was served every Sunday.

Father Cyril, meanwhile, soon got weary of his three-hour commute by suburban train and bus, and eventually moved his family to the village where his church was located. He settled down, planted a large apple orchard, led services on feast days, preached to old ladies and carried out various priestly duties. In his free time, he read extensively and wrote under a pseudonym on the history of the Church in the famous *Messenger*, publisched in Paris by YMCA Press. His articles were full of astute observations and penetrating thoughts. Gradually, he became known in some circles. Visitors from the capital began to come his church, mostly members of the intelligentsia. They wanted to breathe country air and hear a learned discourse. The priest visited Moscow often and there saw his old friend Vitya. They exchanged forbidden literature and discussed repressions against the Church by the authorities. They also talked about ways to deal with intrusive state supervisors and KGB-appointed elders. Sometimes they shared a bottle of red wine.

Then, suddenly, perestroika began.

Underground literature appeared at bookstores and priests began to be published in newspapers and shown on television. They were invited to lecture in schools and at universities. John of Kronstadt was canonized, and, soon after, so was the Tsar. The two friends suddenly had nothing to talk about. They saw each other less and less frequently, and when they did meet they felt awkward. The one who cultivated his apple trees and wrote articles grew close to Catholics, placing benches in his church (a decision which drew no objections from the old women, to say nothing of the visitors from Moscow), reading the Scriptures and conducting parts of the service in modern Russian – a sure sign he was lapsing into the Latin heresy.

Father Victor, meanwhile, remained faithful to Holy Russia. He kept the benches and the modern Russian out, delivered fresh, emotional sermons and soon was transferred from his near-Moscow region to a parish church in the capital. He was given a church building that had been returned to the Church by the state and under his skillful management it rose from ruins and turned into a pretty picture. He joined various Orthodox commissions, committees, editorial boards and societies. In short, he rose to a position of authority. Even his posture changed, and his body acquired a certain solidity.

Father Cyril, meanwhile, spent so much time rubbing shoulders with Catholics that he was banned from leading services for six months and became a subject of a small public *auto da fe*. It took place at a learned Orthodox conference, where Father Victor, the admirer of Holy Russia, gave a particularly scathing speech.

His former friend paid little attention to the ardent denunciations. He kept thinking instead, "There used to be more love in the Soviet Union. Perhaps I should run off and join the Jesuits."

He also continually mumbled to himself, "There you have it!" shaking his head and quietly grunting now and then.

The Darkness

A teacher asked an applicant during the seminary entrance exam, "On which day did the Lord create light?"

"It is unclear."

"What do you mean?"

"It was so dark."

Faster, My Lad!

Father Varlaam, the teacher of apologetics, was known for his impatience, "Come on," he used to say, hurrying a student along whenever he didn't answer a question right away. "Push the baby out already!"

The students nicknamed him Obstetrician.

A Beard

Third-year student Deacon Oleg had trouble growing facial hair. All he could muster was two or three thin tufts instead of a real beard. For that reason his classmates called him Aaron's Beard.

Not long before graduating from the seminary, Father Oleg shared his chagrin with Father Cyril Pavlov, "I'll soon be a priest and look at what I have instead of a beard. It's like a desert with a few cacti. Could you say a prayer for me, Father?"

The priest smiled brightly at him and cited Peter's first epistle:

"Let it not be that outward adorning of plaiting the hair, and of wearing of gold, or of putting on of apparel. But let it be the hidden man of the heart, in that which is not corruptible, even the ornament of a meek and quiet spirit, which is in the sight of God of great price."[1]

Father Oleg laughed happily when he heard this and felt utterly at peace. The most interesting thing is that, at the age of thirty, when he had been a priest for a long time and a father of a large family,

---

1. 1 Peter 3: 3-4. Yet Peter is here addressing the adornment of Christian women, not priests' beards. Verse 5 continues: "For after this manner in the old time the holy women also, who trusted in God, adorned themselves, being in subjection unto their own husbands."

his beard and mustache suddenly thickened and gave him a highly respectable appearance. Clearly, Father Cyril's prayers had had an effect.

"Finally, you've become a grown-up," his sharp-tongued wife said.

She was the one who wore the pants in their household. The priest was even-tempered and never responded when his wife poked fun at him. He merely thanked the Savior for all His favors.

Ninth Cycle

Orthodox Miracles in the 21st Century

A Sinner's Death is Terrible

There once was a fellow who decided to go on a pilgrimage. He got the idea from a neighbor, a woman whose name was Sergeyevna. She had returned from a pilgrimage herself, which had cured her leg. She had traveled to a nearby monastery at Bobrenev. There were no miracle-working relics at Bobrenev, except for the Fyodorov Mother of God icon. It was an ordinary icon, painted at Sofrino, but there was a persistent rumor that it worked miracles. Sergeyevna, when her turn came to approach the icon, had no idea what to ask the Theotokos, because her mind had gone blank. Suddenly she felt a sharp pain in her leg and so she prayed, "Mother of God, please make the pain in my knee go away."

In the morning her knee didn't hurt any more. The pain was gone. Sergeyevna could walk as easily as a young girl. When she came home, she shared the story with her neighbor. The neighbor remembered that Sergeyevna had walked with a limp before going on the pilgrimage, thought about it and, even though he didn't believe her, decided to try it for himself. Why not? It could be an interesting test.

He got to the monastery but discovered that he couldn't approach the icon. He was prevented by some unknown force. He tried different ways of getting close to it, coming up from the right and from the left, as well as straight down the middle. He was stopped every time. He could not get closer than a meter away. No one else had any trouble whatsoever getting near it – kids, women, even a miserable, disheveled young man. He alone was quite unable to draw near.

The man became so angry that his face darkened. He decided to ask the monk selling candles at the church to explain what the problem was. Perhaps there was a secret word he needed to say.

The monk looked at him through the thick lenses of his glasses and said, "The Theotokos is not allowing you to came near Her. Apparently, because of sin."

"Because of what sin?" the man shouted.

The monk looked at him again, eyes gleaming through his lenses, and said, "Do not shout in God's temple."

The man had to stop shouting, but the monk kept the pressure on. He was developing a taste for it, it seemed. "You must repent. Tomorrow we will have our usual service, and then, at eight o'clock, we will hear confessions. Come to confession. Have you ever confessed your sins?"

"Never."

"Then it's high time you did. The only thing is, you should remember everything thoroughly."

The man wanted to respond that he had nothing to remember, but he shrugged and spat on the ground instead. Of course, after he had left the church. Then he suddenly turned around and ran full speed toward the icon, hoping to take it at full gallop.

But at the distance of one meter from the icon it was as though he hit a wall. The fellow hit his head hard on something, something like a tree trunk, even though there was nothing there, just thin air. He grabbed his forehead and went straight to the train station without looking back.

"What kind of an icon is that? These people are like dogs," he said to himself as he headed home.

When he returned, he saw his neighbor Sergeyevna on the other side of the fence. She was digging potatoes and showed no sign of a limp. The man decided to sneak up behind her and strangle her. But Sergeyevna spotted him, greeted him happily and ran up to the fence to chat.

"How are you? And how was my beloved little icon? Did you feel its divine grace?"

The man stood there for a while but said nothing. Then he turned around and went away. He walked around with a darkened face and said nothing to anyone. A week later he was dead.

Sergeyevna, of course, couldn't resist returning to the monastery and asking around about what had happened to her neighbor. It must have been something terrible, since he died as a result of it. There, they learned from her how her neighbor had died and shook their heads in awe. Many people had seen him run into the invisible wall. As to the learned monk, the one who wore glasses and sold candles, he merely shrugged, "It does not surprise me at all."

From the Lives of Young Mothers

Tonya got pregnant. He was a future parachutist attending a military school. They met at a dance club. Of course, he had no intention of marrying her. Tonya was just 17 years old. It was clear she was pregnant by the time her senior dance rolled around. Her mother was supportive when she heard the news.

"I'm glad you didn't decide to get an abortion, darling. Don't worry. We'll raise the child together."

The doctors said, "The umbilical cord is twisted around the fetus's neck. It's very unfortunate. The baby might suffocate at birth."

They advised Tonya to get a Caesarian. Tonya's mother agreed with the doctors. But Tonya didn't want to have her belly sliced. She liked the way it looked and didn't want it to be cut with a knife.

Tonya told the doctors, "I'm afraid."

"You'll kill the baby," the doctors replied.

Tonya grew depressed. Somebody suggested to her mother that they go to Bobrenev, the first right after the Ring Road. The monastery had a Fyodorov Mother of God icon. All that was needed was to pray to it and everything would work out. Tonya was already in her ninth month and might go into labor at any moment. And they had no way to drive themselves to Bobrenev. The only public transportation available took them as far as the turn-off. After that, it was a three-kilometer walk through a field. It was the end of November and the weather was getting cold. But her mother took Tonya by the hand, they got on the bus, got off and began to walk. A strong wind blew and the ground was slippery, but they pressed on.

They barely made it. They got to the cast-iron gate, pushed on it and found it open. They entered the monastery and went to the church, but it was closed. Tonya began to cry. Her mother went all around the monastery looking for help. A monk came out of a stone building and said that they held services only on Sundays, but that they always allowed access to the icon to those who wished to pray to it or light a candle. He unlocked the church with an enormous key. Tonya came in and ran to the right icon, even though she had not been told which one it was. In her heart, she knew which was the right icon.

They stood in front of the icon, made a sign of the cross and lit a candle. What next? Tonya was sad and in tears. And they still had to make their way back through the field. The same monk who had opened the door for them came up to her and said, "I have no idea what your trouble is. Stay here a while, or take a seat over there and pray. Everything will work out."

Tonya took a seat on the bench and her mother sat next to her. They sat there and rested, and then started on their way home.

Two months later Tonya's mother returned to the monastery and recounted to them what had happened.

"We came out of the monastery and Tonya suddenly screamed, "'Mother, something is happening to me.'

"I thought her contractions had started.

"'Do you feel like something is pulling down at the bottom of your stomach?' I asked.

"'No, Mother. Something is pulling me up.'

"She began to run. I started after her.

"'It's slippery over there, Tonya. Wait.'

"We reached the turn-off just as the bus came. Two days later the contractions started. She gave birth to a baby boy. A healthy, strong baby boy who weighed four kilos. All the maternity ward doctors came by to look at Tonya and the baby. One of them, some kind of professor, said, "'It is a first in my entire medical experience.'

"The moment we came home from the hospital, a student from the military school came to see us. He was a friend of that loser, the baby's father.

"'Do you happen to need a father?' he asked.

"We were completely at a loss.

"'What about a husband?' he asked then.

"It turned out that he had had his eyes on Tonya for a long time, and would have come to her earlier, but his parents had been dead set against the match. However, he had managed to convince them, and the moment he did, he ran to see us. They got married two days ago."

A month later, the baby was brought to the monastery to be baptized. This time, Tonya looked very different, very calm. The baby didn't cry, only made baby noises. Her mother wanted Tonya to recount again how it all turned out so well, but Tonya was embarrassed. She only said, "Back then, in the field, when we left here, I felt as though I had been swept up by some force. I felt so light. It was then that I knew that I no longer had anything to fear."

Pansies

Father Antipas received permission to live at a retreat five kilometers from the monastery. Trained as a gardener in his past life in the world, Father Antipas transformed the retreat into a splendid garden. All kinds of flowers bloomed in its flowerbeds, starting in early spring and late into fall. On a windy day, the smells from his garden reached the walls of the monastery. He built a small greenhouse in his cell. He corresponded with the Agricultural Academy and they sent him seeds for new flower varieties. Nevertheless, he never stopped praying and remained cheerful and full of energy. Monks who visited him in his isolation admired the fruits of his labors, to which Father Antipas usually replied, "I wish I could smell the flowers in heaven."

One day, a wise holy man paid him a visit. He said, "You don't have much longer to wait."

A few months later Father Antipas died. It was late fall, the first snow of the season had fallen and the Lord revealed a miracle to the monks. On the day after their brother the gardener was buried, a bunch of pansies grew on his grave and the flowers opened. They bloomed for several days and didn't die despite the cold and the wind, until they were completely covered with snow.

Never in Vain

Nina Andreyevna found God when she was 40 years old. Her beloved husband had left her and her heart had turned to God. She had three kids and she felt very sorry for them. Like any mother, she wanted their lives to be happy and easy. She was afraid that God would punish them for her and her late husband's sins, which, as she had read in one book on faith, accumulated and weighed heavily on future generations. She was certain that the two of them had plenty of sins. Her own father, as well as her grandparents, had all been atheists. As to her husband's family, there had been plenty of non-Christians there who had not even been baptized.

One day, a dying woman gave her a strange old icon which bore the inscription "Tsar." This was in the early 1980s, which was a difficult time for the Church. Real icons, painted on wood with real pigments, were a rarity. You could only find cheap Sofrino images. Nina Andreyevna was very happy to receive the icon.

The icon depicted a saint holding a spear and wearing a royal purple tunic. He must have been the tsar of the inscription, but it was not clear which tsar he was, since no name was given. Nina Andreyevna decided to show the icon to a priest. He looked at the strange word and explained to her that it spelled Uar, not Tsar. It was an inscription in Church Slavonic and in that language the letters that made up the word did make it look like Tsar. Nina Andreyevna looked up his life story in the Euchologion and discovered that one prayed to the Holy Martyr Uar for relatives who had not been baptized, both living and dead. Thanks to the martyr's intercession, your family tree, which may have accumulated many sins, could be cleansed of its oppressive weight of filth. This was exactly what she needed.

From the same priest who had helped her read the inscription she received a benediction to daily read the canon before the image of Holy Martyr Uar, listing her family members, both her blood relatives and her husband's. This she should do throughout Lent. Every day. The priest had blessed her.

Every day Nina Andreyevna waited impatiently for evening to arrive. In the evening, once she had finished her chores and put the kids to bed, she would light a candle before the image of Uar, open the canon and say her prayers. After every psalm of the canon she mentioned her and her husband's relatives, both the living and the dead, all whom she knew and whom she could remember, as well as those whose names she had learned from other relatives.

She rather liked praying. After reciting the canon, she felt joy spreading through her soul and the world becoming infused with light. The only thing she was not sure about was whether or not all those whom she had mentioned had had their sins forgiven. Three weeks passed and Holy Week began. Nina Andreyevna continued to pray. But she was plagued by doubt, "Oh, Lord, what if it is all in vain?"

On the fifth week of Lent, late at night, she was awoken by a terrible scream, "Mother, come open the window."

It was her youngest son screaming, seven-year-old Vanechka. Nina Andreyevna came running to the children's room and threw open a transom. Vanya was sitting in bed, rubbing his eyes.

"There is a terrible smell here," he said softly.

"Did you have a bad dream?"

"It didn't seem like a dream. It was so real. I was lying here, in my bed, and then suddenly he appeared over there in the corner."

Vanya motioned with his hand.

"He wore a violet crown, except he wasn't real but made of light. He was very small, no larger than a hand. He walked up to me and said, '"Cursed be the day when you learned the name of Christ. Cursed be the day when you were baptized.'"

Vanya sighed.

"Then, suddenly, Martyr Uar appeared. He was just as small, except he emitted bright rays of light. One of the rays hit him, and the violet one began to twist and tried to spin away from the rays, but he couldn't. Then, he just popped."

The room began to stink and Vanya woke up.

His mother kissed him on his forehead, patted his head and the boy fell fast asleep, sniffling softly in his sleep.

Nina Andreyevna told everyone she knew this amazing story, concluding each time, "Never test the Lord or ask Him stupid questions, because no effort is ever wasted."

The Damaged Bookcase

There once was a young woman who prayed in secret from her parents. When they went to bed, she would remove the books from the bookcase, light an icon lamp and begin to recite the daily prayer and read from the Book of Psalms. One day she was so caught up in her prayers that she didn't notice when the flame of the icon light got too high and began to burn the bookshelf. She blew it out, but it was too late. The top shelf had a black hole burned through it.

The young woman was terrified. What would her parents say? She began to pray for the hole to be fixed by some magic, so that the bookcase would be like new again.

"I believe that the Lord can do it," she kept repeating.

She stood there praying for an hour, then another, closing and opening her eyes and hoping for the miracle to happen, but the black mark was still there. Disconsolate, she went to bed.

In the morning, she took a look at the bookcase, and saw that the hole was still there. It was impossible to hide it, as even the tallest books didn't quite cover it. The young woman waited for a disaster to strike. But her mother came into the room and noticed nothing. Then her father came in and also said nothing. They stared at the bookcase, and said nothing. It was only three years later that the young woman's mother noticed that the bookcase had a hole burned into it, but by then she too had started to go to church and she was able to understand her daughter. Besides, they soon bought a new bookcase, anyway. The old one had started to fall apart.

Father Paul and Agrippina
1. To a Distant Land

Once upon a time there lived a girl whose name was Grunya. She was being raised in a respectable merchant family, and she said to herself: "When I grow up, I will be a nun." Soon she did, in fact, more or less grow up, and she started her studies at the nursing school at the Convent of St. Martha and St. Mary. She received a habit and began to minister to the sick. She was very happy. One time, Grand Princess Elizaveta Fyodorovna, on her Saint's Name Day, gave Grunya her photograph, which she had personally inscribed. But then the Bolsheviks came, murdered the Grand Princess and chased everyone out of the convent.

Grunya began to visit the Monastery of St. Daniel, where she met a young hieromonk. His name was Father Paul. He was an ascetic and spoke sternly with his followers, which appealed to Grunya, since she absolutely hated sweet talkers. She had a strong personality and she liked a firm hand.

In due course, the Bolsheviks laid their hands on St. Daniel's as well. They arrested Father Paul and transported him to the camps. At first he had no idea that a young woman, a devotee, had followed him. Twenty-eight-year-old Grunya traveled with him in order to look after him and to keep him from dying. An elderly ascetic at St. Daniel's, Father Simon, gave her his blessing to follow Father Paul and Grunya's parents also accepted her decision. Grunya took to the road, traveling as best she could. There was one type of train car for inmates and another for ordinary passengers. No one knew when the inmates would be taken off one train and put on another, so she had to be alert. Grunya stared out the window, listened closely and stayed awake. She always managed to get off the train at the right moment. But then there was the problem of having to wait for the next train and to get on it in order to keep following the transport. Each time she had to cajole and beg the conductor to let her on, and she always managed to get into the car that was next to the inmates. But she was able to see Father Paul only from afar and rarely.

Then, in one of the transfer prisons she was allowed a visit. When he saw the young woman, Father Paul didn't crack a smile but frowned and said, "Who blessed your journey?"

"Father Simon and my parents," replied Grunya.

Only then did the priest relent a little.

2. Following a Sleigh

Grunya followed Father Paul further. The final 200 kilometers to his place of exile, the town of Akmolinsk (now Astana), had to be covered in a sleigh, into which were loaded some female convicts, Father Paul and the guards. The horse started. Grunya started to walk behind the sleigh. The horse was straining to pull the sleigh full of people and trotted slowly, but still faster than a human being could go. Grunya broke into a run. The female convicts took pity on her. They asked the soldiers to allow her into the sleigh. They stopped the horse and called the young woman over. She came up to them:

"Do you plan to run the entire 200 versts?" they asked her.

"I do," she replied.

They let her into the sleigh.

She and Father Paul rented a room in town. They hung a rope across the middle of the room and partitioned their two halves with a bed sheet. Father Paul performed the liturgy. Grunya chanted along with him and cooked their food, did the housework and washed their clothes. One day a drunken policeman, an ethnic Kazakh, came into their room and demanded money from Father Paul. Father Paul had none. The policeman then shot at Father Paul point blank. He missed Father Paul but hit Grunya, because she jumped in to shield him with her body. The bullet hit her on a cheek. It was not a serious wound, but they had to take her to the hospital. Father Paul kept scolding her:

"Why did you do that? You have no idea what you're doing."

3. Go One More Time

One winter they ran out of water. Grunya picked up the bucket. There was a blizzard outside and carrying a full bucket over the slippery ground was difficult.

"Bring half a bucket," said Father Paul.

But when she got to the river, Grunya thought, "What's the point of taking half a bucket and coming back a second time. I'm going to take a full bucket."

Father Paul saw that the bucket was full and that Grunya had disobeyed him.

"Go back and pour half a bucket back into the river," he said.

4. Not a Word

Father Paul spent more than 20 years in exile and in the camps. In 1955, he settled as a hermit in Tver region. Only two monks served him, besides Agrippina Nikolayevna, which was what Grunya was now called. No one else even knew where he lived. In isolation, he wrote letters to priests and some laymen. The persecution of the Church had eased, but the life of the clergy was still very hard. Father Paul helped them choose the right path and his letters were awaited as eagerly as a meeting with the Lord, because the Reverend Father knew God's Will. One person to whom he never wrote was Agrippina Nikolayevna.

"What is the point of writing to you?" Father Paul used to ask her. "It is clear that I love you and pray for you. The rest you'll know from your confessor."

Agrippina Nikolayevna never took offense. She believed that he was right and knew she could survive without his letters.

People often said to her, "You saved his life, you know."

To which she would reply, "What is the point of writing? It is clear that the Reverend Father loves me and prays for me. The rest I'll learn from my confessor."

5. Save Me from Agrippina!

When Agrippina was 56 years old, Father Paul gave his blessing for her to marry an ailing old man so that she would minister to him and so that he would not die without human care. They did not wed and were husband and wife only on paper. Agrippina Nikolayevna took care of him until he died.

Then she went to live in the house of an elderly priest, who was a good man and a famous one, too. Agrippina Nikolayevna became his maidservant and spiritual daughter. Father Paul wrote letters to the priest. In almost every letter he comforted the priest and asked him not to be angry with Agrippina. Because Agrippina had become impossible to bear. Her unyielding personality had an edge to it. The old priest, an experienced, wise and cultivated man, could not get along with her. He complained about her to Father Paul. Father Paul replied to him, "It is God's will. Be patient. It is God's will."

Finally, he grew tired of repeating the same thing over and over again and wrote that the priest could let her go if that was easier for him, even though... Even though tolerating her was God's will.

6. The Passing

Agrippina Nikolaevna died in extreme old age, in 1992. Fifteen priests performed the funeral service. They couldn't decide who would carry her casket. Everyone wanted to take part in the procession. The casket was carried around the church, St. Nicholas at Kuznetsy. People chanted and shed tears.

7. *He Saw What He Wanted*

Those stories were about Agrippina Nikolayevna. It is not possible to write about Father Paul. It makes you tremble.

He lived the final thirty years of his life as a hermit, but he knew what was happening thousands of miles away. He could hear conversations held in other cities and could read thoughts which a person kept hidden from everyone. He wrote letters to people whom he chose himself, and sometimes sent them cables, as well. The letters recounted those unheard conversations, named men whom Father Paul had never met and were posted to addresses which he had no way of knowing. Or, to put it another way, he saw everything and was present everywhere, but in his own way, spiritually. But this doesn't make it easier to understand. In his letters, he often answered questions which people had only intended to ask him. It was like something out of science fiction.

Here is one such story. When Father Vsevolod Spieler was undergoing surgery, Agrippina Nikolayevna visited Father Paul. While serving her tea, Father Paul casually asked her about Father Vsevolod's son, "Why is Ivan Vsevolodovich standing by the door of the surgery?"

Then he caught himself.

"Oh, I'm sorry. Of course, you can't see that."

Indeed, it happened exactly as he had said. The entire time his father was in surgery, Ivan Vsevolodovich had stood by the door of the surgery.

Father Paul died in November 1991 at the age of 98. No one knows where he is buried or even under what name. He seemed to have been transported into the twentieth century from the time of Abraham and Isaac, when the Holy Spirit breathed through the nostrils of our forefathers and they heard the Voice of the Lord just as we now hear the radio or the sounds of motor vehicles outside our windows.

Tenth Cycle

American Stories

Hatred

Sasha Gundarev hated priests. The sight of them filled him with such deep revulsion that whenever they were shown on television or when he spotted one in real life – but mostly on television, of course – he would switch the channel immediately, full of bile. On several occasions he even had to run to the toilet to vomit.

"Why do you hate them so much?" his Orthodox wife Vera asked him, tears welling up in her eyes.

"You know why," hissed Sasha.

Indeed, Vera did know why, yet she repeated the question time and again from desperation. Sasha had long ago told her what he thought of priests. He had read all of Vera's religious books and was well-versed in such matters. He used Vera's own books to defeat her in their arguments.

"To start with," Sasha asked, "why are they so damn pleased with themselves? What have they done that is so great? Nothing. Therefore, there is no reason for them to be so damn haughty. Then, why is it that one half of them hate Jews, while the other half are great nationalists of the "land of the Rus" and fans of all those nationalistic programs shown on Channel Three? England and France are also holy, by the way, not just Russia, and so are Spain and New Guinea. Besides, Christ was the first internationalist. The priests pervert his teachings, Vera, his Scriptures. Moreover, why is that that they love power, both secular and spiritual? They love most of all to order all the lost souls around, which only further damages those souls, and they also love to venerate the odd icon in the company of the President. Finally, why do they love money so much? Why aren't they embarrassed to drive around in fancy foreign cars and build four-story "cottages" for the clergy while harping all the while on how much the church is persecuted? Meanwhile, ordinary people are starving."

At this point, Vera sometimes could counter Sasha's arguments by asserting that far from the capital, in remote villages, the people and the clergy starve together.

"They get a pile of rubble and are told to rebuild it into a church. They get no money for it. Young kids, straight out of the seminary, also starve," Vera screamed.

"Sure, at first those kids starve and then they grab power, so as not to starve any more," Sasha responded cuttingly. "They save money to buy a bishop's mantle. All I know is that everything is bought and sold."

Vera knew nothing about that and so she fell silent. Sasha, meanwhile, went on and on. The only concession he would make was that he could forgive ordinary priests, and especially the young ones, but not bishops and metropolitans.

One day, Vera rather carelessly convinced Sasha to travel to the –sky Monastery with her and attend a hierarchical liturgy. Vera had hoped that Sasha would be overwhelmed by the beauty and solemnity of the feast-day service, but Sasha hated everything. He especially disliked the expression on the bishop's face, which to Sasha seemed particularly supercilious. He also hated the fact that everyone was fawning before the bishop, handing him a comb and running behind him with candles. In other words, Vera failed to change Sasha's mind. She cried and prayed to the Lord for her husband.

One day Sasha went to the United States for a two-month work project. There he happened to meet a Russian whose name was Peter Grigoryev. Peter turned out to be Russian Orthodox and, when he heard Sasha criticize priests, suggested that he meet their local bishop.

"I have no wish to meet any of them," Sasha responded tersely.

"Look, we've arrived," said his new friend.

He stopped his car next to a nice green courtyard. Sasha noticed a golden dome rising above the trees tops.

Once Sasha and Peter got out of the car and opened the cast-iron gate, they saw an attendant. An elderly man with a white beard was sweeping the courtyard with a broom, wearing a leather apron. It seemed to be a primitive painting by Pirosmani rather than a scene in present-day Pennsylvania. When he saw that his guests had come, the attendant grew extremely embarrassed. He tossed down the broom and invited them in for tea. However, by the time they sat down to tea, the attendant had exchanged his apron for a black cassock, because he turned out to be the bishop. While they had tea, Sasha said nothing, whereas the attendant, or rather the bishop, regaled his guests with stories about his Russian grandparents, laughing heartily at his own jokes. He was a great nephew once removed of a famous Russian Itinerant painter and a nephew of an equally well-known composer. However, Sasha had no desire to hear any of his stories. He went to a service the following Sunday to confirm that the whole business of sweeping his own courtyard had been nothing but a performance put on solely for his benefit.

But the bishop conducted the service differently from the archpriest at the Monastery. He acted like an ordinary priest, very down to earth, just as Peter had promised Sasha. There were no candles, choir boys or combs.

Nor was there a special meal served after the service. Only tea and donuts, similar to Russian *ponchiki*. The bishop, according to Peter, preferred oatmeal, which he prepared himself every morning.

"Does he really make it himself?"

"We have tried to help him, of course, and sent various cooks to assist him, but he keeps sending them away gently."

"Does he drive a nice car at least?"

"He does have a car. You can't live in America without one," replied Peter, pointing to an ancient Volkswagen that was parked nearby.

"It's a 1976 model," added Peter. "The Bishop got it as a gift when he was ordained. He has yet to change it. He keeps replacing various parts, but it has a good engine and it still runs well."

"But he must be embarrassed to drive around in such a car. He is a bishop, after all."

"Do you think we didn't try to give him a nicer one? Each year one of our parishioners gives him a car on his Saint's Day. He usually thanks the donor and even drives the new car for a week or two. But then" – Peter sighed – "he gives it to someone. Nobody knows exactly to whom. Whenever we ask him about his new car, he pretends to be stupid. I'm sorry, brothers and sisters, he says, you must forgive me. I've smashed your beautiful car, it's been totaled. It is nothing but a heap of scrap metal now. He even falls on his knees and asks us to forgive him because he's grown senile."

Sasha liked such stories. He also liked the bishop's modest services. He liked the man, too, and found him bright, happy and energetic – even though he was a trickster, which was obvious.

The following Sunday, Sasha came to the service again, but he arrived toward the end, in order to talk to the amusing cleric once more. This time the bishop spent a long time talking to Sasha, asking him about mathematics and about his American colleagues. Without butting into his affairs, he gave Sasha an important piece of advice. At first, Sasha didn't understand why the bishop told him a particular story, but later on he figured out what it was about and acted exactly as the bishop had advised him to. As a result, Sasha was invited to return to the United States the following year and to work on another project. Sasha happily accepted the offer.

Certainly Sasha did not immediately begin to believe in God and attend services, or fall in love with priests. But he did become more tolerant. Then he returned to his native Russia, where his wife Vera was eagerly waiting for him – she was his wife, after all, albeit a religious one. From then on, Sasha no longer hated all priests. He put a picture of the bishop on his desk and whenever he saw a priest on television he no longer changed channels but headed straight for his desk to get a breath of fresh air. After taking a good look at the bishop, he would become tolerant again. Sometimes he would even say to Vera as a way to comfort her, "Their mindset remains Soviet. In another ninety years we too will have bishops like this one. Do not despair, my dear Vera."

Father Basil

Father Basil was a very humble man, even though he was a bishop. But, truth be told, he was an American bishop. When he visited Russia from America, after services he would pat kids on the head, give them candy and smile at them, and people would marvel that so many different kinds of bishops existed in this world.

One day, Father Basil was traveling by car to visit a priest somewhere near the ends of the Earth. The priest had a parish in a distant village, and he had invited the bishop to visit him and to see his church, which, incidentally, dated to the sixteenth century. The bishop finally accepted the invitation. The road was terrible, the car was bouncing up and down, but no one complained. Suddenly, the driver stopped. They could not go any further because of a traffic accident. A motorcycle smashed into a truck. There was a body of a gray-haired man lying face down next to the motorcycle. Another man, holding a helmet, was looking at him and crying – it was his father lying on the ground. He had been killed on impact.

"If your father was a believer we could hold a service over the body," the bishop said.

"Yes, yes," nodded the young man. "My father always believed in God and prayed. He didn't go to church because all the churches in our area have long since been destroyed. However, he used to say that he had a confessor."

His vestments were brought over from the car and Father Basil put them on. But before commencing the service, he asked, "It is a little strange. Your father never went to church. Then, how could he have a confessor?"

"He listened to Christian broadcasts from abroad on foreign radio stations. He listened to them almost daily. The priest who hosted his favorite program was called Rodzyanko. I don't recall his first name. He was the one my father regarded as his confessor, even though he had never met him."

Father Basil slowly knelt at the side of the spiritual child whom he was seeing for the first and last time.

Father Michael

Father Michael was a priest in New York City and conservatives considered him a dangerous liberal. Liberals considered him a good priest. He didn't allow his parishioners to kiss his hand, he never harangued them and never told them how to raise their kids. He lead vespers and Lenten services in an abridged form. Reactionaries attacked him, but everyone else loved him. He didn't criticize anyone. He just loved all kinds of people. Whenever he told funny stories, he was the first to burst out laughing and to slap his knees. He used to say that if he conducted services unabridged, his congregation would flee.

"We are dealing with spoiled Americans. This way they at least attend an abridged service."

Eleventh Cycle

Readings for Orthodox Parents

1 Most people knew Grisha as an ordinary and somewhat quiet member of the congregation, a middle-aged man attending church. He seemed to have a job, working either as an engineer or a computer programmer. He was married but he and his wife had no children. His wife was not a believer. She came to church once a year, on the Saturday after Good Friday, to have a *kulich* blessed. Then his wife unexpectedly died and Grisha dropped out of sight for nearly six months. Then, all of a sudden, he came back. But what a change had taken place. He wore a mud-spattered light summer coat, even though it was already very cold outside. His hair was long and unkempt and he smelled. Yet he still had kind, clear eyes. And there was no tint of liquor on his breath. Grisha was politely asked to stand in the vestibule and he did as he had been told. People asked him how he was and tried to give him money. He refused the money and didn't answer their questions.

It became his new routine. He went to church and stood in the vestibule, doing nothing but praying. He was always dirty. He no longer had a home and slept in doorways, shifting into the street and city parks during the warm season.

Several years passed. Grisha became a familiar figure, part of the landscape, especially since in the beginning he mostly kept quiet. Then, one day, a young priest at the church where Grisha came to pray began to sin. Naturally, no one knew anything about it. One day, the priest passed by Grisha, who stood by the front door, as was his custom. Suddenly, Grisha blocked his way and shouted obscenities at him, threatening him with Divine Retribution and naming the priest's secret deadly sin.

The priest ignored Grisha's harangue. Then Grisha urinated on his car, right on the windshield, and punctured one of its tires. It so happened that after the service the priest had been planning to go to that place where he went to commit his sins. So he couldn't get there this time. But still he did not mend his ways. He got his car washed and the tire fixed, and resumed his usual rounds, just as before, going both to church and to the other place.

Grisha then punctured his tires again, all four of them this time, and smashed all the windows in the bargain. The priest came out of the church and saw his car vandalized yet again, and suddenly he had had enough. He felt sorry for himself and for his car, and he had no money for repairs. Grisha, meanwhile, was protected by the head priest and could not be touched. Besides, he could easily denounce him to the head priest. At first, the priest wanted to punish Grisha and get him thrown in jail as a vagrant, but then, thinking it over some more, he decided to give up sinning instead. He never told Grisha about his decision, but when Grisha saw him again, he suddenly handed him a red tulip. When the priest saw the tulip, his heart melted and he never regretted giving up his sin. When Grisha died, the priest humbly told this story in public. Everyone listened with bated breath and, naturally, they expected the priest to tell them what sort of sin he was talking about. But he never did.

2 One day Grisha put on a Pokemon hat and a child's sweatshirt with a yellow Pokemon face on it and stuck hair pins in his hair that also had Pokemon faces on them. He wore boots decorated with Pokemon faces. He picked up a notebook with a Pokemon face on it and placed a stuffed Pokemon toy on his shoulder. This is how Grisha went to Sunday School. The classes had just begun and the kids ran outside and stood there laughing at Grisha. Grisha took out a yogurt with a

Pokemon painted on the container and began eating it with a special Pokemon spoon. As he did so, little Pokemon balls began to tumble from his pocket. This made the kids laugh even harder.

The parents politely asked Grisha to leave. Grisha took the large Pokemon toy off his shoulder and began to coddle it like a baby. Then, suddenly, he threw it on the ground and also threw down the notebooks, the sweater, the boots, the hat and the hairpins. He ran away barefoot. The kids joyfully began to pick up the notebooks and the balls, but their parents explained to them that the blessed one was ridiculing the universal obsession with Pokemons, and that they should not pick up the toys. Roma's father even shouted out that Pokemons are devils. The kids promptly stuffed the toys into their pockets and went home.

Roma, the best student at Sunday School, spent Sunday evening thinking and at last said to his mother before going to bed, "Mom, Grisha was criticizing not only us kids who are obsessed with Pokemons, but also you parents. He left us those toys to play with. He didn't want parents to be so terribly afraid of Pokemons."

His mother put a finger to her lips and said: "Hush."

In the next room, his father was reading an evening devotional.

3 Little Senya didn't like going to church. But his mother and father made him go anyway. They made him stand during services from beginning to end, even though he was bored to death. He would try standing on one leg, then on the other, closing and opening his eyes, counting candles and talking to his friend Vovka Avdeyev in sign language. But the service would not end.

One day, during a Sunday liturgy, Grisha came up to Senya and handed him a silver flute.

"Play," said Grisha.

"But the service is on. Why do you tell me to play?" Senya asked in surprise.

"So what if the service is going on? Play the flute if you're bored. Any time you get bored, pick up the flute. It's a magic flute, this one."

Having said that, Grisha disappeared into the crowd. Nevertheless, Senya was scared of his parents and didn't play the flute during the service. He made up for that by playing a lot at home. His parents, when they learned that it was Grisha who had given him the flute, endured the torture of his practicing in silence. In time, Senya learned to play various tunes, both other people's and those he had composed himself. He became so skilled on the flute that his parents allowed him to join the children's orchestra at the local Culture Club. Senya quickly became a star and the orchestra never performed without him. The problem was that, since all the concerts were scheduled for Sundays, Senya attended services less and less. His parents were sad, but they knew that the boy had talent. Senya eventually graduated from a music school and the conservatory, and he now plays in an orchestra in London. Every Sunday, whenever he is not away on tour, he goes to church, to the same parish where the late Metropolitan Anthony used to conduct services. Senya heard him preach many times before he died, and he always stood stock still during the service. As to Grisha's flute, which is now all scuffed and hoarse, he keeps it in a special velvet-lined case in his desk.

4 One day in the middle of vespers Grisha started singing a Russian folk song:

"Why do you sway so, thin rowan tree…"

He also started dancing. They escorted him from the church, scolding him, "Why do you sing in the middle of the service, Grisha. It is rude."

Grisha shouted, "Everyone should amuse himself as best he can."

That was his way of pointing out that people were not paying attention during services.

5 One day in early spring, Grisha picked up some twigs, lit them and began running around the church yard holding them high.

"Grisha, stop running around," they asked him.

But Grisha went on running and shouting, "Fire! Fire!"

His words and actions came back to people late that summer, when peat bogs began to smolder and the smoke hung over the city. That was when people began to develop respect for Grisha.

6 Grisha had a special affection for children. He even gave up his usual playing the holy fool when he was with them, and gave them candy, sometimes even before they took communion. Parents repeatedly asked Grisha not to give their children candy before communion, because kids didn't know any better and would eat it right away.

"You had better watch yourselves, not your kids," Grisha replied.

Sometimes he was even more direct, "You ought to think of stuffing your own faces a little less."

Many parents, when they heard this, gave in to temptation and told their kids to stay away from Grisha.

7 Sometimes Grisha would hug a married couple, pat each person on the shoulder and say to them very humbly and sweetly: "Please, please, stop fighting. Your Petya (he would use their child's name) is watching you and he gets very upset." Yet their child might be no more than two months old. Sometimes, the Petya in question might not even have been born yet, and would still be in his mother's womb. In that case, Grisha would use a random name, but the parents had so much respect for him that they sometimes gave that name to their newborn child.

8 On Christmas Eve, Grisha always came to church wearing a red Father Frost hat. He also had a beard, but it was his natural one, and it was reddish and not very thick.

9 Some parents, knowing about Grisha's love for kids, asked his advice about raising their children. For instance, how to teach kids to pray or to fast. Grisha gave the same answer to all such questions, "Teach yourself first."

Twelfth Cycle

Cautionary Tales to be Read in Sunday School

Pray Constantly

There once was a girl who didn't like to pray.

Her mother would call out to her, "Dusya, come over here and pray."

But Dusya would go on playing. Her dolls, rattles and inanimate stuffed animals seemed more important and dear to her than an encounter with the All-Merciful Lord. Even when she could be persuaded to stand in front of the icons, she kept shifting from one foot to the other, picking her nose, leaning against the wall and sometimes even attempting to sit down. That was how she behaved during the reading of the morning and evening prayers, even during the prayer before communion.

Her loving mother tried all sorts of things to arouse an enduring love of prayer in her child's heart. She sprinkled holy water on her stubborn daughter, touched her with a piece of the Oak of Mamre, anointed her with holy oil from the grave of a great holy man. All to no avail. Dusya hated praying as much as before. When the girl was a little older, she became even more stubborn and disobedient. She began to run away before half the devotion had been recited and no amount of persuading could soften her obdurate heart. If her long-suffering mother tried punishment, the obstinate child would start to scream and scratch at her like a mad person.

In the end, her long-suffering mother could bear it no longer. One day she picked up a kitchen knife and, moaning bitterly and reciting numerous prayers to our forefather Abraham, stabbed her insufferable daughter. Dusya fell silent and remained silent forever.

Children, this is what happens to anyone who prays half-heartedly or without requisite zeal.

Questions and Assignments

1. Why did Dunya's mother pray to Abraham while killing her daughter?
2. Explain the correct way to behave during prayer
3. Define the word "obdurate."

The Tale of a Christian Hedgehog

Once upon a time, in a warren at the foot of an old oak tree, there lived a Christian Hedgehog. Up in the same tree lived Squirrel, who was not a believer.

"Dear Squirrel," Hedgehog would call out to her. "You're not a Christian. Awaken. You must be baptized in the river."

"I'm scared of water," Squirrel replied, cracking another nut.

"You must overcome your fears."

But Squirrel could not understand the great good that would come to its squirrel soul once she turned to the True Faith.

In time, Hedgehog baptized all the animals, beetles and spiders in the forest and taught them to say a simple prayer.

"No matter what happens or doesn't happen," explained Hedgehog, "you must always say one thing: 'Praised Be the Lord.'"

Even Squirrel learned to say this uncomplicated prayer. Hedgehog taught her to make a sign of the cross and commanded her to bow repeatedly facing the East while holding on to a tree branch with her tail. Squirrel agreed to bow, because she liked all kinds of physical exercise, but she still refused to be dunked in the river, even for the sake of getting baptized.

However, the Good Lord sent Hedgehog a helper to assist him in his missionary work. One day, Hedgehog's warren, hidden in the roots of the tree which was also home to the Squirrel's hollow, was visited by Ladybug. Ladybug wore a kerchief over her head with a polka dot design. She was holding a string of black prayer beads and she looked rather humble. Hedgehog told her about his fruitless attempts to convince Squirrel to become baptized.

"Ever since I found out that I'm no ordinary insect but Our Lady's Bug, I constantly pray to God," Ladybug told Squirrel. "Believe me, Squirrel, nothing could be sweeter than life in Christ and God's prayer recited with the help of prayer beads.

But Squirrel did not wish to listen to Ladybug. She just hopped from branch to branch, cracked nuts and giggled.

"I think I've got an idea," Hedgehog shouted. (Despite being very respectable and serious most of the time, he was jumping up and down with excitement.)

Several days later, he finished making a string of unusual prayer beads. He strung a number of nuts on a long string and showed the new prayer beads to Squirrel.

"These beads will be yours the moment you overcome you fear of water," he said to her.

Squirrel promptly came down to the foot of the old oak tree. All three of them, Hedgehog, Squirrel and Ladybug, set out for the river, which was very near their wild strawberry meadow. Squirrel shivered repeatedly and tried to turn back several times, but the Hedgehog showed her the prayer beads and Squirrel continued moving forward.

Finally, they got to the bank of the river. Ladybug volunteered to be Godmother, and Hedgehog stood as Godfather. They dunked Squirrel in the water and read all the necessary prayers, but when they finished reciting their prayers they saw that Squirrel was no longer breathing. She had drowned.

"No problem," Hedgehog said, waving his paw. "Praised Be the Lord."

"Indeed," Ladybug agreed. "She died a Christian. Praised Be the Lord."

"Praised Be the Lord," echoed the leaves, the flowers, the birds, the bugs, the animals and the tiny black insects all around them.

Questions and Assignments

1. Do you approve of Hedgehog and Ladybug's actions?
2. What would you have done if you were in Hedgehog's shoes? In Squirrel's?
3. Assign roles and perform the story in character.

True Repentance

Vitya Ivanov was a bad Christian. He didn't listen to his teachers, didn't do his homework, harassed girls and fought during recess. He brought chewing gum to school, as well as a slingshot and a pea shooter pipe, propelling bits of chewed up paper across the room at other students. On New Year's, he brought in firecrackers and set them off right under the principal's window. In short, Vitya was a delinquent, even though he attended a Christian school.

Teachers tried repeatedly to bring Vitya to his senses, telling him that those who behaved badly ended badly, but Vitya was stubborn and didn't listen to them.

What do you think happened? Soon enough, Vitya's mother got cancer, then his sister went blind, then his grandmother was struck by paralysis and finally their house burned down. As to Vitya, while running down the stairs he fell down and broke his leg. Only when he was in the hospital, lying in traction with his leg lifted high toward the ceiling, did he understand that it was all his fault.

"Forgive me, O, Lord," he exclaimed, shedding bitter tears on his pillow.

That very moment his mother recovered, his sister regained her sight, his grandmother rose from her sick bed and started walking again, and some friends donated a new house to Vitya's mother. (They happened to have a spare one they didn't need.) The bone in Vitya's leg mended instantly. The doctors could only shrug in amazement.

Children. This is what true repentance can do for you.

Questions and Assignments

1. Why did Vitya's mother become ill with cancer, his sister go blind and his grandmother become paralyzed?

2. Was Vitya's repentance genuine?

3. When was the last time you have been to confession, eh?

A Christian Heart

O, God-fearing, obedient child. Touch the left side of your chest with your dear, soft little hand. Do you hear something beating in there? It is your heart. And now, my child, let us see whether you are a true Christian. Does your heart ache when you see the downtrodden, the miserable, the oppressed, the persecuted, the lepers, the weeping, the suffering, or those who are in mourning? Do you distribute alms to beggars? Would you give up what you value most, for instance your toys and favorite clothes, to poor homeless kids who live in railroad stations? Do you shed tears of repentance whenever you are sorely tempted to eat a candy and fail to resist this revolting desire, approaching that cupboard, climbing on a stool with your tiny feet, opening the door and promptly snatching that miserable object of temptation, colorful wrapper and all? Do you realize, my lovely child, that the colorful wrapper is wrapped about your ruin? Does your heart begin to beat faster at the thought that you have spent all day sinking deeper and deeper into the abyss of your trite and mundane existence, that you have played, jumped, screamed and not once thought of the Great, Wondrous and Glorious Creator of the Universe? Do you thank the Lord for every minute of your life and every breath you take? Do you bear without complaining various illnesses, such as measles, influenza, chicken pox, mumps and vitamin deficiency? At night, as you climb into your comfortable bed and hug your beloved mother who blesses you softly before you go to sleep, are you aware that you might die in the night and your soft bed will then become your grave, for the ways of Divine Providence are concealed from man?

Question and Assignments
Check: Is your heart is still beating?

Two Daughters

There once was a pious woman who had two daughters, Anya and Tanya. Anya was obedient in every way, listened with bated breath to every word her mother uttered, gladly carried out every request her beloved mother ever made, daily fed the crumbs left over from her meals to the Lord's winged creatures, greeted everyone with a sweet tender smile, assisted the elderly and every Sunday attended services in the Lord's Sanctuary with her mother, where she made sure to light a candle before an icon and stood straight and still throughout the service, as though she herself were a candle.

Tanya could not have been more different. She was often rude to her sweet mother, refused to help her with chores, climbed trees, tore her clothes, hated to be in church for long, running out into the street during the Holy Liturgy. She often beat up her good sister for no reason at all and stuck her tongue out at strangers. At school, Anya was a straight A student, while Tanya got Ds and even Fs. Her poor mother shed copious tears on account of her wayward daughter, endlessly appealing to her, but it was all to no avail. Tanya remained incorrigible.

Time passed. The girls grew up. The Lord rewarded Anya richly. She got married to a nice man and together they had beautiful, healthy, apple-cheeked kids. Their kids prayed to God daily, giving thanks for everything He had given their pious family. As to Tanya, she spent her entire life completely alone and when she grew old she lost all her teeth. She went to live in a forest, in a house on chicken feet, and turned into the ugly witch Baba Yaga.

Questions and Assignments

1. Do you want to turn into an ugly old witch?
2. Raise your hand if you think you resemble Anya
3. If a girl at your school resembles Tanya, don't be friends with her.

Harry Potter Is Bad

Larisa Yepifanova went to a Christian school. Students were not permitted to read Harry Potter books, because he was a wizard and the Church didn't approve of magic. Students were given several warnings about it, at general meetings, by the school's Father Confessor Vladimir and by their teachers in class. But stupid Larisa didn't pay attention to her wise teachers and borrowed a book about Harry Potter from a neighbor, who went to a regular school. One by one, she read all the books and then watched all the movies, and each one more than once at that. It all ended badly. One night, Harry Potter came to visit Larisa Yepifanova astride his broom. He was a nice little boy, wearing glasses. He flew into her bedroom through an open balcony door, quickly circled the entire room, said "peekaboo" to Larisa and flew out through the window like he had never been there. After that incident, Larisa developed a stammer and had trouble sleeping.

Questions and Assignments

1. Did Harry Potter do well by visiting Larisa late at night astride a broom?
2. Do you think he was unable to visit her by some other means, but only astride a broom?
3. Why did Larisa develop a stammer? Think it over carefully before answering.

Thirteenth Cycle

Christian Conversations

1 Father Basil called Father Vincent, his neighbor in the next cell, on his cell phone.

"What are you doing, Father?"

"I'm eating in secret. And you?"

"I'm almost asleep."

"Well, may you sleep without dreaming."

"Dine with the angels."

2 "Father, I feel enough strength in me to embark upon the life of the spirit. Give me a chore to do."

"Very well, my son. Rise at six o'clock every morning and bow ten times while praying to Our Lord Jesus Christ."

"Father, God Bless you. I feel I have enough strength for the life of the spirit only toward evening. But I sleep through the early mornings."

3 "Father, my classmate with whom I share a desk bullies me and pinches me in class. He chants 'Petrov, bug off' and calls me various bad names."

"Change seats. But do it lovingly."

"Father, I have changed seats. He now taunts me during recess."

"Have a serious talk with him, but do it lovingly."

"Father, I have had a talk with him, but he keeps taunting and now even punching me."

"Then, why don't you make a fist and punch him back? But do it lovingly."

4 "Know that if you judge someone, you will suffer the temptation of the flesh. It seems to be a fitting punishment for judging people."

"Give me an example."

5 "Father, may I start reading spiritual books?"

"While you're still in school, you should stick to reading good books."

6 "Father, when you baptize my Vanya, don't dunk him in the water."

"Why not? You have come here to have him baptized, have you not?"

"I didn't know you were going to dunk him."

7 "Father, during the service I stand there and think of all sorts of extraneous things."

"If you can't give your heart to the Lord, at least be content that you are giving him your feet."

8 "Dear brothers and sisters, before taking Holy Communion, fold your arms over your chest, say your name clearly and take out your dentures in advance."

9 "I forgot it was Wednesday yesterday and I had two pieces of chicken. Am I lost?"

10 "Father, here is my donation for the construction of the church."

"God Bless you, pardon my French."

11 "Yura, have you ever tried to use a screwdriver to unscrew the alms box?"

"No, Father. But thank you for an excellent idea."

Fourteenth Cycle

Readings for Christian Ladies Searching for a Husband

A Marriage Made in Heaven

Kolya and Olya got married. They were young, but they were already religious, and for such a serious undertaking they wanted to ask for a blessing from the very top. At least, they wanted a blessing from a person of high spiritual authority. Their good friends, who went to the same church, advised them to visit an old lady who was, despite living in the Smolensk region, a true holy woman leading a holy life. Everyone called her the Blessed One. The Blessed One had been bedridden for four decades, went nowhere and could barely see. Nevertheless, she could predict the future and whenever she gave a blessing to an undertaking, it invariably came off well.

Kolya and Olya had many misadventures, but they eventually arrived in the Blessed One's village, and they immediately went on their knees to her, declaring that they wanted to unite their destinies. The Blessed One was having breakfast, eating raw cabbage. Crunching on the cabbage and not looking at the couple – she was nearly blind anyway – she said, "Your bride, Kolya, is still in preschool. Wait for her. Your bridegroom, Olya, is right here. His name is Vovka and he's a tractor driver. He's been waiting for you for a long time."

They looked out the window and saw a peasant dressed in leather boots and a gray cap walking by. Apparently, it was Vovka. Kolya and Olya were a little surprised. After all, they loved each other. But what were they to do? Such was the Blessed One's verdict. Kolya went back to St. Petersburg, whereas Olya married Vovka and came to live in his hut. Vovka, when drunk, beat Olya up, even when she was pregnant, but that was apparently how it had to be if Olya wanted to find salvation. Whether or not that was so is pure guesswork, because the Blessed One, who lived in the same village, only moaned unintelligibly and didn't permit Olya to enter her house. Most of Olya and Vovka's kids were born idiots and died promptly, except for one girl who came out normal. She was clever and sweet and took after her mother. Olya protected her and once the girl grew a little older Olya and her daughter left Vovka. Leaving almost all her possessions behind, Olya came to St. Petersburg, where she found Kolya who, while waiting for his preschool bride (by then she was likely in middle school), lived with a woman eight years his senior, drinking hard. Olya had nowhere to go. She had originally come to St. Petersburg from Biysk to attend college. She could have returned to Biysk and stay with her parents, but Biysk is the sort of town that is repeatedly flooded.

Olya found a job at a factory in St. Petersburg and lived in a factory dorm, sharing a room with five equally half-homeless women. She sent her clever daughter to a music class at a local library. There, a great enthusiast, Anton Mikhailovich, taught her to play the accordion. She began to play in pedestrian underpasses and on busy street corners, earning a decent living and supporting herself, her mother and even Uncle Kolya – once Olya took pity on him and agreed to see him again. But eventually Anton Mikhailovich proposed to Olya. He saw how beautiful she was and besides she was 32 years old, practically half his age.

They now live happily in Anton Mikhailovich's three-room apartment. Olya resolutely refused to have a church wedding, even though Anton Mikhailovich wanted one. Church weddings are so beautiful. Olga's daughter soon graduated from high school and started university. Suddenly, she began to attend church, pray and go to confession, all completely in secret from her mother. Her mother always had a strange reaction whenever she saw an icon or heard talk of the Patriarch, the Orthodox miracles of the twentieth century, holy fools, and salvation. She would start to scratch her arms and weep hysterically.

The Normal Person

Zhenya Snegireva had a hard time finding a husband. She had graduated from college three years before but still she was unmarried. Zhenya had only two joys in life. She went to the theater on opening nights, because she had loved the theater since childhood, and she went to church, because in her freshman year in college she had found God and been baptized. In church, Zhenya prayed to find a husband, and once she even fasted for three full days, but she still didn't find anyone. She only had Vanya Sinitsyn, a colleague at the travel agency where she worked, but he didn't count because he was a non-believer. Zhenya's confessor refused to give his blessing to a union with Vanya. On the other hand, Vanya had not even proposed to her. All they did was spend their lunch hour together every now and then, but Zhenya still decided to ask her confessor for a blessing – just in case, so that if the time ever came she could respond to Vanya properly. She didn't receive a blessing.

"It would be torture to live with a non-believer," the priest told her.

All Zhenya could think of was to visit a holy man. She decided to go to the Trinity-St. Sergius Monastery to pray, to pay her respects to the relics of Saint Sergius and to visit a holy man.

The holy man was old, gray and sighed deeply and repeatedly. He looked at Zhenya closely and said, "My child, you have to pray to Saint Sergius. He will help you.

Zhenya came out reassured and went straight to the Trinity Cathedral, bowed to the relics and prayed, "Father Sergius, pray for me to find a Christian bridegroom."

She lit a candle, listened to an akathistos hymn and caught a suburban train home. In the train car seat across from her sat an extremely good-looking young man. He had a thin mustache and he wore a black uniform jacket. He cast an eye at Zhenya every now and again. Zhenya blushed and shifted in her seat. Suddenly, the young man spoke to her, "Are you returning from the Lavra?"

Zhenya said nothing and nodded silently.

"It is where I study."

They began to talk and it turned out that Gennady attended the seminary. He was on his way home for the weekend.

He had not entered the seminary right after high school. He got a job first and did his military service, which meant that he was close to Zhenya in age.

"This is what happens when Saint Sergius prays for you. This is what happens when a Saint takes up your case. Why not? I could certainly be a priest's wife," Zhenya thought while she was giving Gena her telephone number.

Zhenya and Gena began dating. Just as she had asked Saint Sergius. Gena turned out to be quite the Orthodox Christian. He loved to talk about the salvation of the soul, the Saints of the Land of the Rus and the Masonic Conspiracy. He took Zhenya to services, the liturgy, vespers and public prayers. He hadn't proposed to her yet, clearly taking a good look at her. But in the meanwhile he began to treat her as a wife to be, just for the sake of practice.

For example, he told her what she had to wear: nothing but skirts and a kerchief over her head, even indoors. He berated her when she ate a piece of chocolate during a fast. He grew angry whenever she tried tentatively to argue with him, timidly saying that she didn't believe in the Conspiracy. When Zhenya once suggested they go to a play, he rolled his eyes and screamed, "It's the work of the Devil. Naked women! Perverts! That's what the theater is all about."

Zhenya began to worry that her husband to be was a bit insane and decided to go to the theater all by herself. When Gennady found out about it, he said to her, "You know, I've decided to become a monk, because a monk's calling in the service of the Lord is higher than a priest's."

He stopped calling her.

There was nothing for her to do but to go to the holy man again.

"Reverend Father, I found a bridegroom in response to my prayers. He was Orthodox sure enough, just as I requested, but there was something definitely wrong with him."

The holy man smiled and said nothing. Zhenya realized that he had nothing else to say to her and turned again to Saint Sergius for help.

"Father Sergius, please help me find another bridegroom. I no longer even care if he is Orthodox. I need a decent, normal person."

She set out for the city in the suburban train and looked carefully all around. But there were only old women in her car, drunken peasants, and mothers with young children. Not one suitable person. The next day Zhenya went to work and there too she met nobody new. Vanya Sinitsyn kept smiling and giving her looks, as usual. Finally, he came up to her desk and said, "It's been a while since we went to lunch together."

At lunch, finishing his fruit drink, Vanya suddenly asked Zhenya, "Listen, there's a new play opening at the Fomenko Theater tonight. Let's go and try to buy tickets at the door. We could get lucky, you know."

Zhenya accepted his invitation. They began to go to the theater and attend interesting exhibitions together. Vanya turned out to be very interested in art. He bought Zhenya flowers, sometimes took her to cafes, held her hand but never tried to kiss her, which appealed to Zhenya. Sometimes they entered a church and listened to the chanting of the congregation. Zhenya talked to Vanya about the church and Christianity. Vanya listened and sometimes asked questions. Other times he said nothing. He didn't argue with her.

One evening, walking Zhenya home, he said to her, "I'll get straight to the point: I'm in love with you."

It is torture to live with a non-believer.

But in the end Vanya got baptized and on Saint Thomas's Sunday, the first Sunday after Easter, Zhenya's priest married them. They lived happily ever after.

The Folk Art Collector

Anya Mokrousova was interested in folklore. She acquired the hobby from Sergei Parmin, who explained to her that folklore is all around us. All you need to do is to write it down. Which was what Anya did, and then some! For example, when she went to visit her grandmother at the hospital, she collected hospital folklore. After she had spoken to her younger sister, she had school folklore. Standing in line at the store, she gathered store folklore. While her apartment was being painted, she gathered house painters' folklore. All the while, Sergei courted her and in the end he proposed. Except it was a very strange way of proposing.

"You see, my dearest Anya," said Sergei. "A month ago I was baptized and I want you, hopefully my bride to be, to be baptized as well, and to start attending church. In time, we'll get married."

Anya had long noticed that something was going on with Sergei. One time he turned down his favorite meat pie, another he refused to come to see her – not to mention the fact that there came a time when he almost entirely stopped kissing her. But Anya had not asked him point blank what it was and waited instead, hoping that events would take their course. And now they had.

"What do you mean I should start attending church?" Anya exclaimed. "Only crazies go to church. Not on your life, not me."

She refused to go to church or to get baptized. Sergei, of course, tried to make her change her mind by sneaking her tapes of Metropolitan Anthony's sermons, brought her to meetings to his congregation and introduced her to the priest. All was in vain. Finally, he broke up with Anya. Actually, it was not even clear who broke up with whom. They broke up with each other. But Anya was hurt, because she was convinced that it was religion that came between them, that it was Russian Orthodoxy – the girls in black skirts and the red-cheeked priest in metal-framed glasses – that was to blame.

She went to graduate school. By the time Anya started, Sergei had already finished. Soon, she completely changed. She started to wear a black, full-length skirt and a kerchief on her head. She kept her eyes downcast and often traveled somewhere. Soon rumors began to circulate that she was visiting holy sites. Only Anya and her graduate advisor knew that the masquerade was merely a way to get in character, and that she traveled not to visit holy sites but on research trips. While traveling, Anya gained the confidence of various pilgrims, holy men, holy fools and ordinary Orthodox folks and listened carefully to everything they talked about. It was easy to get them to talk. They talked about the Savior, the virtue of obedience, and the End of the World. What they didn't know was that Anya had a portable voice recorder, which they could not see, under her jacket.

Three years later, the academic world was shaken by a small earthquake. Anya wrote her doctoral thesis on the poetics of modern para-ecclesiastical folklore and its social and cultural aspects.

Everything she had heard at monasteries and religious communities had been included in her dissertation. Young women who associate themselves with church, Anya wrote, always speak in a special soft voice, keeping their eyes down. It denotes their humility and meekness. Young para-ecclesiastically-minded men wear their hair long and gather it into a knot in the back. They speak mournfully, hoarsely and have a slightly manic stare. This is meant to reflect an inner flame, devotion to church doctrine and, possibly sleepless nights spent in prayer. Everyone has to make a sign of the cross everywhere and on all occasions, in the street, at a café – everywhere – never feeling any embarrassment at doing so. It is also important to prepare for the imminent end of the world.

Anya meticulously took down when and under what circumstances she had heard various predictions of the coming world catastrophe and the Apocalypse, its timing being pushed back again and again, and how religious people, including Saint John of Kronstadt, hated yids, but adored Holy Russia and eagerly awaited the return of the Tsar, the nation's savior. She recorded also how the Church was not embarrassed to publish the *Protocols of the Elders of Zion*. In short, she put into her dissertation everything that would make a normal person puke. She was naturally very pleased with herself, all the more so since one of the persons chosen to publicly review her dissertation defense was Sergei Parmin. Yet Sergei praised her dissertation highly. She had collected unique materials, he asserted, and described what had never before been described. The author showed rare perception and remarkable depth of knowledge. All the while, Anya cast surprised glances at Sergei. The unanimous verdict was that her dissertation defense was a great success.

At the reception, Anya was approached by Sergei, who had by then had a few drinks. He was very happy. He squeezed her elbow and said, "I'm so sorry. I was a fool."

Soon they got married. Sergei said nothing about his faith. Anya, overjoyed by the way things turned out, got baptized almost immediately, even though she still hated wearing skirts. At the wedding, Anya wore a white pantsuit and they were married by a progressive priest in the center of Moscow. Six months later, Anya became a true believer, an Orthodox Christian.

However, she is not one of those para-ecclesiastical crazies who hang around churches. She is a regular parishioner. She attends church in blue jeans, not wearing a kerchief, and still goes to the same progressive church. To all appearances, she is now expecting her second child and she has been collecting young mothers' folklore for over three years.

The Difficult Life of a Woman

There once was a young woman who loved a priest. She simply couldn't go on living without him. He didn't seem to be such a big deal to fall in love with. His hair was long and unkempt, he was piebald and not very handsome. But she knew why she loved him. A long time ago, when she was in her second year at university and began to attend church, she went for confession to him. She revealed to him that she was a drunk. The day before, she had been at a party to celebrate a friend's birthday and they all got drunk as pigs. In reality, she hadn't drunk too much, but she needed something to confess and, besides, she had got out of bed several times during the night to get a drink of water because the alcohol had made her thirsty. She went to church in the morning.

The priest didn't tell her that drinking liquor was sinful. He merely inquired what they had drunk and who paid for it. The young woman was taken aback. No one had ever asked her such questions. What does it matter to most people who paid for the drinks? The young woman saw fatherly concern in this and fell in love with the priest.

The priest tolerated her love, but he also often told her that the best path for a woman was to get married and to have children. Soon, the young woman actually did get married to a nice, kind man who was working as a computer programmer and they quickly had three children. But she didn't stop loving the priest and still couldn't live without him. She missed him whenever he was away traveling for any length of time.

Did she love her own husband as well? Yes, very much so. But she loved the priest even more. The priest taught her things her husband had no idea about. Or, at least, he never discussed such subjects with her. Besides, the priest understood her soul, whereas all her husband ever said to her was that she had great tits. He also kissed her on the corners of her mouth. Of course, other young women would have cried for joy had they been in her shoes, but this particular young woman, who was no longer so young, wanted something more. On the one hand, she had a husband who worked day and night writing computer programs in order to put food on the table, demanding only one thing in return, and on the other hand she had a priest, the soft chanting of the church choir and celestial joy. But the husband was a big problem and the woman grew very tired of it. She left her three kids, who were by then, respectively, two, four and five and a half years old. She left behind a pretty incoherent note, the long and short of which was, in so many words, that she was begging everyone's forgiveness, and was going away, destination unknown.

Two months later, her family found her at a remote Siberian convent, where she had been readily welcomed because the convent had opened only recently, was half empty and could certainly use another pair of hands. Besides, she was from Moscow, so that her arrival was almost equivalent to a visit from the Patriarch. Naturally, the woman had concealed her true family status. But very soon it all came out. The woman's loving father, who was already quite advanced in age, came to the convent, fell on his knees before her, spoke of her kids and her sacred maternal duties, and begged her to return home. Her mother could only sob during the entire trip. Her husband had stayed behind in Moscow to watch the children. The Mother Superior, who had been given a charitable donation by the woman's wealthy father to ensure a favorable outcome, also encouraged her to go home. Not because of the charitable donation, mind you, but because a mother of three was supposed to be with her kids. The mother of three agreed to return.

The only problem was that she seemed barely alive. Of course, her husband forgave her and hugged her when he came out to greet her, even shedding a few tears. The kids were so happy to see their mother that another woman in her place would have also burst out crying and understood everything. But she was not any other woman. She was Mrs. Tatyana Alexandrovna Pushkareva and Mrs. Tatyana Alexandrovna Pushkareva didn't burst out crying. She kissed them all and smiled at them, but shed no tears. Then she returned to her housework, ironing a pile of wrinkled laundry, mopping the floors, making soup and cherry compote and frying chopped meat patties. The kids ate and even forgot to misbehave at the table, staring at their mother. To them, it was as though the sun had returned to their lives. That sun shone in every face except Tanya's. She no longer wanted to be married, no longer wanted to bring up her children and, most of all, no longer wanted to go back to work. She only wanted one thing: to lead the secret life of the spirit and have no one interfere with her.

The priest soon reappeared, as well. He tried to reason with her and said all the right things that had to be said – about responsibility, the need to bear one's cross and to fear the Last Judgment. All Tanya wanted to do in response was scream. But she didn't. She returned to taking care of her kids, listening to her husband rave about her tits and attending church on Saturdays and Sundays. A year passed. The following summer she disappeared again. She was found once more, even faster this time, even though she had gone to a completely different place and to a different convent. Except this time on the way home she bolted. During a long stop on the train, she didn't return to her seat. She had no money, nothing. When they found her and brought her back home, she recognized neither her kids nor her husband. Instead, she went down on all fours in the corridor and began to bark. The kids laughed and the grown-ups took her to the insane asylum. At the asylum they treated her for a long time, giving her shots and conducting therapy sessions. In the end, she got to be more or less herself again. But from then on she was always a little strange. She didn't go back to her family and went to live next to the church instead – the same one, in fact, where her favorite priest led services. She lived in a tiny room with no windows and became a charwoman. She continually mumbled something under her breath and sometimes whined pitifully. But she washed the floors well and polished all the candlesticks until they shone.

Tanya's former husband found another mother for their children. The older ones still remembered their old mother and at first they asked about her. But they were told that their mother had transformed into a little dog and now lived somewhere very far away. She had sent them a new mother, who was very kind. The new mother was indeed very nice and the kids soon grew to love her. They also soon received a new brother. Twenty one years passed. Tanya's back became bent, she faced the ground now, and she mumbled to herself all the time. At night, soft weeping sounds could be heard coming from her room.

People began to revere her as a blessed one and even asked her for advice. But Tanya only responded with a crazy smile, and if that wasn't enough to send them away, she would woof like a dog. The priest, with whom Tanya no longer spoke and whom she only approached to receive his blessing, had grown very weak. His hair was white and he walked with a pronounced arthritic limp. Tanya's kids, meanwhile, grew up having not seen their mother since she had transformed into a little dog.

One day, when Tanya's youngest daughter was returning home from work, she was approached by an old hag with a crooked back. She was dressed in black and she asked the young woman to tell her her name. The young woman did. The old hag, who seemed slightly mad, smiled, and the young woman saw that her eyes were bright and sane. She felt like the old hag could see right through her. The old hag gave the young woman two envelopes, explaining to her that one letter was for her, but that she could not unseal it before nightfall. The other had to be taken later that evening to the two-story building next to the church and given to the lame priest. The old hag pointed to a distant onion dome among tall buildings. Then the old hag kissed the young woman's hand and went away. The young woman was a little surprised but did what the crazy old hag had asked her to do. She did it out of compassion, because she was not a bad person.

That night the lame priest opened his letter and the young woman read hers. The letters were short and very similar. Tanya had written that in the night God would call her to Him and asked them to pray for her. She wrote to the young woman that she was her mother and asked her forgiveness. She revealed to the priest that she had overcome the pain of her love for him only two years ago, by becoming a holy fool. In the morning, Tanya was found in her room. She was kneeling before the icons, stone dead.

The Gentry Girl Peasant[2]

Slava Sorokin was lonely and unhappy. He went to church and all that, of course, but he had trouble making friends. People said to him formulaically: "God bless you," or "Happy Holidays," or "Happy Communion," and smiled piously and bowed to him, and that was all. That made Slava sad. He never succeeded in making Orthodox

---

2. The title, in Russian *Барышня-Крестьянка*, sometimes translated as "Mistress into Maid," is an allusion is to a story by Alexander Pushkin.

friends, but in the meantime he drifted away from his college buddies, who had other interests.

He sometimes shared his woes with a kid in his German class, Lesha Pirozhkov. His real problem was not a lack of male buddies, but the absence of a woman in his life. At college, the girls smoked and wore miniskirts. They all seemed too loose to Slava. At church, on the other hand, the skirts were too long and the kerchiefs covered everything except for their eyes. The women in church seemed forbidding. Slava didn't know what to do. He was already 20 years old.

One day, Lesha Pirozhkov told Slava that he had gotten a job as a guard at a popular night club. The club offered its customers a service: it could match them with a girl to suit any taste.

Slava recoiled.

"You mean a prostitute, don't you?"

"No, they're not really prostitutes," Lesha replied a little vaguely. "They're nice girls."

"No, I can't do it," insisted Slava. "I'm a church-going Christian."

Lesha didn't try to change his mind. He only noted that no one would force Slava to sleep with such a girl. They could spend an evening together, chat and go home, and everyone would be happy.

He didn't revisit this subject again, but Slava didn't forget it. Then, suddenly, he changed his mind. It happened on a Friday. Classes were over, there was a full month before exams would start and all the other students were making plans and getting ready to go off to different places together. They laughed and were happy, whereas Slava walked to the bus stop all alone.

That was when Lesha caught up with him. It was a day when he was scheduled to work at the night club. Slava said, "I'm game. Find me a girl. But all I want is to talk to her. Let me know how much it will cost."

Lesha nodded and replied that the club didn't charge for conversations.

Several hours later, Lesha took Slava to the club and got him in without a membership card. He put him at a table and told him that a woman would join him shortly.

Soon a young woman came up to Slava. Nothing indicated that she was a lady of the night. She was dressed modestly and nicely in a black dress and a light white blouse. She had an open, cheerful face and wore very little makeup. Slava even thought for a moment that he had seen her somewhere before.

"I'm Sonya," she introduced herself simply.

"I'm Slava."

Sonya joined Slava at his table. A waiter silently approached.

"Just some ice cream for me," said Sonya smiling.

Slava repeated this childish order to the waiter. He ordered a bottle of beer and some salted nuts for himself.

The conversation picked up quickly. A few minutes later, Slava could have sworn he had known Sonya for years. The girl was no simpleton. Her conversation hinted at an excellent education, her manners revealed good upbringing. When Sonya used a few French words, Slava, who knew French from childhood, wanted to hug her. But he restrained himself. Embarrassed, he explained to her that he attended church, which meant—

He let the sentence trail off, but Sonya understood what he was trying to say.

They began to talk about the Church and whether the heart has room for both piety and vice. Naturally, it was mainly Slava who spoke, enthusiastically explaining the basics of Christianity to his new friend, trying to instill in her the notion of sin and the most important Christian virtue, humility, which trumps even – er – chastity.

The young woman appeared to be an extremely quick study and even anticipated some of Slava's ideas. Slava wished to comfort her and to let her know that, despite the differences in their social status – he a student at a prestigious college and she a creature of the night – they were equals. Yes, completely equal.

He felt inspired. Sonya was beautiful and her eyes stared at him with such pure devotion. She was better than he. Yes, she was a thousand times better, and more noble. Music played softly, other customers around them sipped their drinks, waiters glided by and it was business as usual at the nightclub. Slava and Sonya went on talking.

At some point, Slava suddenly began to recount to her a story he had written once. Because he occasionally wrote fiction. This particular story was especially relevant for the occasion.

"It takes place at a time when people already knew how difficult it is to serve God in this diseased, ugly world, which constantly distracts us from spiritual joys," he began in a voice that was so soft and infused with feeling that Sonya had to put aside her second dish of ice cream. "Some people had decided to flee the world. They went to the desert, high in the mountains, dug underground dwellings and built simple huts for themselves to live in, to hide themselves from human eyes and ears for years on end. They subjected their bodies to great ascetic trials, squeezing their souls in the fetters of prayer. Those were the best of the best, the most honest ones of the lot, and the bravest, too. The world was not worthy of them, but they hid, concealing themselves like criminals, because the world had chased them away with the whip of evil and vice, it had expelled and banned them, not being able to live side by side with such great purity and amazing holiness. One of those chosen ones had spent many a year in his cave. He was noble by birth, he was from a wealthy and famous family in Alexandria, but he disdainfully threw all his advantages away. Supple and energetic in his youth, he had by then become a hoary old man. His skin had been wrinkled and his body had grown weak. His ascetic life had not only brought him fame – people knew about his holiness and flocked to his cave to ask him to instruct and comfort them – but brought for him celestial glory, as well. Things invisible lay open before his spiritual gaze. He saw angels and conversed with the Lord as easily as with a friend. Heavenly visions often descended upon him. But, strangely, the nearer he got to perfection, the more he was assailed by vague doubts and even fears. One day he turned to the heavens and asked a question which had been bothering him more with each passing day:

"'Tell me, O Lord,' he asked. 'What is the measure of my perfection?'"

Sonya listened to Slava, forgetting to breathe. She seemed to understand and feel his every word. The waiter, who had been coming up to them every now and again to ask whether they wanted anything else, was staying away.

"The Lord didn't answer him for a long time," Slava continued. "Days went by, then months, but the holy man did not receive an answer. He repeated his question daily without respite, revealing to the Lord his great desire to know how high he stood on the spiritual ladder. But at least he knew that he had been heard. One night the ascetic heard a voice which told him clearly: 'Go to the nearest big city. The first person you speak to is superior to you.' Being an experienced and cautious hermit, the holy man did not hurry. He wanted to make sure that the voice he had heard in the night was the true voice of the Lord. Twice more he heard the same words in his heart. Twice more the same strange statement was uttered: 'The first person you speak to is superior to you.' Only then did the old man set out on a journey. He started early in the morning, taking nothing along.

"In the middle of the third day he came upon a city and, moved by a vague fear, decided to remain silent and not to talk to anyone unless he had no choice. His will was strong, but his heart was fearful and tender. As he entered the city, the old man saw a woman walking on the road and carrying a heavy basket. The woman could barely lift her load, and had to stop frequently, breathing a deep sigh. The day was hot, the sun was beating down upon her head and the poor wretch was sweating profusely. Remaining silent, the old man came up to her and placed his hand on her basket in order to help her. But the woman began to scream, fearing that the hermit wanted to steal her belongings. No one was around. The old man kept tugging at the basket while the woman kept screaming. Finally, wishing to calm her down, the hermit said: 'Do not fear. I don't want to take anything. I'm only trying to help you.'

"The woman stopped screaming, looked him up and down and allowed him to take her basket. The hermit silently carried the load to where the woman had indicated, silently bowed to her, waved away the payment she tried to offer him and only when he started on his way again did he realize that he had already spoken to her at the side of the road when he had first met her. The hermit turned back and knocked on the door of the house where the woman had entered. No one answered the door for a long time, but he persisted. Finally, the door was opened and the same woman stood at the threshold. But she was dressed differently. The place turned out to be a brothel. A regular brothel.

"The old man was shocked. He tried to question the woman about her life, but he learned little from her.

"'I'm ashamed to talk about the particulars of my trade in front of you, a stranger who seems to be a holy man,' the woman replied to all his inquiries.

"Greatly saddened, the hermit returned to his cave without achieving any result.

"For several days he remained as though in a trance. It had been his first visit to the city in many a year. But when he finally recovered, he implored the Lord to enlighten him.

"'In what way is this woman superior to me, O Lord?' the old man repeatedly asked, perplexed.

"This time, he didn't have to wait long.

"'In humility and love,' came the response from up high."

Slava fell silent. He called over a waiter and ordered green tea. Sonya sat motionless, lowering her eyes and not daring to look at the young man.

"Sonya," whispered Slava. "What is the matter?"

Sonya raised her eyes. They shone with humility and love. At least that was how it seemed to Slava. He was sure he was not mistaken. Once again, he had the impression that he had seen Sonya before.

"I love you," said Slava. "Marry me."

"When?" asked Sonya, suddenly becoming animated.

"Tomorrow."

"Come to your church tomorrow," said Sonya. "We'll talk about all that there."

Even when he heard her say those words about his church – how could she have known that he had a church which he attended regularly, since he had not mentioned it to her – Slava had no inkling of the truth. He left the club in a haze, barely saying goodbye to Lesha and forgetting to thank him. He spent half the night thinking of the mysterious and wonderful young woman whom he was going to save from the abyss. Or would it be the other way around, and she was the one who would save him? He felt he was in love with Sonya. He fell asleep with that sweet sensation.

The next evening, Slava went to church, but there was no trace of Sonya. In vain he stared at every young woman entering the church. None looked like his friend from the night before. He was crushed and shocked as he stood through vespers. Finally, the congregation was dismissed and the parishioners began to leave. Slava cursed himself. How could he have been taken in by some whore? She had been laughing at him.

Then, young women began to come down from the cleros –the choir balcony. One of them, wearing a dark kerchief low over her forehead, came up to Slava. It was Sonya. Except she was hard to recognize in a long skirt and a kerchief that nearly covered her eyes. But it was definitely she. He knew now why her face had seemed so familiar to him the night before.

"Is it you?" was all that Slava could say.

"Let's go," the young woman said to him.

They came out of the church holding hands. It was a gentle evening. Light snow fluttered in the air and kids were slipping down an ice slide.

On their way to the metro station, which lay through a small city park, Sonya revealed to Slava that she had been deeply in love with him for a long time and had been watching him from the choir balcony, but he had never even lifted his eyes to look at her. He had stood there like a column, staring at the floor.

As Sonya's love for Slava grew deeper, she resorted to a subterfuge. Lesha Pirozhkov, the guard at the night club, was her older brother. From him, Sonya knew that Slava suffered from loneliness but had made no attempt to break free of it. Lesha proposed a simple plan. It took him a long time to convince Sonya to go along with this dubious project, but eventually her patience had run out. The rest was a matter of execution and good luck. A month later Slava and Sonya got married. Lesha was best man at their wedding.

The Russian Schi

Nastya Trofimova got married after answering a personal ad. Life was boring in the old Soviet Union, and she responded to an ad placed by a foreigner. He wrote back and came to visit her for four days. Rob had just turned 50. He was short and bald, but he was well off. Besides, he had a nice smile, flashing his white teeth. He had a strange hobby. He collected Russian political jokes and he could even read a little Russian. In his day job, he was a real estate broker.

Nastya sold her apartment and moved to Canada as a permanent resident, along with her five-year-old son Andrei. Once she settled down, she discovered that her life was totally boring. She cooked dinner for her beloved husband, but he had become so used to eating at restaurants during his bachelor days that he didn't enjoy even her most sophisticated dishes. Nothing she cooked could measure up to what he used to get in restaurants. She took Andrei to preschool and picked him up again, and attended an English class twice a week, which was the sum total of her activities.

Then Nastya met her Russian neighbor, who took her to church just to have a look around. It was a Russian Orthodox church, except everyone had better clothes than they did back in Russia. Middle-aged men were dressed in jackets and white shirts, middle-aged women wore silk dresses. Families brought along their well-dressed kids. Women didn't wear kerchiefs. Services were conducted half in English, half in Russian. That was how Nastya became a believer and even began to sing in the church choir. Andrei followed in her footsteps. Rob didn't object. Sometimes he even came to the Russian Church, usually at the end of the service, in order to join the congregation in a Russian supper of *schi* and *kotlety* – and, of course, to take down in his notebook a new joke or two told by some recent emigré or visitor.

Love Story

Petya Borisov got married early to his high school sweetheart. He had been staring at Lyuda Antonova ever since they were in eighth grade together, without ever taking his eyes off of her. Even his teachers sometimes admonished him for it. In ninth grade he began to write her love letters in verse. Lyuda didn't reply. She liked Zhenya Simonov. But Zhenya soon started to date another girl and, to spite him, Lyuda began to go out with Petya. Soon she forgot all about Zhenya because Petya turned out to be very nice. Soon after Lyuda and Petya got married, they began attending the Institute of Steel and Steel Alloys.

They lived in peace and harmony. Petya wasn't especially jealous, whereas Lyuda was in love with Petya and had eyes for no one else. Three years went by, and after finishing her third year at the Institute, Lyuda gave birth to a daughter, Anya. She didn't even have to take a year off. Both grandmothers were very helpful. Everything was going very smoothly. Petya adored his daughter, took care of her and let her sleep in their bed at night.

But in their fourth year of college something happened to Petya. He found God and very soon became such a zealous Christian that

Lyuda could only groan. She had no desire to become a Christian, the smell of incense at church made her sick and priests seemed phony. Petya's long discussions with her failed to make her change her mind, and eventually they began to annoy her. She was killing herself trying to combine school with taking care of their baby, and she wanted Petya to come home as soon as possible. But Petya went to vespers and vigils, look at him! On Sunday, the only day when they could take a walk in the morning, all three of them together, he was also absent, because he who doesn't attend liturgy loses his connection to the church.

Lyuda's displeasure had no effect on Petya, of course. He gave up trying to change her mind and, except for attending church, he was even better than before, as far as the rest of their life together was concerned. But his wife was unhappy.

Eventually they graduated from college. Lyuda barely managed to earn her degree, whereas Petya got straight As. But instead of going to work at the research lab – at the invitation of Petya's research adviser – which didn't take just anyone, Petya decided to turn down the lab and entered seminary. Now, he almost never came home, whereas Lyuda by then had had another child, a boy. Her displeasure with her husband began to wane, perhaps overshadowed by family concerns. Petya graduated from the seminary and invited his wife and all his friends to attend his ordination. Lyuda decided to come. During the ceremony, she cried because her beloved Petya seemed so far away from her and paid her no attention at all. Instead he kept bowing and dropping to his knees. He was carried around the church by two handsome young men who held him under his arms. At last, when Petya emerged dressed in white and brimming with joy, he had become a complete stranger to her. Along with everyone else, Lyuda approached the cross, which Petya held in his hand, and kissed first the cross and then her husband's hand. As she did this, she felt that he was no longer her husband.

She then realized that his hand seemed like a stranger's hand because he no longer wore his wedding band. For the rest of the day,

Lyuda didn't exchange a word with him. But he seemed not to notice. It was no surprise if he didn't. Their house was full of people and everyone had to be greeted and fed.

The next day, Petya left early in the morning and returned only late at night, saying to Lyuba, "Training. I need to learn how to lead services." Lyuda started speaking to him again, because she had to prepare supper for him and to ask if he wanted his dressing to be mayonnaise or vegetable oil, since Petya was observing all the fasts. Training continued for a month and a half. Two weeks after that, Father Peter was sent to Mozhaisk region, to the village of Pypino, to rebuild an abandoned church. Lyuda had no choice but to go along. For the time being, she left her kids in the care of their grandmothers, because they could not take them to a place where there was nothing.

Petya was given a house, small but sturdy, right next to the church. The church was a scary sight. It was all blackened and fouled inside, but Petya said that the walls were still solid and that the stone floor slabs had held up, which was better than in many other church buildings. The Mayor of Mozhaisk allocated money to Petya because there had been a directive from above to support the restoration of old churches and there was a short period of time when such initiatives were actually supported. Petya happened to be in the right place at the right time. He did what he had never done before: hired builders, purchased building materials and instructed workers how to do their work better.

Lyuda worked to make the house comfortable. She hung new wallpaper, painted the floors and washed the windows. Some friends of theirs who were emigrating to Switzerland helped with furniture. They were such good friends that they even delivered the furniture to them by truck from distant Moscow. The house was now ready for the kids, and the kids were delivered. Summer had just arrived and it was better anyway for them to be in the country for the summer.

Summer went well. From working on the construction site, Father Peter's skin tanned black and he looked rather bedraggled, but he joked a lot. He had been quickly transformed from a promising student into a businesslike, shrewd villager. Perhaps it was the beard that added to this impression. It had grown long over time.

Their daughter Anya made a friend, six-year-old Varya who lived in the next street. They were inseparable, so that she could barely be called in for dinner. Their son Fedya spent all his time with his mother. He didn't bother her, playing in a corner all by himself, but he wanted her to be near. He never seemed to notice that his mother was always sobbing.

Fall came and brought with it constant rain. Lyuda grew even sadder. Churned up clay outside, Father Peter spending all his time God knows where. She sat at home all day, all by herself. And no future whatsoever.

At college, she had been the best singer and sang in the choir. Now, Petya kept saying that she had to learn to sing in church. But all Lyuda wanted to do was to go home to Moscow. She was tired of her life with Peter and the kids. She wanted to take a break from it all – not for a week or two, and not even for a full month, but, say, for a year. Finally, they got a telephone and Lyuda called everyone she knew in turn, to give them her new number. People were surprised to hear from her and invited her to come and visit them, but not too enthusiastically. They all asked her whether she planned to get a job, but that was completely out of the question. Father Peter wanted her to have another child, but Lyuda cut him off rudely, "I'm not your sow."

For the time being Petya left her alone.

Even though everyone in Moscow knew their phone number, they got very few calls. Only the closest friends called, and mostly for Father Peter. Lyuda became something like a receptionist for him.

Another year went by like this. Father Peter began to conduct services in his church, but Lyuda almost never entered the building. She still didn't like it, and she thought instead about what school to send Anya to, the one in their village or a little farther away, to a private school. Then Petya's mother visited them one day and declared that the child had to get a normal education. She insisted that Anya go to Moscow with her and attend a good school in the city, one which had a good student body and where kids learned foreign languages.

At first, Lyuda didn't want to part with her daughter, but in the end she yielded. Anya loved her grandmother and wanted to go with her at once. She even ran off and started packing her toys and books.

The house felt completely empty.

Then the phone rang at last and this time it was not for Father Peter but for Petya or Lyuda. Their high school class was having its tenth reunion – time passed so quickly. Father Peter declared immediately that Lyuda absolutely had to go and take a look at their classmates.

"Otherwise you'll get totally bored in this backwater," he said. "Fedya can be on his own one evening, without his mother."

Lyuda no longer had any desire to do anything. But she decided to go to the reunion. At the party, it turned out that all their classmates had stayed pretty much the same, except a little older. Zhenya Simonov was there as well. He had already been through his second divorce, but he was still the most appealing person at the party, maybe because he kept asking Lyuda to sing. Lyuda sang repeatedly. She was inspired, and the cognac that she drank made her voice softer and larger. By the end of the evening, Zhenya was by her side constantly and he even took her to the train station. When Lyuda's train arrived and it was time to board, Zhenya said, squeezing her elbow like a character in a B-movie, "Stay."

But Lyuda, like a character in a slightly better film, said nothing, pulled her elbow free of his grasp, boarded the train and took a seat by the window.

Father Peter met her at the station. Lyuda had caught the last suburban train out. It was dark as dark could be, and very cold. Petya's hands were like icicles.

Little is known about what happened from then on. What can be said for sure is that soon after Lyuda's foray into society, Father Peter, returning late one night from a trip to Moscow, where he had gone on business, found neither his wife nor his son at home. In the kitchen he found a detailed note describing what he could make himself for supper and no other explanation. Father Peter ate nothing and, despite the lateness of the hour, ran over to his neighbors. The neighbors told him that earlier that day they had seen Lyuda and little Fedya heading for the station. Father Peter called Lyuda's mother. She gave some vague answers to his inquiries but he heard what sounded like a child crying in the background. Father Peter began to scream at his mother-in-law and she finally owned up, "Lyuda is here. That is all I can tell you."

Then Lyuda took the receiver and said calmly, "Dear Petya. Don't call here ever again, please. I am not going to live with you any more."

Two years passed. What Lyuda did during that time is unclear, but in the end she decided to return to the village of Pypino. As she walked from the station carrying her suitcase in one hand and holding Fedya's hand in the other, she spotted the golden domes. It was Father Peter's church, except it had been completely rebuilt. Lyuda picked up the pace and Fedya trotted after her, laughing. He thought that his mother wanted to play a game with him by running ahead.

Lyuda rushed into the church and saw her Petya right away. He stood on the ambo holding a cross, and the faithful approached him to kiss it. Lyuda stared at him and was at a loss what to do next. It was her Father Peter, but he had changed in some way.

Then Fedya said loudly, pointing at the priest, "I want a hat like that."

Lyuda realized that it was the hat that had changed. Before, Father Peter had led services bare-headed, and now he wore a hat. She even remembered what it was called. A *klobuk*.

While she was away, Petya had become a monk.

Alepius and Anthony

Hieromonk Alepius got married. If it had been an angel who got married, it would have been a great surprise. In this case, however, there was nothing to wonder about. What's the big deal, an Orthodox priest getting married? The surprise was that even after he got married he retained a large, and steadily growing, spiritual following, just as in his celibate, ascetic days. Naturally, he never told his spiritual flock that at night he went back not to a lonely, spare Moscow apartment but to a nice home and a wife. Merciful God disposed that they would have no children. The lie didn't seem to interfere with his mission and the breaking of his vows didn't affect his religious responsibilities. Father Alepius was as kind, warm and diligent as ever. Why was he able to preserve these good qualities, and how? Maybe because he had a gift of humility and didn't judge others. (He was, indeed, very humble.) Or maybe he didn't preserve them at all. But people were so desperate for someone to lend them a sympathetic ear and hear what they had to say that they didn't want to inquire too deeply into various nuances, nor did they care to investigate. Or maybe the story was completely different. Anthony, Anthony, these are matters for God's Providence.

Little Lyuba

1 Little Lyuba was old. She wore a clean kerchief and stockings. She remained standing during services and didn't fall asleep. At night, she hardly slept at all and cried all night long. The tears that rolled down her cheeks were as clear as water. With her finger, she constantly traced letters on the palm of her hand, as if she were writing something down. But she never revealed what she was writing. Whenever she was asked to say a prayer for someone, she always wrote the name down on the palm of her hand. It was her daily list of names to commemorate.

Occasionally, she would stop writing and become angry, brushing something invisible aside with her left hand and saying: "Get away from me."

No one saw what it was she was chasing away, but it was easy to guess.

2 There once was a man who got drunk often and abused his wife. While sober, he was quiet, but whenever he got drunk he became a wild animal. Once, his wife got so upset that she left him and went back to the city to stay with her mother. In the morning, the man woke up and found the fridge empty and his wife gone. He had to go out to the store. He opened the gate to go out and found a pile of excrement in front of his house. It stank something awful. While he was cleaning it up, a neighbor told him what had happened. Apparently, an old woman came up to his house and stood there, talking to herself. Then she squatted down and shat on the ground. When she saw the neighbor, she said to him:

"Tell him Grandma Lyuba has paid him a visit."

She said this and left.

"She was a small woman," the neighbor said, almost laughing out loud. "Hard to believe she could make such a huge pile."

The man was offended and started to make inquiries about Grandma Lyuba. Soon he discovered that it was the holy fool, Little Lyuba. As to shitting in front of his gate, it had been her way of accusing him of committing a major sin, he was told.

The man grew mad. He drank a quarter liter of vodka to screw up his courage and headed for the church for the first time in his life. This was where Little Lyuba was likely to be found. Along the way, he picked up a heavy stick in order to teach the hooligan a lesson. Little Lyuba was not in church, but they were expecting her any moment.

Soon the holy fool arrived and the man nearly dropped his stick in surprise. Little Lyuba was a very old woman, all bent over and wearing a white kerchief. She was barely able to walk, holding two heavy bags in her hands. Loaves of bread stuck out from her bags. As she walked past the man who was still holding his stick, she looked at him humbly with her childlike blue eyes and said nothing.

"It is obviously all wrong," thought the man. "She has nothing to do with this business. I bet it was my neighbor who did it."

He turned around and headed home. But after this incident he was no longer able to drink liquor, to which he developed an aversion. His wife soon returned to him. Several years later, she told her husband that she had asked Little Lyuba to pray for her, and that Little Lyuba had replied, "Your Lyona is a good man. You have to be patient."

"She was right, of course, when she said you were a good man," said the wife. "But I wonder how she found out your name. I had never mentioned it to her."

3 In the city of St. Petersburg there lived a priest who in his sermons was very critical of the United States, calling it the Kingdom of the Antichrist. Natasha Anisimova, a biology student at the university and the priest's spiritual daughter, listened to his sermons in considerable bewilderment. Her uncle had recently gone to live in America and he seemed to like it very much. But Natasha trusted her priest. Her uncle, although a biologist of international renown, was a nonbeliever. Perhaps he didn't see everything, or couldn't draw the right conclusions. But one day her biologist uncle invited her to transfer to Harvard University, where he was teaching, because the university had received funds to offer scholarships to students from Russia.

At first, Natasha was excited, but then she became frightened. After all, it was the Kingdom of the Antichrist and the land of perdition. On the other hand, her uncle, her flesh and blood, lived there. Besides, she wanted to see the world.

Naturally, Natasha shared her doubts with her confessor. The priest suggested that she get advice from Little Lyuba. Little Lyuba greeted the young woman very kindly and when Natasha asked her whether she should go to study in America, Little Lyuba replied, smiling, "Go study. Go study."

The young woman thought that Little Lyuba had not heard her question properly and explained to her again that she was thinking of going to study in America. Yes, indeed. In America.

But Little Lyuba insisted, "The Lord's grace is everywhere."

Natasha went to study at Harvard. She graduated and stayed on to work at her uncle's lab. Unfortunately, because of politics and backbiting in his field, her uncle never got nominated for the Nobel Prize. He was so depressed by it that he fell ill and suddenly died. Thus, the prophesy of Natasha's St. Petersburg confessor was not uttered in vain.

4 Whenever she spoke about herself, Little Lyuba said: "The Kazan Mother of God will come for me in person, dressed in white."

5 She also said, pointing to the icons, "These are not pictures."

She spoke to the icons as if they were living human beings. She could feel joy and sorrow while talking to them, but usually she tried to persuade them to grant assistance.

6 When Little Lyuba came to the Diveyevo Convent, they gave her a large cell, displacing the nuns who lived there to make room for her. Nuns were common as dirt, whereas Little Lyuba was a national celebrity. But the nuns' clothes had been left in the wardrobe.

Little Lyuba opened the wardrobe and started tossing out the clothes, shouting: "It stinks."

She refused to stay in that cell. The nuns were offended and many of them decided that she was no holy fool, just an ordinary crazy old hag.

7 When Little Lyuba was asked to take the veil, she refused and said, "I'm a pilgrim."

Father Nahum from the St. Sergius Trinity Monastery even sent her a doll dressed in a nun's habit, but it was no use.

8 Little Lyuba died not in the St. Petersburg suburb, among those with whom she had lived side-by-side for the last twenty-plus years of her life, but in Vyshny Volochek, in the Kazan Mother of God Convent. She was buried there. Many people complained that she had died among strangers, far away from home. But she didn't have a home. Nor was any man a stranger to her.

Fifteenth Cycle

Letters to a Priest

Father Seraphim of Sarov

We are strangers here. We ended up at Diveyevo Convent by the grace of God. It was all due to Father Seraphim. When I read about his life, I couldn't recover for three full days. My life was changed completely. It had already been changed after I found religious faith, but after reading about his life everything became different.

I had come to religion gradually, by the path of many sorrows. Father John, a local priest here in Diveyevo, says it often happens this way. The Lord uses sorrows to knock at the hearts of men. My great sorrow was that Andrei left me when Sergei was little. I was very upset about it. For the first time in my life I began to pray, asking the Lord to give me back my husband. That may also have been the first time that God began to show His mercy to me, a sinner. Andrei left the other woman quickly, then knocked about for a while and there was no news of him for three months. But then he came back to me. He even asked me to forgive him. I forgave him.

Sergei was four years old. We lived in peace for several months and I became pregnant. Then, in my fifth month, I had a miscarriage. No one knew why, but Tonya, my next-door neighbor, said that it was a punishment for my sins. I had had an abortion before I had Sergei, when we shared a room with Andrei's grandmother. His grandmother, may she rest in peace, had had a stroke and had been paralyzed on the right side of her body. She couldn't get out of bed and screamed all night. We couldn't handle having a baby in such conditions. I had no doubts about it back then. I didn't realize that they were already alive in there, in their mother's womb, and had a soul. I thought nothing of it, like that the baby was nothing but a worm. But now Tonya told me that an abortion was a horrible sin and that I would have to pay for it my whole life.

When I had a miscarriage, I became depressed. I knew by then that it was my living child that had died and not a worm, and I didn't want to go on living. Andrei even had to take me to a psychiatrist and I was treated with antidepressants, which made me feel a little better. But what really sustained me was my faith in God, Mother of God, and all the saints.

I began to pray again while I was still in the hospital, asking God to comfort me. I was all alone and covered with blood. I was so terribly weak I couldn't get up, and no one ever came to help me, neither a nurse nor Andrei. Andrei was barely able to keep his head above water taking care of Sergei. My roommates in the hospital were post-surgery patients and couldn't get up. Had my mother been alive, she would have come to be with me, but she had died after heart surgery before Sergei was born. I was lying there all alone. The Lord helped me get up and go to the bathroom. But on my way back, in the corridor, I had a fall. Two other women called a nurse and helped me back to my bed. I was lucky the way I had fallen. I had not a scratch on me and only a few small bruises. Thank God, Father Seraphim was already protecting me back then.

When I returned home and finished a course of medicines the psychiatrist had prescribed, I felt a little better. I could even smile a little. Little Lyuba advised to me to start going to church. There, I was overcome with such warmth and repentance that I went to confession for the first time and took communion.

Before that I had read only the *Life of Saint Seraphim* and a little bit of the Scriptures. At church I bought several other books, such as *How to Prepare for Confession, Advice to a Young Mother, The Prayer* and *The Lives of Russian Saints.*

When I read about the life of Saint Xenia of St. Petersburg, I understood that I had not lived my life correctly, and that I had been following the laws of the flesh and of the world. I realized that I would be happy to leave my old life behind if only I could hope that my life would someday be worthy of the little finger on the hand of this holy blessed saint. The moment I realized this, I felt that Saint Xenia would become my patron and assistant, even though my name is Olga, and not Xenia.

At the time, we lived in Kazakhstan, in Astana. I told Andrei that I had to go to St. Petersburg. Andrei said that he was no longer going to stay with Sergei all by himself, but I had neglected to tell him that I was going to take Sergei with me. Sergei was very glad when he found out that we were taking a trip to another city. I explained to him that it was not going to be an ordinary trip, but a pilgrimage to a holy site, to the resting place of the Holy Blessed Saint Xenia of St. Petersburg.

During our train ride, I told Sergei how Little Xenia used to help people when she was alive and Sergei paid very close attention. We had a wonderful trip, even though we were tested. My wallet was stolen on the train. I began to talk to a woman who seemed very nice. She told me a lot about herself and offered us some of her food, including her compote. When we woke up in the morning the woman was gone. She had gotten off the train in the night. I felt a kind of jolt. I immediately went to check my purse. My wallet was no longer there. When we got to the Smolensk Cemetery in St. Petersburg, we didn't have a penny.

At the chapel in the cemetery I came upon the priest and told him of our misfortune. He suggested I stand by the entrance to the chapel and beg for alms, because the parish had no money to spare. I hadn't expected to get any money from them and I stood by the entrance, begging. Sergei was very embarrassed and began to cry, calling on me to stop asking people for money. But I wanted to spend the night in St. Petersburg before going back home. We needed money for food, and for the return ticket as well. People gave me some change, and I kept praying to the Holy Blessed Saint Xenia. Suddenly, a woman who sold candles and books at the chapel came up to me, saying that the priest gave permission for us to have supper in the refectory. Sergei and I had a very nice meal. The food was abundant and blessed by the Saint. Sergei happily ate the fish and the buckwheat, even though at home he always refused to eat buckwheat and complained about it. There, he finished a full plate. That was the power of the Holy Blessed Xenia.

In one day we collected half the money for one return ticket. I decided that we would collect the rest on the following day. It was getting dark and we still had to find a place to spend the night. The kind woman who sold candles – her name was Maria – advised us to go back to the train station and to sleep there, with God's help. That was what we did. We found a decent, comfortable place, a long bench. Once we said our prayers, Sergei fell asleep almost immediately and I also began to nod off.

That was when a great miracle occurred. I had a vision. I saw a large church with black domes and all around it there were nuns in black habits going to a service. The nuns were in a hurry and the bells were chiming. I looked up and I could see the black figure of a nun striking the bells in the upper stories of the belfry. I joined the nun and entered the church. It was vast and bright and I spotted the Holy Blessed Xenia's image right away. She was looking at me from an icon as though she were alive. That was when my dream ended. I woke up and understood that the Saint wanted me to go to that church with black domes. But I didn't know where it was.

In the morning I woke up Sergei. Together we read our prayer for the morning and went back to the chapel. Maria, God bless her soul, treated us even better than before and right away took us to have something to eat. She asked us many questions and then gave us the rest of the money we needed for the train tickets. I couldn't thank her enough. That was the second miracle that occurred after I prayed to Saint Xenia. I told Maria about my amazing dream and she said that it must have been some convent.

Sergei and I got home without further misadventures, but his father, while we were away, committed a horrible crime against the Church and the Lord. He destroyed my entire iconostasis with its holy images, a bottle of oil from the relics of Saint Pantaleimon, and a jar of holy water. All the icons were gone.

"How could you have done it, Andrei?" was all I could say to him.

My husband replied that he was not going to tolerate such things in his house any longer. He added that I was stuffing his and our son's heads with nonsense and that he had made a mistake when he allowed us to go on the pilgrimage.

I felt as though he had poured a bucket of icy water over me.

A few days later Andrei calmed down and apologized, but it was clear to me that if he didn't get baptized and didn't find faith in the Savior, there would no longer be the Lord's blessing for us to go on living together. I said to him that I would forgive him if he got baptized. Andrei began to shout that he would never do such a thing and he called me several foul names. He even raised a hand against me. Thank God, Sergei was outside at that moment.

The apartment in which we lived was mine. It had been left to me by my aunt, who died in 1998 from a massive heart attack. She had been single and she left the apartment to me. I told Andrei that he would have to leave.

Six months of fighting followed before our divorce. Andrei didn't want to divorce me. When he saw that my mind was made up and that I would divorce him if he didn't get baptized, he yelled at me and sometimes even beat me up. It was a severe test and a time of great sorrow. I even had to go to the doctor again, because I developed serious psychiatric problems and I was also diagnosed with an irregular heartbeat. But in the midst of this hidden and open strife, the Lord comforted me with fabulous good tidings. A woman gave me a thick book to read, which was titled *The History of Saint Seraphim's Diveyevo Convent.*

Every night after I put little Sergei to bed, I read this wonderful book. Closer to the end, I found a small calendar that had been placed between the pages with a picture of a church that looked familiar. When I looked more closely, I saw that it was the very same church I had seen in my dream at the train station. On the back of the calendar there was an inscription: "The Trinity Cathedral of St. Seraphim Convent at Diveyevo. Contemporary view." I burst into tears and spent the entire night praying. O, my Lord! Andrei and I were divorced by then and I was free. It was the Holy Blessed Saint Xenia who had given me her blessing to visit Saint Seraphim.

But the way Saint Ksenia blesses is specific. It occurred to me that I had to leave the world behind in the same way she had done. Father John from Diveyevo told me that it was my pride that had got the better of me, but I never dreamed of ever equaling the Holy Blessed Xenia. I merely wanted to imitate her in some little way. A priest in Astana, Father Valerius, told me that it was not a sin. It may be presumptuous, but I even believe that it might have been the Lord who had instilled in my heart the idea that I must leave my town.

I put an ad in the paper saying that my apartment was for sale and I put a very low price on it. A day later I had signed the sale contract. Thank God I found a buyer very quickly. I gave Andrei a portion of the money from the apartment, observing the Lord's commandment to love my neighbor, and to make peace with him before I left. However, Andrei didn't even want to talk to me and I had to pass the money to him through his mother. Sergei and I gave the rest to churches in our district and distributed it as alms to beggars. To do that, we visited all the churches in our city. We left ourselves just enough to buy train tickets to Diveyevo. Little Sergei was very happy. He kept taking those useless scraps of paper from my hand and giving them to the poor. They were grateful and kept bowing to us. Some were even in tears. I couldn't stop crying either. My old useless life was coming to an end before my very eyes. My soul was filled with such joy that I felt weightless. When I closed my eyes, I felt as though I could fly. Glory to Thee, O Lord. Glory to you, Holy Blessed Xenia. Glory to you, Saint Seraphim.

I still had furniture and some other wordly possessions in my old apartment. I had plenty of old clothes, too. I called all my friends and in a week's time I gave away everything I owned. Many of them were amazed and refused to take anything. They tried to persuade me to change my mind, but I explained to them as best I could that I would have no need for anything from my old life. Sergei was sorry to part with some of his toys, but that was just the Enemy of Mankind tempting him, because we do not take anything along when we go to Heaven. Sergei kept some toy soldiers and a toy Jeep. My confessor, Father Valerius, advised me not to object. I merely told Sergei that he would have to carry it himself, in his own backpack. In my own backpack I packed a copy of the Bible, the *Diveyovo Chronicle*, the prayer book, two towels and two undershirts, as well as a change of underwear for Sergei and myself. My backpack was very light. That was how we set off for the fourth earthly estate of the Mother of God, which, according to Saint Seraphim, also included Jerusalem and Mouth Athos.

We arrived in Arzamas early in the morning of May 16. It turned out that we still had to take a bus to Diveyevo, but we no longer had a penny. We had spent everything on tickets and on food along the way. We paid our respects to all the holy relics in Arzamas and entered every church – there were three that we were able to locate. I prayed to all the saints and to the Mother of God, and Sergei also said his prayers as I had instructed him. Since Andrei and I were divorced, Sergei had become much more mature.

But it was time to start walking to Diveyevo. Darkness had fallen unexpectedly quickly and we had not been able to find a place to spend the night in Arzamas. We had asked several people in the street and in the churches, but no one had a place for us.

We left Arzamas and ate some bread. By then it had grown completely dark. We found a place surrounded by a long wooden fence. It was some kind of hill with a tree on top of it, and that was where we spent the night. Sergei gathered some branches, we made a small fire and got warm next to it. I prayed constantly to

Saint Seraphim and the Holy Blessed Xenia, who had both suffered far greater privations and cold in their time. In the morning, the Lord in his mercy allowed us to witness a miracle. Our poplar tree burst into leaf overnight and in the morning was all covered with tiny green leaves. It was the only tree that had any leaves on it anywhere in the neighborhood. The branches of all the other poplars around us were still bare. Sergei suggested that it must have been our campfire that had warmed the poplar tree, but I'm convinced that the campfire had nothing to do with it. It was clearly the Lord's blessing for our journey. God be thanked. The Mother of God protected us and watched over us. After a night in the cold and after sleeping without a roof over our heads we didn't even catch a cold. That was clearly because the Holy Blessed One and the Saint had interceded on our behalf.

Early the next morning we neared Diveyevo. When I saw the same church with black domes that I had known since my dream, I began to cry so deeply that Sergei became frightened. The service had started and we went to liturgy, paid our respects to the relics of the Saint and heard the akathistos. A nun came up to us and asked, "Are you here on a pilgrimage?"

"No, Mother, we're no pilgrims. We've come here to stay."

Once again I couldn't keep myself from crying. The nun advised us to go and find the Mother Superior, and to ask her for permission to stay at Diveyevo.

The Mother Superior greeted us very kindly when we came up to her after the service. When she found out that we were from Kazakhstan and that we no longer had a home, she allowed us to stay in a small peasant hut that belonged to the convent. When we moved in, it was dirty and untidy. No one had lived there for many years. Two windows were missing windowpanes, and I don't even want to mention how filthy it was inside. Some people who came to visit us said that we would have probably been better off living outside. That was because there was a bad odor in the house. But that too was temptation. It was a true miracle, wasn't it, that we, a pair of homeless vagrants, got a real house as a gift on our first day at the convent? Besides, the bad odor could be aired out. The problem was that there were rotten rags and vegetables in the cellar. I threw it all out and cleaned the cellar, and things got a lot better.

At first we used an electric heater to warm up, but it got very cold in winter, and during the coldest nights we were allowed to sleep in the church, because it was heated. But those problems and trials are now all in the past. Now, thank God, we have a stove and windowpanes, and there is even running water.

We share the house with one other person, a middle-aged woman and the mother of one of the nuns at the convent. Her name is Svetlana. She had been thrown out of her own house by her husband, who is a drunk. Svetlana takes care of Sergei when I do my chores. My mother is dead, but the Holy Blessed Xenia sent Sergei another grandmother instead. I do my chores daily, and Sergei often helps me out, even though he gets tired quickly. Two weeks ago he turned eight. I have not sent him to school, of course. At first, the nuns tried to convince me to send him to school and I even went to talk to the principal of the local school at Diveyevo. But when I came into the building I saw that they had television sets in all the classrooms. My son doesn't need that. Thank God, his soul remains unspoiled and pure. He doesn't read any secular books, but he knows all the prayers by heart. What will he see on television but Sin and the Devil? The most important thing is to have a penitent heart, Little Sergei, the rest will take care of itself, you'll see. He has friends and he doesn't need school for that. There are plenty of kids around, both locals and the children of those who come to pray to the Saint. The nuns love my Sergei and they recently bought him a pair of new boots and a jacket. They complain to me that I don't take good care of him. But I have no way of taking care of him, because I don't get paid for my chores, and even when I'm offered money I refuse it because I would rather get my rewards in heaven. That's how we go along by the grace of God and the prayers of the Holy Blessed Xenia and Saint Seraphim.

When Sergei grows up, God willing, he will enter a monastery. Perhaps even the Sarov Monastery will be rebuilt by then and he will take the orders. I will stay here, next to Father Seraphim, for the rest of my life. Maybe in the course of time I will be allowed to become a nun, and if I ever take the veil I will be called Xenia in honor of the Holy Blessed Xenia of St. Petersburg. But it is too early to think of such things. My confessor here in Diveyevo, Father John, says that while Sergei is little it makes no sense even to think of joining the convent. But I do think of it a lot, sinner that I am. I should offer my thanks to the Lord for allowing us to live here, on such holy soil, close to the relics of a great Saint. I have no fears here. Even if the Antichrist comes to rule elsewhere, he would never be able to cross the sacred ravine where the Mother of God had trodden. That was Father Seraphim's prophecy.

Saint Seraphim, Our Holy Father, please pray to the Lord on our behalf.

A Funny Little Miracle

The Holy Week sticks in my throat. The black wind blows into my eyes. I shut them so as not to go blind and not to see, because I can't look any more. It's time to shut my eyes and freeze. I absolutely hate those blindingly sunny, volatile, wind-swept days in the middle of April. There is still snow on the ground and the blinding, ailing sun keeps shining.

For a year, despair has weighed heavily on me, pushing me deeper and deeper into a black tunnel without windows. What windows could there be, anyway, in a tunnel? I can't breathe. Don't understand why it is that if I have despair in my soul and in my heart, my lungs can't breathe? But the only breath that would alleviate my suffering is a puff on a cigarette. All I need is to inhale the bitterness, the smoke with its strange aftertaste of death or grass, to get healthy again and to know once more what I live for. It is as though someone keeps kindly offering me a simple solution, a mouthful of bitterness that will banish the tunnel.

I'm driving, and in my mind's eye I keep smoking one cigarette after another with the car window down, exhaling the smoke outside and knocking the ash into the ashtray. I'm waiving aside the thick curtain of smoke to make it easier to see. If anybody smokes next to me, in the street or indoors, on the landing between floors, I don't try to sniff the smoke and I don't inhale it greedily. It's their smoke, not at all tasty, disgusting, other people's.

But I have had enough of the temptation, as you call it in church, quite enough. I asked you when I came to confession – remember? – whether I could smoke just one cigarette. Just one. Only to put an end to this obsession. Let it be a defeat, I don't care – as long as it ends. But you said to me with a smile, "By the authority vested in me by the Lord, I do not allow it."

I said to you then, as though I was still playing the same role that had long stuck in my throat, "I'll break your ban."

You said coldly, "Try and see if you can."

I thought yet again, "Damn it, this man says so few words, but each one has weight."

There are so few things that have any effect on me, but this still does, thank God. The man's words still have power over me, even if not a lot of power. I'm glad they do, and I have never even tried to violate your prohibition.

But then Dima went away. The sudden freedom always affects me in the same way. It is as though for some reason a weight is taken off my shoulders. (Is it the cross of marriage?) But along with the freedom, depression sets in. An unbearable depression. At least I had Dima to talk to and he would listen to me, but now it's all over, nothing but void. The kids don't fill this void, they are different. I felt the same desire, at times more sharply and at other times less, but I was too lazy to go and buy myself cigarettes. I felt a strange weakness the moment the push came to shove. I couldn't even decide which brand was better or tastier.

That morning I went to get my car fixed. For the first time in a long time I had put it in the garage, because its door locks had been vandalized and the tape player had been stolen. With the doors unlocked there was no way I was going to leave the car out in the courtyard. I had to call on Sasha the Janitor, who looks like an intellectual and charges 50 rubles for his help. He cleared the ice from the garage door, I put the car in and locked it up. But apparently somebody had stood next to the garage late at night, smoking. Or rather it must have been two of them, a guy and a girl. His pack was empty and when he threw it away it went a considerable distance. She, on the other hand, had not finished all the cigarettes in her pack. There were quite a few left, because when I kicked it to make sure that no trash was lying in front of my garage, long thin white cigarettes fanned out from the pack.

Surely it was fate.

When I last smoked, we didn't have such such beautiful white cigs. We used to smoke the Bulgarian BT brand and we thought it was a great piece of good fortune when we could get our hands on them. Once, I tried a Marlboro cigarette because I wanted to see why everybody was so crazy about them. I was 15 years old then. I can hardly remember that time now, and I don't think it was good. At the time, I didn't smoke much, but I used to show off a lot. Even when I was alone, I was still posing. Like, look at me, how deeply I suffer.

But then it all came to an end, because the church disapproved of smoking. It was easy for me to quit, I hadn't yet developed a habit. But it probably was like the travails of the Holy Blessed Theodora, which they say we all undergo after we die: any sin leaves a trace upon the soul and we'll have to answer for each one. If I used to smoke, it didn't all simply air out, and now I have to battle it for real. But on that sunny April day I suddenly had a thought: why did I need to fight it at all? Was it really a sin? No, it was not a sin. No apostle ever said anything about smoking. Forget it. Compared to taking one's own life, is smoking a sin? Then again, I was just going to try it and at least put my mind to rest.

I picked up two of the cigarettes scattered on the snow, but one had gotten wet. I kept the dry one. I sniffed it. It had the nice smell of a good cigarette. I held it between my lips.

I pulled the car out of the garage, locked the door behind me and drove down the hill to a side street. There it was, my blonde friend, sitting there waiting for me. I pushed in the lighter and waited. But the lighter failed to pop out. I pulled it out and checked it. Instead of a red-hot spiral inside, it was cold and gray. It was broken. OK, I was headed to the repair shop anyway. I'll tell the guys about the lighter. But then I spent so much time telling them about the doors and we discussed the disgusting druggies who break into cars for so long that I completely forgot to mention the lighter. When I came back to pick up the car, I was embarrassed to tell them about it. Even though it might only take a second to fix a car lighter. The cigarette was still sitting there between the front seats, under the hand brake. Then again, there were plenty of matches in the city. And there were plenty of lighters, too. I was in a rush to get home to relieve Mother, who was watching the kids. It seemed stupid to stop in order to buy matches. I could easily take some from home next time. I even had a thought to smoke the cigarette at home, but with the kids around it wouldn't be much fun. No, it was better to smoke it in the car.

Before slamming the door, I took one last look at my only hope sitting under the hand brake and I went home very happy. The manic stage was clearly upon me. The evening passed well. I yelled only on two occasions, which was actually very good for me. Only once did I slam the kids' saucepan against the floor. The handle came off right away. It's a joke. They can't even make a decent pot or pan any more. Everything says Made in China.

Grisha got overexcited. Lisa went to sleep quietly, but Grisha kept screaming and calling out to me. He called to me in his sleep, and I couldn't tell whether he was awake or not, so I kept running to him as he moaned. Maybe it was those magnetic storms again? After running to him four times in three hours, I thought that if I didn't fall asleep right away and Grisha didn't stop shouting, I was going to die. I began to pray, "Lord, I promise never to smoke under any circumstances. I promise that tomorrow, the moment I unlock the car, I'll throw away that cigarette. Let me sleep. Let Grisha not scream any more, so that I can take a little nap too. I'm very sorry."

Grisha fell silent right away. I don't know whether the prayer had something to do with it, but next time we saw each other again it was morning.

After breakfast the three of us went to take a walk. We put on our coats and went downstairs. We had to drive a short distance to the Neskuchny Gardens. I unlocked the car and started the engine. The car rolled across the courtyard and a dove flew out from under my wheels. That was when I remembered that I had to throw away the cigarette. Yes, quickly. I couldn't find it anywhere. It had been there only the day before, right under the emergency brake, a white stripe against the black plastic. There was nothing there now. I stopped in the middle of the courtyard and looked for the cigarette under the seats and shook out the mat. I asked Grisha and Lisa whether they had taken a long white tube stuffed with brown crumbs. They said they hadn't.

"Are you telling the truth?"

"Yes, Mom."

I know they didn't take it. There wasn't enough time. We had just gotten into the car. Where did it go then? Lord, did You not trust me? Did You take the cigarette from me? I would have thrown it away, honest, but if it was a miracle, then I thank You. It was a funny little miracle, Father. That's all.

The Fruits of Repentance

This was how it happened. I was studying for an exam and stayed at home while my parents went to the dacha over the weekend. I got a bit brain dead from studying and in the evening decided to go for a walk. There is a bookstore near my house, located in a cellar. They know me there because I often buy books from them. It's a good bookstore and they get many books earlier than the large chains. I went in that time, and an assistant, Leva, came up to me right away. He is a rather strange guy, long-haired and spaced out.

"Look," he said. "Here is a new book. It's cool. What year were you born?"

"Nineteen eighty one."

"You look older."

"Many people say I do. It's probably because I have a beard."

"Then it may not be for you. Your time was different. As for me, that was exactly how we were. The author is twenty-nine years old, just like me. I too used to live in a small town. I could have written this book myself."

"What is it about?"

"Buy it and read it. It doesn't cost much. It's about nothing in particular, just our shitty life and high school."

I bought the book. It was titled *A Town*. I read it that same night, because it was well-written, with a nice rhythm to it. I just couldn't bring myself to read another textbook that day. The book is about a guy who is in his last year of high school and he lives in a small town. All he does is smoke, drink beer and think of girls. But thinking is only the half of it. The girls in his town are easy, and he goes and picks one up. After the second date she invites him over to her place. The book doesn't describe what they do in much detail, but all the same while I was reading it I felt this kind of pressure. I should have thrown away that stupid book like a viper and got under a cold shower, because it helps a lot. I actually did go to the bathroom, but I took the damn book with me. It was as though it had become glued to my fingers. I sat on the edge of the bathtub and finished reading it. And did exactly what they did in the book, except without a girl.

At first I sat there as though I had been struck by thunder. I had not done anything like that for four years, ever since I was baptized. Now, it happened just like that, for no reason. I looked at myself in the mirror. Just to make sure it was still me. It was indeed me, but my face seemed disgusting. I started striking my own face, hard, taking a long windup. It hurt and I burst out crying.

In the morning I went to confession. It happened to be a Sunday. I didn't go to my own church but to a different one. The young priest who heard my confession said that it was a great sin and that I couldn't yet be admitted to receive communion. But I didn't want to receive communion, I just wanted to have peace. But I couldn't. All the parishioners stood there, praying and then they went to receive communion and to kiss the cross. The choir was singing and the priest was giving a blessing to the people, while I alone stood there, as if I were glued to the floor. I felt that I had been separated and cut off from the normal world and existed in a black, transparent box, like in a casket. My sin was my casket. The others were lucky because they had not committed as great a sin as I, whereas I was like an animal, Father. I even decided, in order to lessen my guilt, that it had happened because you were out of town. When you are away I feel like I don't have anyone to watch over me. It's as though everything is permitted, when the Reverend Father is away. I do not really think so, not consciously at least, but a thought like this lives somewhere in the subconscious. Perhaps I do not have enough of the Lord in me. He looks after us too, but I do not feel His eyes on me as distinctly as yours.

Then I went home and while I waited for the trolley car I felt as bad as before. There were people all around me, and they walked and talked, frowned and laughed, shouted and smiled. There was a little girl on a park bench, and kids riding their bicycles, the sky was very blue and covered with clouds, and a smell of fried food wafted from windows, but I was still separated from it all. I was on my own planet called Sin, from which I was not permitted to return to Earth. That was a reminder to me how little I was worth.

I came home and I could not do anything. Confession had been no help at all. I wanted to hide somewhere, to disappear and cease to exist. I was a pig, a bastard. I had a drink of water and didn't eat any food. I decided to pay for my sin by fasting. Then I opened the closet and tossed all the clothes out. I sat in the closet and covered myself with a blanket so that the Lord wouldn't look at me so sternly and would forgive me. That gave me some relief. I sat there for a long time. Then the phone began to ring, but by the time I got out of the closet it had stopped ringing. It rang again right away – my parents were calling me on their cell phone to check how I was doing. I was doing very poorly.

I had no desire to get back into the closet, and I stuffed the clothes back into it haphazardly. I stood in front of the icon of the Savior and began to pray with my eyes closed, "O, Lord, cleanse me and forgive me. I have fallen, but please restore me."

I bowed to the ground and began again, "O, Lord, cleanse me and restore me..."

And another low bow.

I don't know how much time passed. I was sweaty and tired when I sat down at last. But my casket was still there. There was no ticket for me to return to Earth. My eyes met the orange cover of the book that I had read the night before. I grabbed it and tore up its pages. A minute later I heard it rustle down the pipe of the trash compactor. The rustling smoothed my wrinkled soul and I was cheered. I realized that I had to do something decisive in order to pay for my sin. Not just pray and bow, but do something radical. I put on my sneakers and went out.

I walked along the courtyard and then in our neighborhood park. It is very large and you can spend hours walking in it. I saw mothers with strollers, an old lady with two dogs on a leash and heavily made-up girls in miniskirts and high heels. By the square where there are slot machines and a kebab joint, I finally saw a group of kids my age. There were two girls and three guys, one of them clearly a muscleman. I could have easily picked a fight with him, but I suddenly thought I didn't want the girls to see them beating me up. I kept walking. Then I saw them. They were exactly the right group. They sat on a bench by a narrow path, about five of them. They were kids, 16-17 years old, all pretty drunk by then. They were smoking and drinking beer.

I approached them and asked them in a loud and insolent voice, "Hey, kids, have any beer for me?"

One of them, who had a shaved head and an earring, got up right away and cursed me. The others guffawed. I gave him a little shove to get him mad, but he was so drunk that even a light push was enough to make him sway and sit down on the bench again. The other kids, instead of coming to his aid, laughed again, "Come on, Flea. You can do it. All you gotta do is throw up."

Flea seemed to have been the weakling among them and no one wanted to help him. Suddenly, he turned very pale and headed for the bushes.

"That's right, go on. That's right, go retch."

They didn't pay me any attention. I was like a piece of furniture to them. I turned around and went on, walking very slowly in case Flea wanted to chase me. But no one followed.

Again I couldn't find anyone to pick a fight with, so I left the park and began walking around apartment buildings. Finally, I saw two men. One was younger and the other older. Both had a mustache and they looked like traders at our neighborhood market. They sat on a cardboard box and ate from paper plates, drinking something that looked like beer. Next to them was an empty bottle of vodka.

I came up to them and said, "We ought to throw you out of Moscow, you filthy bastards. Look at the trash you've left here."

I kicked the bottle over and it rolled down the sidewalk.

The older of the two, the one who was fatter and looked more disgusting, rose quickly and his eyes lit up. The younger one also began to get up, but he was moving more slowly. He clearly wanted to finish his food first. I got ready for a fight. Suddenly, the young one shouted, "Watch out. Police."

I turned around. A squad car, its windows rolled down, drove into the courtyard and headed toward us. The men jumped aside, crossed the courtyard and slipped out through an archway. Perhaps they had reason to fear the cops. I didn't want to run away and began to walk toward the police car. A red-faced cop, who was on my side of the car, looked me over from head to toe as the car passed me slowly. I thought of Cain, whom no one could kill because he had a mark on him and the Lord didn't allow anyone to kill him. I felt sorry for Cain.

My head was spinning and I could barely walk. Suddenly, I realized that I had had no food since morning. I had only had a drink of water. It was almost evening. I went to the market and bought myself four hot dogs. I ate them right away. Forgive me, Lord, I'm a sinful glutton.

Father, I'm so happy you're back. Perhaps you could help me repent truly and reap the fruits of my repentance. I want to break this horrible casket. I beg you to pray for me. Your sinful Vasily.

Benediction
Christ Is Risen

Everything ended like no one expected.

Mother Anna and the nuns washed the floors, polished the candlesticks so much that they shone like the sun, placed red Easter candles into them and fetched a bag of still-warm communion prosphoras from the bakery. Father Antipas brought in bunches of white roses and lilies from his garden and the nuns placed them around the icons. The smell of freshly-baked bread mixed with the delicate scent of flowers; a light rain was falling outside and the wet freshness wafted in through the open windows. The nuns gathered in the right choir, placing the holy books on the lectern and sitting down on the benches. Some nodded off, placing their heads on each other's shoulders, while others read their prayers. Mother Georgia leafed through a thick Easter Triodion.

The younger crowd was the first to arrive. Father Theoprepius, his hair uncombed, was all covered in feathers. Clearly, he had been playing some game. The extremely tall Father Dorimedont burped softly and shamefacedly. Father James had his arm in a sling. (He had fallen from a tree.) Father Yehudiel kept shivering, because his cassock, which he had laundered for the holiday, had not dried properly. They were followed by Father Gavrusha and Monk Stepanenko, both very sleepy, since for two straight nights they had been watching thrillers on video. Both looked around with sadness in their eyes.

The monks positioned themselves on the right choir and immediately began pinching and sticking each other with splinters of wood which they had brought along for exactly that purpose. But then a new group of monks, headed by Father Metrophanos, entered the church. The youngsters immediately calmed down and gathered their wits, hiding the splinters in their cassocks and standing at attention. It was widely known that Father Metrophanos would crack upside the head anyone who made noise in church or showed a lack of piety, regardless of who it was. Father Metrophanos left his highly disciplined charges in the choir and headed determinedly toward the altar.

Fedya the Carpenter, who in his previous life had been an actor at a drama theater, brought in wooden benches with carved legs, first one then two more. A middle-aged woman wearing a black kerchief with a silver fringe and holding a purse, sat down on the first pew. It was Fedya's mother. A bespectacled writer scurried to the candle counter. Her eyes were filled with tears and, picking up a pencil, she began writing a long note commemorating the living, "For the health of…" The superman priest, who was manning the counter, took her note and winked at her. He even seemed to sing something to her softly. The young woman brightened, wiped her eyes with a white handkerchief and stood nearby, so that she could cast an occasional glance at the priest who had cheered her and bolstered her spirit.

Mother Theodosia came in and held the door, to make sure Father Abercius didn't yet again hit his elderly forehead against it. Several unknown holy men arrived and softly, so softly, headed to the altar. The old man of the oak tree arrived in a wheelchair, followed by red-cheeked Misha carrying a string of dry mushrooms over his shoulder and a jar of steaming fresh milk. He placed the milk on a stool next to the memorial candles, and put the dry mushrooms there as well. At length, other nice people came in, such as the atheist priest, the drunkard priest and the kleptomaniac priest. They came in with their heads bowed and stood by the door, not daring to go any further. Then two nuns brought in Mother Superior Raisa, who also seemed dejected.

Suddenly, an old man wearing a hat and a gray raincoat appeared in the churchyard, face aglow, emitting a bright calm. He was held up on two sides. He was focused on something inside him and yet he seemed to notice everything that was happening around him. He was helped into the church. He removed his hat, made a sign of the cross and, thanking his assistants, headed toward the altar. Those who were already in the church froze. It was as though a bright trail appeared in his wake. Only Abbess Anna's nuns caught on and, promptly rising from their benches, asked him for a blessing. The holy man smiled, looked at all of them together, such that each thought that he was looking only at her, and blessed them. When the nuns raised their heads, the priest was gone, and only the door to the altar was swaying gently. The writer wiped her eyes. It was, of course, none other than Father Tikhon. He was followed by the holy blessed – Little Lyuba, who kept mumbling something under her breath and taking notes on the palm of her hand, homeless Grisha holding a volume of the latest Harry Potter book under his arm, and the silent, gray Tanya, who had once had three children.

Father Nicholas, who lived on an island, entered, swift and light-footed, and, before anyone could bat an eye, disappeared behind the altar. Then Father Paul the Provider was led in. He was short and sturdy and wore eyeglasses held in place by a piece of string. He looked like a large wild mushroom. He was led to the ambo by a female attendant and a muscular young man. When he reached the ambo, he was assisted up the steps by Father Metrophanos and Father Artemius. No one noticed how the other Father Paul came in, accompanied by his Grunya, but he too was already in the altar, whereas Grunya took her place next to Abbess Anne's nuns.

Suddenly, there was noise and commotion. The kids had arrived. Every mother had four, five, even six. They were energetic and noisy. The boys had closely cropped hair and were dressed in white shirts, and girls of different ages all wore red kerchiefs. Soon their fathers came in, too. They had been locking their cars in the churchyard. The kids immediately grew quiet and even babes in arms pressed harder into their mothers' breasts and dozed off briefly. Then, suddenly, there was a loud din outside and the windows in the church began to rattle. It was the businessman priest landing in the churchyard in his personal helicopter. The chopper hung low over the church, dropping a ladder, and the priest promptly slid down, right next to the church door. He waved his hand to the pilot and the chopper immediately regained height, banked and flew away. The priest put on his cassock and entered the church with a spring in his step. The kids, who had started to fuss, went quiet again and didn't hear the ne'er-do-well priest come in behind the businessman, dragging his foot a little and wearing a shoe with a hole. He walked hand-in-hand with his wife.

The couples began to enter: Kolya and Olya, Petya and Lyuda, Zhenya and Vasya, Nastya Trofimova and her Rob, Slavik and his beautiful Sonechka, Sergei and Anya, who was checking a portable recorder on her belt. Tanya and Grisha came in still carrying their knapsacks. All were young, happy and full of energy. Ever-smiling American priests arrived, light of foot. Both bishops, Father Michael and Father Valerius, were accompanied by their wives and well-dressed children. The girls wore hats and the boys were dressed in three-piece suits. It was, in other words, your typical middle America. Lenya Korotkov came in wearing a red Father Frost cap, but he got embarrassed and took it off.

"I will say it roughly, and in a whisper, because it is not yet time," Deacon Gregory said softly and went forward, to the ambo, where he was joined by Father Misael. Father Misael stopped him and answered him solemnly, "We often forget that the happy heavenly reservoir for the soul is the expanding house of this world."

They understood each other and headed to the altar.

More and more people entered the church. They exchanged greetings, hugged each other and bowed. Some were there for the first time, to see the Paschal Procession of the Cross, but they too, taking their cue from the others, picked up red candles and stood shifting from one foot to the other and talking in whispers.

The church was full and the service began. And some service it was. At first it was nothing special, and it went on quietly, but then it grew louder and more sonorous. The choir began to sing: "Christ Is Risen from the Dead." The procession exited from the warmth of the church into the damp darkness and the raw April air, then circled the church singing quietly, sending small gleams of light to the high, darkened sky and casting the glow of candles on the bent trees that stood frozen and tense and covered in bursting buds. They returned to the church altered, pure of heart and with clear, childlike faces. The choir continued singing and each word came loud and clear as never before. It didn't even seem to be a choir but high waves lifting all those present and carrying them farther and higher. The church was now completely lit up and new faces appeared out of nowhere. With each passing moment there were more and more of them. Who they were and where they came from could no longer be known. There were slim young men and beautiful young women, strong men in white shirts and handsome women in colorful dresses, boys and girls, old men and women who looked like angels. And still more people kept coming.

Patriarchs, metropolitans, archbishops and bishops kept popping out of the altar one after the other. They had on gleaming red outfits, white and black cassocks, and some wore mitres and others did not. There were dozens, even hundreds of priests, martyrs, protomartyrs, the holy blessed, the reverends, saints. They kept repeating: "Christ is Risen, He is Risen, He is Risen!" Countless voices answered them and the crowd sang, gleamed and brimmed with joy. People hugged one another and kissed each other on the cheeks. The priests, whose main feature was that they were "good people, no matter what," got shy, and holding their hands over their hearts, tried to say something. But they were also hugged and kissed and then quickly got lost in the joyous crowd. Suddenly, a gray priest came out to the ambo wearing golden vestments. The church grew so quiet that the cracking of the burning candles could suddenly be heard. The priest looked at the brightened faces of the crowd and said:

"O you, rich and poor, one with another, dance for joy! O you ascetics and you negligent, celebrate the day! You who have fasted and you who have disregarded the fast, rejoice today! The table is rich-laden; feast royally, all of you! Let no one lament his poverty, for the universal kingdom has been revealed. Let no one mourn his transgressions, for pardon has dawned from the grave. O death, where is thy sting? O grave, where is thy victory? Christ is risen, and you are overthrown! Christ is Risen, and the demons are fallen! Christ is Risen, and the angels rejoice! Christ is Risen, and life reigns! Christ is Risen!"

The church responded in one breath, and thunderously: "Indeed He is Risen!"

Little Gosha, who was riding on the shoulders of his very solemn father, shouted "Hurray!" and roared into his father's bald spot as if he were a terrible tiger.

Glossary

Ambo – A raised platform in the middle of the nave of the church, from which the scriptures are read during the Divine Liturgy.

Akathistos – From the Greek word *"akathist"* which means "not sitting." An akathist is a hymn to a saint, the most famous being the Byzantine hymn to the Virgin Mary.

Archimandrite – Head of a monastery; abbot. See *priests*.

Bible – The Biblical text used by Orthodox Christians includes the Greek Septuagint and the New Testament. It also includes the seven Deuterocanonical Books, which are generally rejected by Protestants and a small number of other books that are in neither Western canon. Orthodox Christians call the ten books that they accept but that are not in the Protestant 39-book Old Testament canon *"Anagignoskomena"* (a Greek word that means "readable," "worthy of reading"). They regard them as venerable, but on a lesser level than the 39 books of the Hebrew canon.

Bishop – Overseer and leader of a region or diocese. Bishops are almost always chosen from among monks and are thus celibate. An archbishop denotes some form of leadership of other bishops of the local church.

Deacon – Literally a "servant." A deacon censes the icons and people, calls the people to prayer, leads the litanies, and has a role in the dialogue of the Anaphora. He is not permitted to perform any sacraments on his own, except for Baptism in extremis (in danger of death), conditions under which anyone, including the laity, may baptize. Deacons can also be archdeacons (serving among the monastic clergy) or protodeacons (a distinction of honor awarded to senior deacons, usually serving on the staff of the diocesan bishop). The position of deacon is often occupied for life. The deacon also acts as an assistant to a bishop. Deaconesses exist in nunneries, but do not assume the liturgical role of male deacons in the Divine Liturgy.

Holy Fool – The *yurodivy* (юродивый), or Holy Fool ("Fool for Christ"), is one who acts intentionally foolish in the eyes of men. He or she often goes around half-naked, is homeless, speaks in riddles, is believed to be clairvoyant and a prophet, and may occasionally be disruptive and challenging to the point of seeming immoral (though always to make a point). Fools for Christ are often given the title of Blessed (блаженного), which among the Orthodox does not necessarily mean that the individual is less than a saint (as in the Roman Catholic Church), but rather points to the blessings from God that they are believed to have acquired.

Icon – Orthodox believers do not consider icons to be idols or objects of worship. Instead, they are a way to venerate the individual depicted or represented. Icons are rich in symbology and are meant to convey information about the person or event depicted, particularly the individual's spiritual aspects.

Fasting – All Orthodox Christians are expected to fast following a prescribed set of guidelines. They are not to view fasting as a hardship, but rather as a privilege and joy. Orthodox Christians usually have one of three types of fasts in mind when they speak of fasting. *Ascetic fasting* is done by a set monastic rules. The rules mainly consist of total abstinence from certain foods and a substantial dietary reduction. *Eucharistic fasting* means fasting from the Holy Eucharist celebration itself. This is done during the weekdays of Great Lent along with an ascetic fast. *Total fasting* is a total abstinence from all food and drink for a short duration. This is done for one or even just part of a day, for spiritual concentration on something that is to come.

Hegumen/Hegumenia – Igumen or hegumen is the title for the head of a monastery, similar to abbot. The head of a convent of nuns is called *igumenia* or *ihumenia* (Greek: *hegumeni*). The term means "the one who is in charge," or "the leader" in Greek. An *igumen* is not necessarily a member of the clergy. In the Slavic tradition, the title of *Igumen* also serves as a title for a priest-monk in between Hieromonk and Archimandrite.

Hieromonk ("priest-monk") – A monk who has been ordained to the priesthood. Not all monks live in monasteries, some hieromonks serve as priests in parish churches thus practicing "monasticism in the world."

Hierodeacon ("deacon-monk") – A monk who has been ordained to the diaconate.

Metropolitan – In the Russian Orthodox tradition, a rank above archbishop. The title can be used for primatial sees as well as important cities. Metropolitans do not have any special authority over other ruling bishops within their provinces. However, metropolitans are the chairmen of their respective synods of bishops, and have special privileges.

Monk – There are three main types of monastics. Those who live in monasteries under a common rule are *coenobitic*. *Eremitic* monks, or hermits, are those who live solitary lives. Hermits are usually associated with a larger monastery but live in seclusion some distance from the main compound. Their local monastery will see to their physical needs, supplying them with simple foods while disturbing them as little as possible. In between are those in semi-eremitic communities, or *sketes*, where one or two monks share each of a group of nearby dwellings under their own rules and only gather together in the central chapel, or *katholikon*, for liturgical observances. All monks are celibate.

Orthodox – The term is from the Greek and means "correctly believing," or "correctly glorifying." The Orthodox Church, officially called the Orthodox Catholic Church and commonly referred to as the Eastern Orthodox Church, is the second largest Christian denomination in the world, with an estimated 300 million adherents.

Patriarch – The head of certain of the nine autocephalous Orthodox Churches.

Priest – Priests can be *archpriests* (one who supervises a number of priests or parishes), *archimandrites* (head of a monastery or abbot) or *protopresbyters* (a priest is somehow distinguished or ranks above other priests). The Orthodox Church has always allowed priests (and deacons) to be married, provided the marriage takes place before ordination. Widowed priests and deacons may not remarry and it is common for such members of the clergy to retire to a monastery. This is also true of widowed wives of clergy, who do not remarry and become nuns when their children are grown.

Prosphora – Greek for "offering," it is the bread used for the Divine Liturgy. (Also spelled "prosfora.")

Saint – All persons currently in heaven are considered to be saints, whether their names are known or not. There are, however, those saints of distinction whom God has revealed as particularly good examples. When a saint is revealed and ultimately recognized by a large portion of the Church, a service of official recognition (glorification) is celebrated. This does not "make" the person a saint, it merely recognizes the fact and announces it to the rest of the Church. A day is prescribed for the saint's celebration, hymns composed and icons are created. Numerous saints are celebrated on each day of the year. They are venerated but not worshiped, for worship is due to God alone.

Theotokos – Literally "mother of God" in Greek, this is the term used to refer to the most revered of saints, Jesus' mother Mary.

About the Author

Maya Kucherskaya is a literary critic, novelist, biographer and teacher. A graduate of Moscow State University, she received a Ph.D. from UCLA and is the author of more than 100 articles on literature and culture. She has served several times as a judge on Russia's most prestigious literary award, the Booker, and her first novel (recently rewritten and published as *The Rain God*) received the Student Booker prize. *Faith & Humor* was awarded the 2006 Bunin Prize.

About the Translator

Alexei Bayer lives in New York, where he writes in English and in Russian, his native tongue, and translates into both languages. His translations have appeared in *Chtenia* and *Words Without Borders*, as well as in such collections as *The Wall in My Head*, a book dedicated to the 20th anniversary of the fall of the Berlin Wall, and *Life Stories*, a bilingual literary anthology to benefit hospice care in Russia. His writing has appeared in *Chtenia*, *New England Review* and *KR Online*.

Acknowledgment

The author, translator, and publisher all wish to express their particular gratitude to Olga Meerson, who applied her keen linguistic skills and deep knowledge of Orthodoxy to a thorough proofing of the translation.